TIME OF DEATH

TIME OF DEATH

A STILLWATER
GENERAL MYSTERY

Lucy Kerr

CROOKED
LANE

NEW YORK

F

Copyright © 2016 by Lucy Kerr.

Published in the United States by Crooked Lane Books, an imprint of The Quick Brown Fox & Company LLC.

Crooked Lane Books and its logo are trademarks of The Quick Brown Fox & Company LLC.

Library of Congress Catalog-in-Publication data available upon request.

ISBN (hardcover): 978-1-62953-990-4
ISBN (paperback): 978-1-62953-991-1
ISBN (ePub): 978-1-62953-992-8
ISBN (Kindle): 978-1-62953-993-5
ISBN (ePDF): 978-1-62953-994-2

Cover design by Melanie Sun.
Book design by Jennifer Canzone.

Printed in the United States.

www.crookedlanebooks.com

Crooked Lane Books
34 West 27th St., 10th Floor
New York, NY 10001

First Edition: December 2016

10 9 8 7 6 5 4 3 2 1

To Danny and the girls:
You are so nice to come home to . . .

PROLOGUE

Clem Jensen never considered himself a betting man. The riverboat casinos had never held his interest, except for their jumbo shrimp cocktails. Bingo at the senior center was only worth it for the brownies. Seventy-odd years of bad luck left him skeptical that fortune could blow fair.

But he'd held his breath and rolled the dice, just this once. It wasn't right, what he'd done, but neither was what he'd seen. Now his long shot was paying off.

He might not be a betting man, but he'd gambled, and he'd won.

Still, it gnawed at him. He believed in a day's pay for a day's work, more or less. He didn't trust what came easily, and this had come a hair too easily for comfort's sake. The gnawing feeling had grown, and his stomach had protested until he'd finally listened to his daughter's pleas—Laura had always been a worrier—and driven himself over to Stillwater General.

The flu, no doubt. He should have gotten the shot she nagged him about every year, but he'd had other things on his mind. Now he'd have to take his medicine and let

Laura fuss and fret. In no time, he and CJ would be back on the river, fishing for trout and largemouth bass. Next year, he'd get his shot without complaint. Next year, everything would be different. CJ would be healthy again; Laura would finally be rid of her slack-jawed weasel of a husband.

Clem tugged at the brim of his cap and said a quick prayer of thanks that his grandson took after Laura, not the weasel. Spotting an ambulance in the rearview mirror, he wrestled the van to the side of the road. Another rig followed close behind, lights and sirens wailing, and he wished, for an instant, he could hitch a ride. Shifting the rusted blue van back into drive took an effort that left his arm trembling, and the gnawing sensation grew stronger.

The deal had been too easy, he thought, wiping away the sweat streaming down his face. Like hustling pool.

Stillwater General Hospital was lit up like a Christmas tree. The parking lot was full, cars painted red and white, as if it was homecoming, and half the damn town had turned out to celebrate. He managed to find a spot in a back corner and heaved himself, groaning, out of the van. Figured he'd end up here, of all places, but where else was there to go? Stillwater Gen was the only hospital for nearly seventy miles. He'd had no choice.

He lumbered toward the emergency entrance, impossibly far away. Maybe it was time to give up his daily sausage biscuit. He'd already quit his traditional fishing boat cigar, after all. CJ didn't like the smell, and he'd rather have time on the water with his grandson than any stogie. Things were finally looking up for the Jensens—Laura and CJ were

Jensens at heart, always had been—and he wanted to enjoy every minute of the good times heading their way.

The gnawing sensation grew sharper, tearing at his chest, and he stumbled.

He thought back to the last meeting. True, his associate had been running late. Late enough that he'd started to wonder if the plan had changed, if he'd missed something. But in the end, it went as smooth as ever: a simple exchange over coffee and a sausage biscuit. Far enough out of town to avoid the gossips, public enough to be safe. In the end, everyone got what they wanted, though he hadn't expected his partner to be so cheerful about it.

Too cheerful.

Too easy.

He staggered toward the emergency room doors. They slid open with a whoosh, but a wall of people blocked his path. No one heard his croaking pleas over the noise and confusion.

He'd thought he was the hustler, he realized in a moment of knife-edged clarity. Turned out, *he* was the one who'd been hustled.

Fear reached into his chest and squeezed hard.

He shouldn't have come. He lurched outside again, gulped down cool night air that didn't stop his sweating, and fell onto the closest bench. People rushed past, unheeding, and went inside. They'd be crushed, he thought absently, trying to rub away the pain, struggling for air. He'd sit for a moment. Just a moment, to catch his breath, and then he'd go somewhere else. Somewhere safe.

It was darker now. He steeled himself for the long walk back to the van.

Clem Jensen wasn't a betting man. Flush with confidence and righteousness and foolish, foolish hope, he'd forgotten the most important rule of the game: *never bet against the house.* Now he remembered, as the darkness crowded in, that the house always won.

And he was at their mercy.

ONE

On a list of the five most depressing places to end an engagement, hospital cafeterias take fourth. In my experience, weddings take the top spot; I've been told funerals are a close runner-up, and it seems like a surefire way to spoil a birthday. A lakeside picnic on a beautiful late-summer afternoon squeaks into fifth place, whether you're the one doing the ending or not.

But slot number four belongs to hospital cafeterias: they're grim to begin with, and having your wedding called off over bad coffee and a rubbery egg-white omelet tips things right over to despair.

Though to be honest . . . I wasn't feeling as much despair as I should have.

"I'm sorry, Frankie," Peter Lee, my unexpectedly *ex*-fiancé, said in the same voice he used to deliver terminal diagnoses. "I hope we can still be friends. And colleagues," he added as an afterthought.

I took a sip of my so-called coffee. "Let me get this straight. You're breaking up with me because I covered Mindy's shift last night instead of going to a dinner party?"

He paused a heartbeat too long. "Of course not."

"Her twins didn't come down with strep on purpose." I tugged the elastic out of my chin-length, dark-red hair. The unruly mop of curls sprang free, and I brushed them from my eyes so Peter could better see my glare. "You know the ER is always understaffed on Friday nights. I couldn't say no. Why didn't you go without me?"

This seemed an entirely reasonable solution—preferable, in fact, to me attending yet another stuffy dinner with a hospital bigwig. In the six months since Peter had proposed, nearly every weekend had included some sort of charity gala or dinner party or networking opportunity. Good for Peter, a rising star in Chicago Memorial Hospital's pediatric surgery department. Deadly dull for me, especially compared to the frenetic pace of CM's emergency room, where I was a nurse. But I hadn't had the heart to tell Peter so.

"I didn't *want* to go without you." Frustration crept into his voice. "What's the point of spending the rest of your life with someone if they're always too busy to spend time with you?"

I winced. It wasn't flattering, but he had a point. Lately, whenever I thought about our future together, my lungs and shoulders tightened instinctively, the same way they did when I saw a doctor make a bad call. Not exactly a recipe for marital bliss.

"I'm sorry," I said after a long moment. "You're right."

I fished for the necklace I wore beneath my scrubs. The elaborate platinum and sapphire ring was a hair too loose. Rather than risk it falling off midshift, I'd taken to wearing it on a chain, even when I was nowhere near the hospital.

Which probably should have been my first clue that Peter, while a talented surgeon and genuinely nice guy, wasn't The One. "I can't keep this."

"I guess I should have asked about a return policy." He tried to smile but couldn't quite pull it off.

"They'll take it back," I assured him.

"You're handling this . . . well. Better than I expected," he said cautiously.

"Did you think I was going to make a scene?" My first, youthful engagement (lakeside picnic) had ended with caustic words and bitter weeping, but no witnesses. The second had ended, loud and furious, in front of a room full of people doing the hokey-pokey. (Wedding. Not mine, thankfully.)

This time, however, I felt fine. The sting came from wounded pride, not a broken heart. My eyes were dry, my smile was genuine, and my hand, when I held out the ring to Peter, was perfectly steady. Which should have been my *second* clue.

The third clue—the clincher—was the relief that washed over me as Peter nimbly plucked the ring from my outstretched palm. The aching exhaustion of my twelve-hour shift vanished, and my lungs relaxed for the first time in ages.

I'd been an emergency room nurse for twelve years, but I didn't need medical training to realize the truth: I'd been looking for a way out. Peter, gentleman that he was, had given it to me.

"What are we going to tell people? Our families?" he asked.

I grimaced. Even the idea of breaking the news to my mother sent a chill down my back. Still, telling my family could wait. I could probably put it off until Christmas. If I worked over Christmas, I could put it off even longer. But the news would be all over Chicago Memorial by lunch tomorrow.

Judging from the way the cafeteria staff was gaping, it would be public knowledge by lunch *today*.

My appetite vanished, and I pushed my omelet away.

"I'm off work for the next few days," I said, thinking fast. If I wasn't here, Peter could handle the fallout, spin the story however he wanted. I owed him that much. "Tell them I'm too much of a flake."

"Nobody who has seen you work is going to believe that," he said.

No, they wouldn't. My personal life might be a disaster, but I was good at my job, and everybody who entered the ER knew it. "Tell them you want someone taller."

He tapped his fingers lightly on the table—long, slender surgeon's fingers—exasperation clear. "But I don't."

"It doesn't have to be the truth," I said, and then his true meaning hit me, and I could have bitten my runaway tongue. "Oh. You don't want someone taller."

"Or shorter," he said, holding my gaze.

I looked down at my ringless hands for a moment, acknowledging his words. Then I stood, pulling on my fleece jacket, tucking my curls haphazardly under a knit cap, and swinging my messenger bag over my shoulder. "You're going to make a very lucky woman very happy someday."

"But not you?"

I heard the note of hope in his voice but shook my head. I'd given him the wrong answer once; now I was more careful with my words. "Not me."

★   ★   ★

Three broken engagements, I realized on my train ride home. One was understandable. I'd been young and foolish and a little bit scared. Two was slightly harder to explain, but not unheard of, especially after I'd found my fiancé hooking up with a bridesmaid at our friend's wedding. Three, however, was a pattern. An *issue.*

I'd hoped that by choosing the right guy, at the right time, I'd fixed the problem. But maybe the problem wasn't the fiancés. Maybe it was *me.*

I wasn't against the idea of marriage, exactly. Plenty of my friends were married, and some of them even seemed happy about it. My parents had been wildly in love until my father's death; more than twenty years later, my mother still hadn't remarried. Besides, if I'd hated the idea of marriage, I wouldn't have gotten engaged. Three times. But settling down felt like settling somehow. I liked change, and a challenge, which is why ER nursing was perfect for me—no two cases, no two shifts, were ever the same. When I got tired of a city, it was easy to relocate, since nurses were always in demand.

Try as I might, I couldn't envision a decade, much less a lifetime, with Peter—or anyone else.

Peter was a great guy; he'd find someone soon. Smart, funny surgeons had no trouble meeting women. But he hadn't just been relieved by my breezy acceptance of our breakup. He'd been hurt, and rightly so. I liked to think I was a truthful person, but I'd been dishonest with both of us when I'd accepted his proposal. The realization made me feel small and wormy.

I reached my apartment, a third-floor walk-up in funky-but-gentrifying Wicker Park, grateful I'd turned down Peter's offer to move into his sleek West Loop condo. I'd lived here for almost three years, the longest I'd stayed anywhere since graduating nursing school more than a decade ago. I'd decorated it piecemeal—a burnt-orange velvet sofa, a scarred kitchen table from the thrift store, artwork from my travels covering the teal-blue walls and tucked amid my textbooks and romance novels.

It struck me that while I liked to read about happy endings—I saw too many of the other kind at work—I had no idea what my own might look like.

Clearly, it was time to shake things up. Despite my postshift fatigue, I felt restless. Three broken engagements in thirty-four years was not a track record to be proud of, and there was no one to blame but myself.

I needed to get out of town. I closed the blackout shades in my bedroom against the late-morning sunlight, changed into yoga pants and an ancient Cubs T-shirt, and settled into bed with my laptop, intent on vacation browsing. My perpetually beleaguered budget wouldn't stretch as far as an international flight, but I could probably find something in the States. I snuggled under my down comforter and started checking destinations. Peter's schedule hadn't allowed for a true vacation, and it had been too long since I'd gone on any kind of solo adventure. Now I browsed the possibilities I'd ignored over the last year and a half. Whitewater rafting in Tennessee, scuba diving in Key West, bouldering in Utah . . .

Surfing in San Diego. Perfect: sun, street tacos, and plenty of waves. I could even double up on my adventures;

there were plenty of places to rock-climb in that area, too. The nonrefundable tickets weren't cheap, but I'd been saving my vacation time—and my pennies—for the wedding. Peter could field all the questions about our broken engagement and get his side of the story out first. He was too kindhearted to paint me as the villain (though my guilty conscience whispered he should), but he'd definitely earn sympathy points. Fair enough. He deserved them.

My eyelids drooped as I searched for a hotel, my all-night shift finally catching up with me. Pushing the computer aside, I turned off the light and closed my eyes. With any luck, I'd dream of surfing and sunshine, not Peter's disappointed expression. I let myself tumble into sleep . . .

. . . and woke to the sound of my phone blaring.

I rummaged amid the tangle of blankets, finally spotting the electric-blue case near my feet.

"Yeah?" My voice was thick and raspy with sleep.

"Frankie?"

"Yeah." I checked my watch—it was almost three in the afternoon. I'd slept a whopping four hours, and the abrupt awakening left me disoriented. Then I placed the voice. "Charlie?"

"It's me," my little sister confirmed, her words strangely high-pitched and tremulous.

I stood and stretched, trying to dislodge the tightness that had seized my shoulders again. Charlie didn't call me, as a rule. And I didn't call her. "Is Mom okay?"

Her voice cracked. "Mom's fine. It's the baby."

Instantly, I was as awake as if I'd just downed a double espresso. "I thought you were due at Christmas."

"Thanksgiving," she said, and I felt a pang of guilt. Worst aunt ever, but that's what comes of not talking to your family except on major holidays.

I did some fast math in my head. "You should have another six weeks—you're too early."

"I know," she wailed, the words tumbling out in a rush. "Something's wrong. I've been feeling lousy, so I came in for an extra checkup, and the doctor says my blood pressure is too high, and they keep running tests and looking serious, and I keep asking if the baby's okay, but nobody ever really answers, and what if that means—" She dissolved into giant, hiccupping sobs.

"Breathe. Slowly," I said. "Is Matt there? Put him on."

People often commented on how much Charlie and I looked alike—short, with our mom's red hair and brown eyes and our father's round cheeks and freckles. But the similarities ended at the five-foot mark. Where I was low-key, rolling with the punches, and often acting on impulse, Charlie was devoted to routines, checklists, advance planning, and anything else that could suck the fun out of a situation. While my sister might be tightly wound, however, she was also levelheaded. This kind of hysteria—and the fact she'd resorted to calling me—meant things were truly bad.

"Hey, Frankie."

"Hey, Matt." I pictured Charlie's husband, a big, shambling Viking of a man, an English professor at the local community college. His gentle smile and easygoing nature complemented Charlie perfectly, but I could now hear the strain in his voice as well. "What's going on?"

"Preeclampsia," he said. "She was complaining about headaches and not being able to read inventory reports at the store, and when she came in to the hospital, her blood pressure was sky-high."

"When did they admit her?"

"Yesterday."

"Good," I said. "Preeclampsia's nothing to mess around with."

That was putting it mildly. Unpredictable and fast-moving, preeclampsia could—and did—kill mothers and babies. I'd seen it with my own eyes.

"She's doing great," he said, trying to sound upbeat and failing miserably. "Just gotta get that blood pressure down. We'll be home in no time."

"What was her last BP? Do you remember?"

"One fifty-two over one hundred."

I frowned. With those numbers, Charlie wouldn't be going home tonight. Or at all, most likely, until the baby was born. "What are they giving her?"

"I wrote it down." A pause. "Hydralazine. Magnesium sulfate? And a shot. Betamethasone."

"Tell her it *hurts*," Charlie said in the background.

"Tell her that's normal," I retorted, though the spunk in her tone was a good sign. "The magnesium in the IV is going to burn a little, but it should prevent seizures. The shot is a steroid, to help the baby's lungs develop faster."

"That sounds good," he said. "Isn't it?"

"Healthy lungs are always good." I didn't add that if the doctor was giving Charlie betamethasone, she'd be delivering in days, not weeks. "How's she holding up?"

"Oh, she's a trooper, your sister. Doesn't like bed rest."

"I have a business to run," Charlie called. "And an eight-year-old. I can't stay in bed for the next six weeks!"

If Charlie carried this kid for the next six weeks, it would be a miracle on par with the Cubs winning the World Series.

"Then *rest*, and let me talk to Frankie," Matt told her affectionately. Charlie's arguing grew faint, and he said, "Okay. I'm in the hallway."

"How bad is it? Be straight with me."

The cheerful note dropped away. "Not good. She's so worried about the baby she's in a full-on panic. She's fighting everything the doctor tries to do. She doesn't trust the nurses. And the stress isn't helping her blood pressure." He sighed. "I love your sister, but she is a terrible patient."

"I know." Charlie saw hospitals the same way she had when she was six: the place where our father had gone to get better—and instead, he'd died. Even now, more than twenty-five years later, she didn't trust doctors. Or nurses, come to think of it.

I knew better. During my father's final heart attack, I'd been huddled in a corner of the room, hidden behind a chair, watching as the nurses worked frantically to save him. I'd seen how much they cared, and I'd seen how quickly a life could change—or end. That moment had set me on the path toward nursing—and away from both Stillwater and a life in the family business.

I liked to believe my dad would have understood my decision, even if the rest of my family didn't.

"Where's Riley?" I asked, thinking back to my eight-year-old self and wondering how my niece was handling matters.

"Your mom's watching her. Which probably isn't help-ing anyone's blood pressure."

I paced from kitchen to bedroom and back again. "Charlie needs to calm down. The more her blood pres-sure spikes, the more dangerous it is for her and the baby. She could start having seizures."

He dragged in a breath. "Can you tell her that? She might listen if it came from you."

I had my doubts—giant, Everest-sized doubts—but all I said was, "Put her on."

"Why did Matt talk to you outside?" Charlie asked when she was back on the line. "Is it the baby? Did they find something? It's worse than they're telling me, isn't it?"

"It's exactly what they're telling you," I said in the same brisk-yet-reassuring tone I used with my patients. "You have preeclampsia, and it's serious, but treatable. Every-thing they're doing is to help you and the baby."

"It's a girl," she said.

"It's a *Stapleton* girl," I corrected. "Which means she's a fighter. But you have to help her, Charlie. Calm down. Stop fighting the doctors. Rest and let the meds do their thing."

For a time, the only noise was the beeps and whirrs of the monitors.

"I'm scared," she finally whispered. I closed my eyes at the pleading note in her voice. The same one she'd used when we were kids, a pitiful little wheedle that wound itself around my heart. "Tell me she's going to be okay."

I don't lie to my patients. I never promise what I can't deliver, because I've seen what that does to patients and their families. What it had done to mine. I swallowed and tried to figure out the kindest truth I could give my sister.

Because she was my sister, she understood the meaning behind my silence.

"Come home, Frankie." She drew a great, shuddery breath. "Please."

"I'm not sure what good I can do." I glanced down at my laptop, the screen filled with palm trees and beaches and bargain airfare. I'd wanted a break, the chance to clear my head and get some answers about myself. Going home would only churn up more questions. But I knew how hard it must have been for Charlie to ask, and my resolve softened.

"You can *be here*. With your family." She didn't add "for once," but I heard it all the same.

I had a few days off duty. I could stick around long enough to make sure Charlie and the baby were out of the woods. Spend some time with my niece, Riley. I could—perhaps—put to rest some of the ghosts I'd left behind in Stillwater. By the time I returned to Chicago, the gossip about my failed engagement would have died down.

I wanted to shake things up, and this definitely qualified.

I closed the laptop, bidding farewell to my dreams of San Diego and surfing. "I'm on my way."

TWO

Nestled in a bend of the Illinois River, halfway between the state capital and the state line bordering Missouri, Stillwater was the biggest town in the county—which wasn't saying much. It boasted a high school and a junior college, a historic downtown my mother assured me was thriving, and Stillwater General Hospital. I pulled into the hospital close to ten, parking at the far edge of the emergency lot out of habit.

I stood and stretched in the sharp night air, glad for the down vest I'd thrown on at the last minute. Stillwater Gen had transformed since I'd moved away twelve years ago. The modest rural hospital had become a full-fledged medical center—helipad on the roof, office buildings along the perimeter, two new wings towering over the old three-story brick building. Would my father have lived if this new facility had been around twenty-some years ago?

Some questions have no good answers.

Thanks to traffic, I'd spent almost seven hours in my ancient Subaru with nothing but coffee, staticky radio, and raging self-doubt to keep me company. I was no closer to understanding my serial-engagement ways than when I'd set out from Chicago. I'd anticipated plenty of time to think while I was home—Stillwater wasn't typically a hotbed of excitement—but one look at the emergency entrance proved tonight was anything but typical.

Ambulances from neighboring towns lined the ER driveway, lights flashing in a silent, disjointed rhythm. The sound of radio chatter and indistinct shouting carried across the parking lot, and I could hear the rhythmic thumping of a medical helicopter approaching overhead. Stillwater Gen had been hit with a large-scale trauma, and the department was in triage mode. I wondered how many patients they could take. Stillwater was the biggest trauma center around, but the number of rigs parked outside suggested the ER would be stretched to breaking.

The realization was like a shot of adrenaline. My fingers itched to get inside and help out, to run IVs and apply the right kind of pressure, to *do* something, rather than simply watch. Sitting idly by wasn't in my nature, and I instinctively picked up speed.

Then, with an effort, I slowed my pace. This wasn't my hospital. I wasn't authorized to help—I couldn't even take someone's temperature. I jammed my icy hands into my vest pockets. My job was to help Charlie. Nobody else.

In the ambulance bay, paramedics were unloading a gurney. A fluffy ball of red and white—a pom-pom?—tumbled to the ground as they ran toward the entrance. A nurse met them halfway to the door, checking the IV they'd started and nodding as one of the men rattled off vital signs. I cocked my head, trying to figure out if it was the cadence of the words or the voice itself that sounded familiar. Before I could decide, they disappeared inside the building.

An older man—barrel-chested, his shoulder-length gray hair visible beneath a beat-up black trucker hat, his mustache drooping like walrus tusks—sat hunched on a bench near the main ER entrance. A relative, I guessed, or a witness.

"Busy night," I said. "What happened?"

He grunted, rubbing his arms against the cold.

A warning prickled along my scalp. "Sir? Are you waiting for someone, or do you need help?"

Slowly, he lifted his head to look at me, mouth working soundlessly.

"Sir, are you in pain?"

"Elephant," he rasped after a moment. "On my chest."

Up close, his skin was gray. Rivulets of sweat poured down his face, soaking his faded Harley-Davidson T-shirt though the night was cool.

"What's your name?" I crouched next to him.

"Clem," he managed.

His cap, I noticed, was emblazoned with "World's Best Grandpa."

"Clem, my name's Frankie. I'm a nurse, and I think you're having a heart attack. Were you in the accident, or did you drive here yourself?"

He gripped my arm with surprising force. "Not . . . accident."

The prickling sensation intensified. I could imagine it perfectly. He'd driven himself to the ER only to find it swamped; he'd been overlooked in the chaos.

"I need help!" I shouted toward the silent ambulances. "I have a patient in possible cardiac arrest and we need transport, stat! Somebody help!"

There was no response—the EMTs and paramedics were inside, and nobody in the waiting room could hear me through the dual sets of doors. In an instant, I made my choice. Off-duty or not, I wasn't going to leave a man to die. Charlie and the baby would have to wait.

"Let's get you inside." He shook his head, but I dropped my backpack and slipped an arm around his waist. "I'll help you, okay? Up we go . . ."

I hefted him to his feet, straining under his bulk. A muscle in my back twinged in warning, but I ignored it and tried to propel Clem forward. No good. He outweighed me by at least a hundred pounds, and he couldn't support himself. Before we both toppled over, I eased him back to the bench. "I'm getting a wheelchair. Hang on, Clem."

I sprinted through the main entrance, doors sliding open to admit me—and stopped short. A solid mass of people, all clamoring for answers about their loved ones, blocked my way. I shoved my way through the crowd and saw countless teenagers in Stillwater High colors, sprawled in chairs and slumped on the floor. Most had the lacerations and glassy-eyed look associated with car accidents. But there were too many kids for a car accident, I realized. Someone mentioned a game, and it hit me—not a car crash. A *bus* crash. In football season. No wonder the ER was jammed.

Unfortunately, Clem's heart attack wasn't going to wait for a more convenient time.

"I need help!" I cried, but my voice was lost amid the clamor. "Someone get me a wheelchair!"

I spotted a sturdy-looking teenager with mouse-brown hair, a panicked expression, and a deep-purple blazer embroidered with the word *volunteer*. I grabbed her arm. "You! Get me a wheelchair. Or a gurney. Outside. *Now!*"

She stared at me, then whirled away and sprinted down the hall like a scared rabbit. I cursed under my breath and fought my way outside again to check on Clem, who was looking worse. "Clem, hang in there. We're going to take care of you."

What *we*? Nobody else had shown up. The EMTs were still inside. The ambulances stood, lights whirling, doors hanging open, just as before.

Doors open.

I raced to the first rig and hoisted myself into the back. "Nitro, nitro, nitro," I muttered, yanking on drawers and peering at the contents. "There you are."

Nitroglycerine spray won't stop a heart attack, but it can relieve chest pain, at least temporarily. I was hoping it would get Clem on his feet long enough for us to make it inside.

I gave him the spray and counted to sixty. "Is that better?"

He dipped his chin and groaned.

"Clem, stay with me. Tell me about your grandkids. What are their names?"

"Just CJ," he wheezed as I took his pulse: fast and thready. "He's eight."

"So is my niece," I said. "I bet he's a handful."

Clem's smile was more like a grimace. "Wanted . . . to . . . help."

"Don't they all?" I said, dosing him a second time. "Let's try walking again."

He shook his head and tried to twist away. Despite his protests, I hoisted him to his feet, my muscles burning.

We took a step. And another. And another, just as pain tore through my back, so fierce I nearly let go of Clem.

An instant before I crumpled to the ground, bringing Clem with me, a soft voice said, "I found a wheelchair."

I looked up. The volunteer I'd yelled at earlier stood breathless and red-faced, her hands gripping the back of a wheelchair.

"I stole it from admitting."

"Good girl," I gasped as she maneuvered the chair behind Clem.

Together we eased Clem into the seat, and I set off at a run for the ambulance bay, ignoring the burning along my spine, the girl at my heels. The automatic doors slid open, and we were in. I only hoped we weren't too late.

If the lobby had been chaos, the ER itself was a cyclone—noisy and fast-moving, but purposeful. The staff dashed from one room to another, barking information and commands. Sobs and moans filled the air, and the PA system called out a nonstop litany of doctors and departments.

I'm too small to move patients as big as Clem by myself, as proven by the fiery pain in my back, but I've got a good set of lungs, and now I put them to use. "Hey! This guy's gonna code! Somebody help!"

Every hospital has its own lingo and procedures, a language you only learn through experience. But a code is universal—it's like shouting fire in a theater, and it gets you immediate attention.

Although . . . not always the attention you expect.

A doctor, stocky and scowling, shot out of a nearby exam room, halting when he realized I wasn't one of his staff. His ice-blue gaze flickered to the girl beside me, brow lowering, and he snapped, "You're not supposed to be back here."

"This man—"

"I'm in the middle of a multivictim trauma. Get in line."

"Excuse me?" Doctors have egos, to be sure, but this wasn't the time. "He's a classic MI. Chest pain, shortness of—"

"Take him to triage," he said with a wave of his hand, and turned away.

My vision hazed with anger. Clem had been waiting, alone and terrified, in the dark. More waiting wasn't the answer. "Forget triage. I'll take him to the cath lab myself."

When patients present with a myocardial infarction—a heart attack—the best thing to do is take them to the cardiac catheterization lab, so we can find the blocked artery and use a balloon to open it up. Ideally, you do it within sixty minutes—but I had no idea how long Clem had been sitting outside. We could be at the nineteenth minute, or the fifty-ninth. I turned to the volunteer, frozen in terror beside me. "Lead the way. And grab me some defibrillator pads, just in case."

The doctor spun around. I met his glare with my own, my words arrow-sharp. "Chest pain radiating to the left arm, shortness of breath. Pulse thready and 112 bpm. Administered two sprays of translingual nitro at three-minute intervals. You need to—"

"Start a line!" he bellowed to the nurse standing three feet away. "Four milligrams morphine, oxygen, put him on a monitor. I want his troponin levels, stat."

"We're out of rooms," she warned.

"Then do it in the hallway," he snapped. "He won't care about the view."

He was a jerk, but at least he was a competent jerk. In seconds, orderlies were whisking Clem down the hall, transferring him to a gurney while one of the nurses ran for a cardiac cart. The nameless doctor turned to me, his tone coldly polite. "You're a family member?"

"I've never seen him before. He was on the bench outside, and I recognized the symptoms, so I stepped in."

His veneer of politeness vanished. "And you happened to be carrying nitro spray with you?"

I paused. "I pulled it off an ambulance."

"I see." His lip curled as he took in my rumpled sweater and tattered jeans. "I take it you're qualified to diagnose and treat cardiac cases."

"Yes, actually." His sniping and the callous way he'd treated Clem needled me even more than a typical doctor's bluster. I stuck my hand out, matched my tone to his. "Frankie Stapleton. I'm an ER nurse."

"Not here, you're not." He ignored my outstretched hand. "Paul Costello, attending. Now . . . get the hell out of my ER. Both of you."

The rest of the staff looked away, unwilling to meet my eyes or even nod encouragement. It wasn't as if I expected them to throw me a parade, but I had saved a man's life. The cold shoulder seemed a little extreme.

Stiffly, mindful of my injured back and wounded pride, I headed out. My stricken volunteer trudged after me. "Elevator?" I muttered, and she pointed to the correct hallway wordlessly. No doubt she felt even worse—the first time a doctor chews you out is terrifying, especially when you haven't done anything wrong.

"Thanks for your help," I said once we were out of earshot. "I couldn't have gotten Clem inside without you."

"You're welcome," she said with a weak smile.

I pushed the elevator button before realizing I had no idea where Charlie was. "Which floor is maternity?"

"Four."

"Great." I paused, noticing the tears welling in her eyes. "Hey, don't listen to that guy. You did great tonight."

She nodded, tears spilling over.

"What's your name, kid?"

The elevator doors slid open, but she didn't follow me.

"Meg." She sniffled. "Costello."

"Costello?" The doors began to close, but I held them open with my foot. "Costello like that attending?"

She stared at the tips of her running shoes. "He's my dad."

I closed my eyes. "Perfect. Just perfect."

In the twenty minutes since arriving at Stillwater Gen, I'd managed to save a life, make an enemy, and reduce a teenage girl to tears.

Even for me, it was quite a Saturday night.

I tapped my foot, restless as the elevator rose. It felt strange to be in a new hospital, to walk around in civilian clothes instead of my usual scrubs.

Stranger still, nobody had asked for identification. At Chicago Memorial, you couldn't get past the front door without proper authorization. Here, I'd made it through the ER, across the lobby, and onto the elevators without a single person questioning me. Even taking into account the bus accident, the lack of security made me uneasy. Only when I arrived at the maternity ward's waiting room, surrounded by pastel seascapes and parenting magazines, did someone asked for ID.

"Room 422?" said the nurse behind the window, eyebrows lifting. She buzzed me through the security door. "You're the sister, right? The nurse?"

"That's me. Frankie."

"Rachel," she replied. Her smile disappeared as soon as I asked how Charlie was doing.

"She's hanging in there," Rachel replied, running a hand over her sleek brown pixie cut. Her tone suggested it hadn't been easy for anyone. She walked me to the nurses' station, then pointed. "Down this hall, last door on the left."

"Thanks. I'm guessing I missed evening rounds?"

"Yeah, but Dr. K is around somewhere. I'll let her know you're here."

"Great."

Charlie's room was at the end of the hallway, the door standing partly open. I took a breath and slipped inside. Clad in a hospital gown, my sister lay curled on her side, squinting at an outdated laptop, the wide black blood pressure cuff wrapped around her arm like a mourning band. Next to the bed, the fetal monitor whirred as it printed a continuous record of the baby's heart rate.

"You're supposed to be sleeping," I said softly.

She jolted and looked up. I was startled by how dull her complexion was, the way worry and fatigue had robbed her dark-brown eyes of their usual sparkle and surrounded them with purplish rings instead. Usually, Charlie kept her thick auburn hair in a braid—like me, she didn't have the time to wrestle with the unruly curls—but now it hung limp and lifeless down her back. "I needed to look over these invoices. Where have you been? I thought you'd get here ages ago."

It was a split-second decision to lie. I'd spent years deflecting accusations that I cared more about my patients than my own family. Telling Charlie I'd put off seeing her to help a perfect stranger, no matter how ill he was, wouldn't help our relationship or her blood pressure.

"Traffic was lousy," I said, tucking my messy hair behind my ears. "The store can wait. Let someone else handle it."

"I *can't*. Besides, it's not as if I'm getting any rest here. Honestly, we'd be better off at home."

"You wouldn't," I assured her, and took the laptop away. "And you know it."

Her hand rubbed slow circles across her stomach. Even from this position, I could tell she wasn't full term. Emergency room nurses are trained to expect the worst, but I forced myself not to think of all the complications a six-week-early baby could have.

"Everything they say is a jumble," she said. "It's all numbers and medicines, and I can't figure out what any of it means, or why it's happening. How can I let them help me when they won't tell me what's going on?"

It sounded petulant, but I heard the fear at the heart of her words. It made sense—Charlie was scared witless, and just like when we were kids, she was lashing out. My back twinged ominously as I lowered myself into the bedside chair. "Well, now I'm here to translate, so stop giving them a hard time."

She bit her lip. "I'll try."

I gestured to the IV stand where three clear plastic bags hung at eye level. "The bag on the right is what we call maintenance fluid. It's to keep you hydrated. The one in the middle is magnesium sulfate, to prevent seizures. The last one is a blood pressure medication called hydralazine. The bands across your stomach are monitoring the baby's heart rate and any contractions you might have, same as when you had Riley."

"Is the baby okay?"

I glanced at the monitor and saw the regular rhythm of peaks and valleys. "She looks good. Unlike your blood pressure."

She rubbed her temples. "The drugs aren't working, are they? My headache hasn't gone away."

"Give it time," I said as a knock sounded at the door.

A tall, slender woman wearing a doctor's coat and pale-blue scrubs peeked her head in. "Frankie?"

"Garima? You're Dr. K?" Garima Karundhi had been in my class at Stillwater High School, but we'd lost touch, just as I had with everyone else. Her black hair was coiled neatly at her nape, and her eyes behind thick black-rimmed glasses flicked over me in a fast, thorough assessment.

"I am, indeed. I moved back after my residency; they wanted someone to grow this department, and I wanted to be close to my mom and dad. You're at Chicago Memorial these days, aren't you? What level is their trauma program?"

"Level one, adult and peds." The highest designation—the place where the most critical cases, young and old, were sent. A grueling, relentless, exhilarating place. I missed it already.

"You always were an adrenaline junkie," she said with a grin. "I'm glad you're here. Charlie could use a friendly face."

Charlie and I hadn't been friendly for years, but I nodded. "Rachel said you'd rounded already."

Even on the maternity ward, doctors only checked in on patients once or twice a day. Garima's presence this late at night was *not* a good sign.

"What can I say? I like to keep an eye on things," she said, brisk and deliberately cheerful as she lifted the blanket to examine my sister's swollen feet. "How are you feeling, Charlie? Have you been able to get some sleep?"

"Not really," she admitted meekly.

"Head still hurt? Blurred vision?"

Charlie nodded, and Garima examined the same monitor printout I'd looked at, her expression betraying nothing. Finally she said, "We're going to up your dosages a bit—I'll have Rachel come in to change out the IV bags."

"Can't Frankie do it?"

"Not my hospital." I shook my head and tried not to think about the nitro spray I'd given Clem. "I'm strictly an observer."

Before Charlie could protest, Garima added, "Frankie can double-check the medication, if it makes you feel better."

Charlie considered, and I gave her hand a gentle squeeze. She sighed. "I guess that's okay."

"Good." Garima tipped her head toward the hallway. "Let's catch up, Frankie."

I gently drew my hand away and levered myself out of the chair, promising, "Five minutes. I'll be right outside."

Garima shut the door behind us. The bright light of the corridor emphasized the frown lines suddenly bracketing her mouth.

"What happened to you?" she demanded. "You look like you're in pain."

"Wrenched my back transporting a patient." Her eyebrows lifted. "I know, I know. Rookie mistake."

She nodded. "Rachel can get you a cold pack, if you need it."

"I'm fine," I said, waving away the offer. "What about Charlie? Two days before she delivers, you think? Three?"

"I'm hoping for more, but . . ." She took off her glasses, rubbed the bridge of her nose. "She's not responding to the hydralazine, and it doesn't help that her blood pressure goes up every time she sees a stethoscope. Even with an ideal patient, this kind of situation could go either way."

"And Charlie's not exactly ideal."

"It helps that you're here. This is the calmest I've seen her since she was admitted." Putting her glasses back on, she peered at me. "How long are you planning to stay?"

"I've got a few days before I need to be back in Chicago," I said. "You think she'll deliver by then?"

"Probably. The baby will have to go to the NICU for several weeks, at the very least. How much vacation time do you have?"

"Some," I said. "But . . ."

"Take it," she said firmly. "Charlie's going to need you, regardless of when the baby comes. Her husband's a good guy, but between Riley and the store, she'll be stretched pretty thin. And your mom . . ."

She didn't need to say anything more. She couldn't, actually.

"Francesca! What took you so long? Why didn't you call? Where have you been?"

I flinched. Garima sighed.

Lila Stapleton—my mother—had arrived.

★　　★　　★

"This is what it takes to get you home? A medical emergency?" My mother turned to Garima. "Twelve years she's been away. Would you treat your mother like that?"

"Depends on how she treated me," Garima replied.

"I came home at Christmas," I protested.

"Fine. Ten months." My mother—all four feet eleven inches of her, silver-streaked hair pulled back in an immaculate bun—paused to inspect me. "I wish you'd grow your hair longer, Francesca. And pastels wash you out," she said, fingering my pale-blue sweater. "How many times have I told you to wear jewel tones?"

"It's a hospital, Mom. Nobody cares how I look."

"You should care. Just because you're engaged to that doctor doesn't mean you can let yourself go. Did she tell you, Garima? Engaged to a surgeon, not that we've ever met him."

Garima stifled a grin as I slid my left hand behind my back.

Too late. My mother grabbed my wrist, eyes narrowing.

"Where's your ring?"

I shrugged, feigning nonchalance. "I gave it back. We called off the wedding."

"What? Again?" Another nurse poked her head into the hallway, took one look, and wisely retreated.

"Mrs. Stapleton," Garima cut in, "I need you to keep your voice down. This is a hospital, and people—including your daughter—are trying to rest. Now, I'm going to write that order for the nurses; you two should visit with Charlie, but avoid any subjects that might become heated."

My mother's mouth snapped shut, though her eyes promised the topic wasn't closed. "Of course. Say hello to your mother for me, Garima. Let her know book club is at my house next week."

"I will. Lovely to see you," Garima said and escaped. Before my mom could start in again, I ducked back into Charlie's room.

"You have a visitor," I trilled.

"Mom?" Charlie pushed herself up on her elbows. "Why are you here? You're supposed to open the store tomorrow. You should be in bed."

"What's more important? Selling leaf blowers and potted mums or checking on my daughter?"

"We can't afford to lose any sales, Mom. None of this is going to come cheap," Charlie said, tension creeping back into her voice. I remembered the way she was staring at the laptop and wondered if the baby wasn't the only thing stressing her out.

"Charlotte, relax," ordered my mother, in the least relaxing voice possible. "I can set my own bedtime, thank you very much. And now that your sister is here, I can go to sleep knowing you're in good hands."

"She was in good hands before," I said. "The staff here is top-notch."

"Well, she's in better hands. Family hands. Francesca, I've made up a bed for you."

I knew a trap when I saw one. The minute I walked in the door of my childhood home, the interrogation would start. "I'm staying here tonight," I said quickly, shooting my sister a desperate glance. "To keep an eye on Charlie and the baby."

My mother looked horrified. "But there's only a couch!"

"I'd feel better if she stayed," Charlie cut in. The automatic blood pressure cuff went off with a hiss. Conversation halted, and I glanced at the numbers: one sixty over one ten—definitely higher.

"I'm staying," I said firmly.

Charlie exhaled, relief plain on her face, and my mother, for once, seemed to understand. "I suppose it will be nice for you to have sister time," she admitted. She bent and kissed Charlie on the forehead. "Call if you need me."

"I will," Charlie replied.

We both exhaled, audibly, as the sound of Mom's footsteps faded. "She means well," Charlie said.

"I know. But thanks for the save."

She nodded, and the IV stand beeped shrilly. Her hand flew to her stomach. "What is that? What's wrong?"

"Nothing. The bag's almost empty, that's all," I said, and pointed to the digital readout. "Someone will be in to swap it out soon."

Moments later, Rachel appeared with a fresh IV bag in hand.

"See, she scans it to make sure they're giving you the right medication. That's how they know they're giving you the exact thing Dr. K ordered. She'll set the flow rate and infusion times to match the order, so you get a nice, steady dose."

"You're sure the medicine won't hurt the baby?"

"Positive. They're doing exactly what I would do."

She settled back against the pillows, biting her lip. When we were alone again, she said, "Everything seems louder at night, don't you think?"

I listened, hearing the beeps and chirps of various machines, the PA system in the hall, the conversations of the other patients, and the faint, outraged wail of a newborn. I wondered if they'd gotten Clem to the cardiac lab, if they'd found his family, if his prognosis was good. "I guess. It's quieter than the ER."

"You're used to it," she said and yawned hugely. "Thanks for coming home. I know you hate it."

"I don't hate it, exactly. It's just . . . slow." Too full of memories. I stared at the bare space on my left ring finger, but instead of picturing sapphire and platinum, I saw a tiny diamond chip, catching late-summer light.

"And you go fast." She paused, following my gaze. "Noah MacLean is still in town, you know. He never left."

"I'm aware," I said stiffly.

"And now you're in town."

"Not permanently."

She nodded and closed her eyes. "I figured. But I'm glad you're here."

"Me, too," I said. To my surprise, I meant it.

★　　★　　★

Well before dawn, I woke with a start, panic propelling me from sleep. Charlie snored delicately, all her monitors humming along. From the hall came the quiet bustle of late-night nursing—lowered voices, gentle knocks, faint newborn wails. I sifted through the remnants of my dreams, trying to figure out why my instincts were shrieking and my shoulders cramped with worry.

Nursing and rock-climbing have a lot in common. Both require equipment and experience, but those can only take you so far. Sometimes, when you're faced with an especially tricky patient or a rough ascent, you need to rely on your gut to figure out the next move. Mine was warning me that something was off.

"Everything okay?" Rachel asked as I wandered out of Charlie's room.

"Yeah, she's asleep. Her vitals look good," I added. "I just need to stretch."

My back, at least, was no longer throbbing, which I took as a stroke of luck.

"Hey, is this yours?" Rachel hefted my backpack onto the counter.

"It is!" I'd dropped the lime-green bag while I'd been treating Clem and hadn't thought about it since. "Where did you find it?"

"Someone dropped it off. I didn't see who."

I frowned. So much for a locked ward. "Thanks. I'll grab it on my way back."

She flashed me a thumbs-up and returned to her paperwork.

According to the directory on the elevator wall, the second floor housed cardiac patients. I wasn't about to risk the wrath of Costello by checking for Clem in the ER. After this much time, Clem had either been transferred to the cardiac ward . . .

. . . or the morgue.

Despite Costello's abrasive manner, he struck me as a good doctor—fast, decisive, smart. So I took my chances and headed to the cardiac wing.

Once again, I marveled at the lax security as I stepped off the elevators. If I'd known what room I was looking for, I could have walked right in. Instead, I approached the male nurse on duty. He glanced up at me through wire-rimmed glasses, shaved head gleaming under the fluorescent lights.

"I'm looking for a patient brought in tonight?" I tucked my hair behind my ears, but it was a losing proposition—bedhead had turned my curls even more wild. I must have looked like a mess, so I kept my tone brusque and official. "Late sixties, probable MI. Mustache."

"You're his daughter?" he asked, standing to greet me.

I hesitated, and his eyebrows rose.

"No," I admitted, shoulders dropping.

"You're the one who found him?"

"That's me," I said. I shouldn't have been surprised at how quickly the news had spread. It was the curse of a small town—everyone knew you, even when you didn't know them. "Frankie Stapleton."

"Marcus Rollins," he said. "Stapleton like the hardware store?"

"Yep. That's my family," I said and waited for the inevitable response.

"Oh, I get it—Frankie. Cute."

"Yeah, my dad thought so, too." Stapleton and Sons Hardware, founded in 1873. There'd been at least one son in every generation to run the business . . . until I'd come along, and my dad realized a boy's *name* might be as close as he'd be able to get to continuing the legacy. So, Francesca and Charlotte, who hyphenated her last name for the sake of the store. I wondered how much pressure my nieces would feel to carry on the tradition. I wondered if they'd want to escape the way I did.

Of course, the store wasn't the only reason I had fled. *Noah MacLean's still in town. He never left.* Hadn't that been the problem? The knowledge was surprisingly painful, even now. Time, as it turns out, doesn't heal all wounds.

Marcus cleared his throat.

"Sorry," I said. "Long night. I wanted to check on Clem."

"Sleeping," Marcus said. "The man has enough morphine in him to bring down an elephant."

Elephant on my chest, Clem had said, and my instinct prickled again. "I don't suppose I could take a look at his chart?"

"No can do. You all don't have privacy laws in Chicago?"

He was right, but I tried again. "It's just . . . I found him, you know? I feel responsible."

Marcus drummed his fingers on the desk. "Word is, you went at it with Dr. Costello when you brought the patient in."

If scientists could harness the power of the hospital grapevine, our energy crisis would be solved. I smiled weakly. "He's probably not going to invite me for a round of golf any time soon."

"Golf's boring," Marcus replied. "Did you cry?"

It would be a cold day in hell before an egomaniac like Paul Costello made me cry. "Hardly."

"Glad to hear it." He stood, folding his bulky arms and giving me a stern look. "I'm going to check on another patient. That's Mr. Jensen's chart right there on the monitor. I wouldn't suggest looking at it . . . unless you're trying to get on Costello's bad side."

"We wouldn't want that," I deadpanned.

"No indeed." He winked broadly. "Room 214, by the way."

"Thanks, Marcus."

He ignored me and strode off down the hall, humming a Jimi Hendrix song.

I glanced around. The central desk was deserted, though probably not for long. I could hear the murmurs from other rooms—nurses attending to patients or quietly conversing while checking supplies. I had a few minutes at most.

I scanned the chart quickly, ears pricked for approaching footsteps. According to the chart, the cardiology team had put a stent in, opening up Clem's artery and restoring the flow of blood to his heart. I was surprised to see his drug history included anticoagulants; the medications listed should have prevented the clot that had blocked his arteries. The rest of the procedure had gone as planned, happily. Clem's last few rounds of vitals—oxygen levels, heart rate, respiratory rate, blood pressure, and more—looked stable, and the tension ebbed from my shoulders.

Out of the corner of my eye, I spotted another nurse approaching the desk. Before she could ask what I was doing, I swiveled the monitor back into place and headed toward Clem's room.

Clem's snores were audible from the hallway. I slipped inside, careful to move lightly. Patients rarely get an uninterrupted stretch of sleep, especially on a critical care floor, and I hated to be the one who woke him. Everything looked as it should: monitors registering his vitals, clearly labeled bags of IV fluid dangling from the stand, and the infusion pump working at the proper rate. Considering the condition Clem had been in when I found him, this was a best-case scenario. So why did I still feel uneasy?

I settled cross-legged into the bedside chair, letting my thoughts drift, hoping whatever was bothering me would rise to the surface.

The answer didn't appear, but my eyelids grew heavy as the day caught up to me. Sometime later, I woke to the sound of the door opening, light from the hallway slashing across the floor. Slow footsteps approached.

"Hey, Marcus?" I whispered. The footsteps stopped. "Are you sure Clem was taking his meds?"

He didn't respond. I stretched, rolling my shoulders to dislodge the tension knotted there. "I was thinking . . ."

The door closed with a decisive click. Marcus was gone, and I decide to follow his lead, ignoring the whisper of warning that hovered at the edge of my mind.

THREE

I'd planned to slip back into Charlie's room and squeeze in a few more hours of sleep, but Garima met me at the door of the maternity unit, grim-faced and rumpled.

"You slept in the on-call room?" I asked after she'd let me in.

"Yes, and it's a good thing I did. Where have you been?"

"Checking on a patient. What's wrong?"

Garima bit off the words as we strode toward Charlie's room. "Fetal distress on the monitor."

"What? I checked on her"—I glanced at my watch—"three hours ago."

Had I been in with Clem for that long? Guilt twisted my stomach.

"That was three hours ago. This is now." She handed me the tapes, and I scanned the narrow strips of graph paper as she continued, "Charlie's BP is spiking, she's spilling more protein . . . she's not responding to treatment. We can't wait any longer."

"You want to do a C-section?" I asked, catching her arm before she entered Charlie's room. "She's going to freak out."

"Which is why I'm telling you first. I want to go soon. My suspicion is that when this goes bad, it will go bad quickly. I'd much rather get ahead of it than try to catch up. Agreed?"

I traced the peaks and valleys of my niece's heartbeat, too jagged and extreme for comfort. I knew the statistics about premature babies, knew the terminology and the treatments and the outcomes. But this baby wasn't a statistic. She was family.

And she was in trouble.

★　　★　　★

"I don't understand." Charlie's eyes filled. "Is this my fault?"

"Absolutely not," Garima said. "Even with a good night's rest and increased medication, your blood pressure keeps going up. This condition is out of your control, but the treatment isn't. We have every reason to believe the outcome will be good. Dr. Solano is an excellent neonatologist, and he'll be in the OR with us, ready to go the second the baby comes out."

"Doesn't she need more time to grow?"

"The betamethasone shot will have developed her lungs. She's showing signs of distress, and the longer we wait, the more dangerous it becomes," Garima replied.

Charlie dashed at her tears. "Frankie? What do you think?"

I took both her hands in mine, squeezing them tightly. "You trust me?"

She pressed her lips together and nodded.

"Then let's go have a baby."

Things moved quickly after that—Matt rushed to the hospital, the neonatologist checked in, and Charlie was prepped for surgery. I rarely saw procedures outside of the emergency room OR, and the difference was startling—all swift, smooth motion, efficient but not rushed.

We hit a rough patch right before Charlie was taken into the operating suite, when she realized Matt wouldn't be allowed inside.

"It's hospital policy," Rachel the nurse explained. "A regular C-section is one thing, but nobody is allowed in the OR during an emergency C-section except staff."

"You'll be unconscious," I said, before Charlie could respond. "Besides, what if he keels over when they start? Everyone should be paying attention to you and the baby. He passes out, cracks his head on the floor . . . it's a distraction."

"Messy, too." Matt tucked a wisp of her hair beneath her surgical cap. "I'll be in the recovery room when you wake up."

"We both will," I said.

"No!" she cried as Rachel began wheeling down the hallway. "You have to stay with the baby."

"The doctors won't let me see her until she's stable," I said.

"But you can wait outside, right? You can be there when they bring her to the NICU." She twisted to face me, wild-eyed.

"Of course," I said. "I'll go in as soon as I'm allowed."

"Rowan," she said, weeping now. "Her name is Rowan, and I don't want her to be alone. Promise you'll stay with her."

"I promise."

"It's time," Rachel said in a low voice.

I bent and kissed Charlie's forehead. "Hang in there, okay? Rowan and I will see you soon."

Carefully, I pried her fingers from my arm, and they whisked her through the doors, the bright lights and chill air on the other side a stark contrast to the warm pastel hallway I'd been left in.

Matt looked at me, haggard, hollow-cheeked, and speechless.

"Recovery room," I ordered. "When she wakes up, the first thing she sees should be your face. Do you want me to stay until they bring her in?"

He shook his head. "I swear Charlie's got radar. She'll know if we're not where we should be."

He was right, so I left him and went to wait for my niece.

★   ★   ★

I bypassed the main nursery, a cheerful, yellow room with wide viewing windows. Only a few red-faced bundles lay in their clear bassinets; the rest, no doubt, were rooming in with their mothers. Rowan would head directly to the neonatal intensive care unit, farther down the hallway, where state-of-the-art equipment and specially trained nurses would give her constant care. I paced back and forth in front of the NICU doors, reviewing everything I'd ever learned about preterm babies, trying to remember who in the neonatal unit back home could give me a quick refresher.

The brightly lit hallway seemed to narrow as I stalked from one end to the other, over and over again. A stream of random images played on a constant loop in my head: Peter's hand cupping my engagement ring, Clem's "World's Best Grandpa" hat, Charlie's terrified eyes. I checked my phone countless times, but the only calls and texts were from Peter—which I didn't return. I wanted desperately to move, to find a way to burn off the fear and adrenaline coursing through me, but I couldn't risk missing Rowan. All I could do was wait and walk and worry. I discovered a new sympathy for every family member who had ever paced my ER lobby.

Some time later, my mother strode into the ward. Despite the early morning hour, she was immaculate in a fresh pair of tweed pants and an emerald-green twin set, though her eyes were sharp and dark with worry. My niece, Riley, followed behind. She'd grown at least four inches since I'd last seen her, bony legs covered in bruises, wearing a bright-blue soccer jersey and purple leopard-print leggings. Despite my mother's attempts to tame Riley's hair, her fiery-red braided pigtails were coming undone, and her face still bore sticky traces of breakfast. She looked like a fierce, tiny street urchin.

She was probably driving my mom nuts, and I grinned for the first time in what felt like days.

"Hey, Riley." I waved. "How'd you two get in here?"

"Grandma made the nurse let us in."

"I figured. Mom, Charlie's still in surgery. There's nothing to do but wait." I checked my watch, startled to see I'd been pacing for less than twenty minutes.

"Fine. We'll wait together."

"Aren't you supposed to be opening the store?"

She smoothed her sleeves. "Your Uncle Marshall's help-ing out."

"Uncle Marshall is, like, eighty." He also wasn't my uncle, technically, just a longtime friend of my father's. He'd been looking out for us ever since my father died, lending a hand at the store or around the house whenever my mom needed it. "You can't expect him to handle the Sunday crowds."

"What crowds?" she muttered. "Besides, he's seventy. And spry."

"Still—"

Riley piped up. "Is my mom okay?"

"Of course," my mother replied. "Riley, there's a rest-room down the hall. Please wash your face and hands."

Riley didn't move, her eyes fixed on mine.

"Young lady, we are not going to track germs and jam into a place for new babies. Go scrub."

Riley's mouth settled into a mutinous line, and I had a sudden memory of her second Christmas. Toddler Riley had spent the entire day defeating every childproofing device Charlie had installed, and there had been a *lot* of devices.

Riley and I were going to get along well.

"Your mom's having an operation," I said. "They decided it was better for her to have the baby today, rather than wait."

"Is the baby sick?"

"Not exactly. She's just . . . early. She's like a cookie that hasn't been fully baked. Still delicious, but a little fragile."

My mother made a strangled noise.

"Will my mom be okay? Is she going to—" Riley broke off, turning away to wipe her eyes on her shirt.

"Your mother's going to be fine," my mom said, simultaneously producing a clean tissue and sweeping her up in a hug. "Everyone's going to be fine. I promise."

I ground my teeth. My mom knew only too well how quickly a situation could turn catastrophic. She had no right to make promises.

"Riley, look at me," I said, stepping forward.

She wriggled away from my mother and met my gaze.

"Your mom told you what I do."

She nodded cautiously. "You're a nurse."

"I am. I'm a very, very good nurse, so you can believe what I tell you. I won't lie. Even if a lie might make you feel better, I will always tell you the truth. Got it?"

She nodded again, chin quivering.

"Francesca," my mother hissed. "You are not helping."

I ignored her and focused on Riley's tearstained face.

"I don't think your mom is going to die. I really don't. I am ninety-nine percent sure she's going to be okay. But I can't promise, because ninety-nine percent isn't the same as one hundred. Does that make sense?"

Her lower lip trembled. "Okay."

"Okay. Here's what I *can* promise you. I will take care of your mom. I will do everything I can—one hundred percent—to make sure she and your baby sister come home safe and sound. Does that work for you?"

Riley sniffled. "Yes."

"Good," I said. "You two should visit the cafeteria. Grandma can have some coffee, you can have some hot chocolate, and when we know more, I'll find you."

"Hand washing first," my mother ordered. When Riley had scampered off, she turned to me. "She is *eight years old*."

I shrugged. "Doesn't mean we should lie to her."

"She's sensitive. You'd understand this if you had children of your own." She paused and went in for the kill. "What happened with Peter? I thought you'd finally . . ."

"I wasn't one hundred percent," I said as Riley reappeared, only marginally cleaner. "Mom, can we not do this now? We've got more to worry about than my love life."

"I wasn't aware you *had* a love life," she said archly.

I rolled my eyes. "Make sure Grandma gets decaf, Riley."

★　　★　　★

A bit before seven, Garima appeared outside the NICU, a coffee in each hand. I leapt to my feet, ignoring the twinge in my lower back.

"Easy, Auntie," she said, passing me a steaming cup. "So far, so good. Charlie's in recovery with Matt, and the baby—"

"Rowan," I croaked.

She grinned. "Rowan is hanging tough. They're getting her stabilized, but Dr. Solano likes how she looks."

"Thank you," I whispered, and sagged against the wall.

"You're welcome," she replied, draining half the cup in one go. "Busy night, huh? Nice save on that cardiac patient."

The coffee was strong enough to chew, and I inhaled the rich, dark scent. "Thanks. Any fatalities from the bus wreck?"

"Happily, no. A few critical cases, a few staying for observation. Could have been a lot worse. I also heard you and Paul Costello hit it off."

"That's one way to put it. Is he always so charming?"

She raised an eyebrow. "I once heard him refer to his hands as God's gift to emergency medicine."

I tried not to gag. "His kid seems nice."

"Meg? She's a sweetheart. Painfully shy, but who wouldn't be with a father like that?"

Which explained why she'd been volunteering at a hospital on a Saturday instead of at the football game with the rest of Stillwater High.

"Come on," Garima said, tapping her ID badge against a sensor by the NICU door. The lock glowed green, and she hauled the door open. "Let's get you gloved and gowned."

A blonde, middle-aged nurse looked up as we entered. "Hey, Dr. K! Heard we've got an incoming?"

"Yep, and here's her Aunt Frankie. Donna, can you get her settled in? I'm going to check on the new mama."

"Sure thing," Donna said and waved me back.

"By the way," Garima said, "Charlie wanted me to tell you to stay put."

"I am!" I protested.

"She seems to think it's not your strong suit," Garima replied as she left. "Glad to see you're proving her wrong."

Donna gestured to the soap dispenser and passed me a nail brush. "Here you go."

"Thanks," I said. "I'm Frankie, by the way."

Donna's eyes crinkled with mischief. "Oh, I know who you are."

I groaned as I scrubbed beneath my nails. "Costello?"

"He's a piece of work," she agreed, handing me a tissue-thin blue gown. "Who knows how long that man could have sat outside if you hadn't noticed him? You saved his life."

"I hope so," I said softly, remembering what I'd told Riley. No guarantees.

Unlike the main nursery, where the bassinets were lined up at the window, the NICU was much more private. Curtains could be drawn across the main windows to prevent people from peeking at the isolettes. Each clear box was surrounded by monitors and supply carts, an upholstered rocking chair, and a second floor-length curtain that could be used for additional privacy. Classical music played softly in the background, and the few babies already inside rested beneath brightly colored signs bearing their names. It was clear that Donna and the rest of the NICU nurses worked hard to make the unit feel like home—probably because their tiny patients stayed for weeks on end.

As much as I liked the variety of the ER, I wondered what it would be like to spend so much time with a patient. The longest I ever saw my cases was a single twelve-hour shift—by the time I returned to work, they'd moved on.

A flurry of activity from the back of the room caught my attention. A moment later, another nurse wheeled in an isolette, a clear Plexiglass box with portholes lining the sides. Inside, obscured by wires and tubes, a tiny hand lifted and made a fist.

"Told you she was doing great," said Donna, helping maneuver the cart into place.

"She's perfect," I breathed. It was true. Rowan was impossibly tiny, impossibly perfect. Despite all the tubes and wires, I could see a thatch of reddish-blonde peeking from beneath a knit cap. Her eyes were squeezed shut, shiny with antibacterial ointment. Donna gave me a pair of latex gloves, and I tugged them on before reaching through the porthole to touch Rowan's hand.

Her fingers closed on mine, surprisingly strong, but she didn't cry.

"She's doing remarkably well," said Dr. Solano.

Donna placed a small plastic mask over Rowan's mouth and nose, then attached it to a machine on the opposite side of the isolette.

"She'll need that CPAP machine for a few days; she can already breathe on her own, but it will prevent her from tiring herself out," Dr. Solano said. He proceeded to rattle off a list of challenges and protocols, all the things the staff would do to help Rowan develop and stabilize enough to go home. The clinical part of my brain took in his words, asking the right questions, filing away the information so I could translate it for Charlie later. But another part was content to marvel at the delicate, helpless creature before me.

Suddenly, Charlie's panic didn't seem so overblown. It was protectiveness, and I couldn't blame her one bit. Five minutes with Rowan, and I was ready to move mountains for her.

I stayed at her side, marveling at the impressive strength of her grip, until Charlie and Matt arrived a few hours later. They were both suited up in gowns and gloves, Rachel hovering behind them. My sister looked ghostly and anxious as Matt pushed the wheelchair closer. "Is that Rowan? How is she?"

"What are you doing out of bed?" I asked, aghast. "You just had major surgery, Charlie. You shouldn't be up yet."

Rachel drew me aside as Matt maneuvered Charlie directly in front of the isolette. "She was threatening to check herself out against medical advice if we wouldn't bring her down here. Dr. K said it was okay, as long as she stays in the chair and I'm nearby."

I didn't like it, but before I could speak, Charlie made a soft crooning noise, tears rolling down her cheeks as she reached inside the isolette. "Hello, sweet girl."

"She's got my ears," Matt said proudly.

"Let's hope she's got your appetite," Charlie replied.

"She's beautiful." Somehow, I kept myself from ordering Charlie back to bed. "The neonatologist said she's doing great."

She spared me a brief glance. "You're sure? Why can't I see her face? What's the mask for?"

"It's to help her breathe—like a sleep apnea machine, but they're using it so she doesn't get overtired. It'll come off in about a week, maybe less. Once she's able to coordinate her swallowing, she'll switch to oral feedings instead of the IV. Dr. Solano will explain all of this to you guys again soon."

"What else did he say?"

I reviewed everything the neonatologist had told me: the various monitors and breathing treatments, the phototherapy for jaundice, other medications Rowan might need. The list sounded daunting, but I knew how lucky we were, and I emphasized that for Charlie. "She'll have to stay for at least a few weeks, but she's doing great."

Matt reached in through the second port to touch Rowan's bare foot, his arm around Charlie's shoulder. She tipped her head against him with a sigh, and it struck me how solid the two of them were.

I was not solid, not with anyone. And it was nobody's fault but my own.

"I'll go give Mom and Riley the scoop," I said and left the three of them there, trying to ignore the jealousy scraping at my heart.

★   ★   ★

I found Garima near the nurse's station.

"Hey," I said, "you let Charlie out of bed already? Are you nuts?"

"Would you prefer she rip out her stitches sneaking down to the NICU?" she shot back, then softened. "She'll be okay, Frankie. We would have wanted her up and moving in a few hours anyway, and Rachel's keeping a close eye on her."

I quashed the urge to argue. This, after all, was why doctors and nurses weren't supposed treat family members—their judgment was clouded. "If you say so. But I'm about to go get my mom and Riley. You might want to tell the staff to brace themselves."

She didn't laugh, and her expression was a look I knew too well—furrowed brow, straight mouth, searching eyes. My hands went cold. That was a bad-news face, one I'd seen—and used—plenty of times in the emergency room.

"You said Charlie was fine."

"Not Charlie. It's your patient," she said. "The heart attack."

"Clem?" The chill spread, and I folded my arms, trying to ward it off.

"I'm so sorry, Frankie." There was no mistaking her tone.

"Clem's *dead*? That doesn't make sense. When?"

She nudged at her glasses. "A couple of hours ago. Maybe less. Respiratory arrest, someone said."

"He was stable last night. He was *snoring*."

She touched my shoulder in sympathy. "You know how fast these things can turn."

"Yeah, you're right." But it didn't feel right. I'd lost patients before—sometimes there was nothing to be done. This time, I *had* done something. I'd found Clem. I'd *saved* him, or thought I had.

"World's Best Grandpa," his cap had read. I thought about CJ, the same age as Riley, the same age I'd been when my dad died, and suddenly I wasn't satisfied with "nothing to be done."

"Make sure Charlie gets back to bed soon," I said.

"Of course." Garima frowned. "Frankie, where—"

I was already headed for the doors.

FOUR

The cardiac ward was bustling, and the air hummed with tension. Losing a patient was always tough on the staff, no matter how much we tried to compartmentalize. Marcus sat at the nurse's station, scowling at a stack of paperwork. He looked up as I approached, his frown softening to sadness. "Frankie! You heard?"

I nodded. "What happened?"

"I don't know," Marcus said. "He was stable, and then . . . boom. Vitals dropped off a cliff, no warning. Happened during shift change."

That figured. Shift change—when one group of nurses went off duty and another came on—was a combination of the witching hour and Murphy's Law. If a crisis was going to hit, it almost always happened during shift change.

"He looked good when I was in with him." The protest sounded feeble, even to my own ears. "Maybe I should have stayed."

"Don't beat yourself up," he said. "You did more than most people would've. Maybe it was just his time, you know?"

"Maybe," I said, not bothering to hide my skepticism. "How's your sister?"

"She's good, and so is the baby. C-section early this morning." I tried not to think about the fact that Rowan's life was beginning as Clem's was ending. "Good thing you woke me, or I might have missed it."

"You fell asleep in there?" He sounded genuinely surprised, and then his face split in a broad grin. "You should be upstairs celebrating."

"I guess," I said. "What are you still doing here? Shouldn't you be off duty?"

"My shift ended at eleven," he said. "But I needed to finish up his chart, and the daughter's on her way in. I wanted to stick around until she got here."

"Long night for you."

He shrugged. "My wife's dad is the same age. Same kind of build. I'd want someone to talk to her, you know?"

"I do," I said, a smile breaking through. "Softie."

He chuckled. "Don't tell anyone."

"I really thought he was on the mend," I said. "Everything looked good last night, didn't it?"

"It did. But the man wasn't exactly in his prime," Marcus gestured to the chart. "He had more history than one of those PBS dramas."

He had a point. It wasn't uncommon for patients to crash so suddenly, especially if they had prior heart issues. I leaned over the counter to get a better view of Clem's chart, my vague uneasiness coming into sharper focus.

"It's like I said last night—he came in with elevated cardiac enzymes, but they shouldn't have been so high if he was on benazepril. And how'd he throw the clot if he was taking warfarin?" I asked.

"You know how those old guys are. The minute they start feeling better, they think they're cured. He probably stopped taking his meds, or forgot to get a refill, and he was too ashamed to admit it. Happens to my father-in-law all the time—my wife is constantly checking to make sure he's doing what he's supposed to." But Marcus looked troubled, which troubled me even more. "Besides, it wasn't his heart, it was respiratory arrest. Didn't matter what he was taking—once his lungs stopped working, his heart couldn't handle it."

"I suppose. Have they taken him to the morgue?"

"Not yet. The daughter wanted to say good-bye before they transported him."

It was such a small thing, but I knew how much it would mean to Clem's family, to have that chance for closure. "Could I . . ."

"Sure thing," he said, eyes warm with understanding.

Working in emergency medicine meant I was plenty familiar with dead bodies. Not comfortable, exactly—I didn't ever want to get to the point that I was *comfortable* with death. But as I entered Clem's room and spied his body, hidden beneath a sheet, I wasn't afraid, or nervous.

I was sad.

The room was still and terribly silent, as if time itself was suspended. I drew the sheet down far enough to see Clem's face. His eyes were closed, and his skin had the ashy pallor of the recently dead. His longish gray hair was thinning on top, but the bushy mustache, drooping over the corners of his mouth, more than made up for it. His "World's Best Grandpa" hat was nowhere in sight.

I swallowed hard and pulled the sheet up again.

Everything was in order. I'd seen cases like this one thousands of times, with outcomes just as tragic. But Clem's death felt personal. I hadn't had time to put up my usual boundaries, and my emotions were already running high, thanks to Rowan's arrival and the end of my engagement. Whatever the reason for our connection, I couldn't shake the sorrow—or the sense of wrongness.

The staff had done a quick cleanup of the room to prepare for Clem's family. Someone, most likely Marcus, had bathed him, arranging his features in a peaceful expression. They'd had to leave his IVs in; by law, those would stay until the coroner signed off on the death certificate. Out of habit, I examined the bags still hanging, half-empty, tubing taken away. They'd run the usual: maintenance fluids, heparin to thin his blood, the standard assortment of cardiac drugs. I'd glanced at them last night, but now I scrutinized each bag, trying to make out the exact dosages. Trying, I realized, to find an explanation.

I should have been satisfied, but I wasn't.

"I'm sorry, Clem," I said softly. "I wish . . ."

What? What did I wish? That I'd found him earlier, that I'd done more, that I'd stayed with him. I wished for all of it, to no avail.

There was a noise at the door. A woman with red-rimmed eyes stood in the doorway. Her shoulders were hunched, thin arms wrapped around herself, as if she'd taken a blow to the stomach. In a way, she had. Marcus stood behind her, eyebrows raised in alarm.

"Who are you?" the woman asked, stepping inside. Clem's daughter, no doubt. Her dark-blonde hair was cut in a sensible bob, but it looked disheveled, her black cardigan crookedly buttoned.

"Frankie Stapleton. I'm . . ." I trailed off uncertainly. Not Clem's nurse, not his friend. A stranger, with a newly discovered sentimental streak.

Marcus stepped in. "Laura, this is the lady that found your father. She was just leaving."

"I'm so sorry for your loss," I said, the familiar words springing to my lips. I made for the door. "I'm sure you'd like some privacy."

Her hand brushed my sleeve. "Wait. You're the one who helped him?"

I halted. "I tried. Everyone did."

She pressed her fingertips to her eyes and took a breath. "Thank you. I . . . I'm still in shock. I was going to come last night, but the doctor said he was stable. He said we could wait until morning, and now it's too . . ." She began to weep. "I haven't even told my son."

"I'm sorry," I said again. Marcus tipped his head toward the door. "I'll let you say good-bye."

As I left, Marcus coaxed the woman toward Clem's bedside. Her shoulders shook, and her sobs rang in my ears even after I'd left the floor.

★　　★　　★

"Aunt Frankie!" Riley bounced up and down in her seat as I entered the cafeteria. "Did you see Rowan?"

"I did." Exhaustion grabbed me by the throat, and I sank onto the hard plastic bench. "She's small, but she's doing great."

"You look terrible," my mother said. "Have you eaten?"

"Coffee," I mumbled. "I've been busy."

She smoothed my hair, the gesture unexpectedly kind. "Let me get you some lunch."

I propped my chin in my hand and closed my eyes. "Awesome. Thank you."

"When can I hold the baby?" Riley asked around a mouthful of peanut butter sandwich.

"Not for a while. They'll probably let you into the NICU, if you're superclean, but they won't let you hold her until she's ready to come home."

"I'm the big sister!" she said, outraged.

"Sorry, kid. Rules are rules."

"Rules are *stupid*," she said.

"Some are," I agreed, not opening my eyes. "This one's not. Kids have germs, and germs are bad for Rowan right now."

"What's bad for Rowan?" My mother had returned.

"Aunt Frankie says rules are stupid."

I opened my eyes and met my mother's frown. "That's not what I said."

Wordlessly, she set coffee and a turkey sandwich in front of me.

"I was explaining to Riley why she can't hold Rowan yet. In a little while, we'll go upstairs and ask if you can visit her."

Riley considered this, her scowl softening. I suspected, after eight years of being an only child, she was a little dictator at heart.

"We saw some babies in the nursery," she said. "They're kind of ugly. Is Rowan ugly?"

"Nah, she's pretty cute. Not a knockout like you, obviously."

Riley nodded, satisfied. She chattered while I ate, carrying the conversation for all of us.

My phone rang again, Peter's picture flashing on the screen. I sent the call to voice mail and ignored my mother's raised eyebrows.

When I'd finished, my mother said, "You should come home and rest."

"I'll crash in the family lounge upstairs. Charlie needs me."

"Charlie can manage without you for a few hours. You'll be no good to anyone unless you get some sleep."

"I've gotten by with less."

"But you don't need to," my mother began, then looked up, directing her words over my shoulder. "May I help you?"

"I . . . um . . . I was looking for Miss Stapleton. Frankie?"

I twisted in my seat. Clem's daughter stood in front of me, clutching a white plastic bag labeled "Patient Effects."

"Is this a bad time?" she asked.

"No, no," I assured her. "Mom, why don't you two check on Charlie? Make sure she's back in bed. I'll be up soon."

My mother was as subtle as a bulldozer, but she could read a room. "Riley, let's go see if we can spot your sister through the window."

Her tone didn't allow room for argument. Once they'd gone, I gestured to the seat across from me. "Sorry about that. My sister had a baby this morning, and everybody's frazzled. I didn't catch your name."

"Laura Madigan." She set her purse on the floor and extracted a fresh tissue. "I wanted to thank you for helping my father."

"You're welcome," I said. "I'm so sorry for everything you're going through. I've been there."

"He's my dad." She dabbed at her eyes. "I thought he was invincible."

"Is there someone I can call for you?"

She glanced up, gave a small wave to a group of nurses two tables over, and shook her head. "No. It's just us—me and my dad and CJ. And my husband," she added with a grimace. "I call him as little as I can. He's not what you'd call supportive."

"Where's your son?"

"At a friend's house."

A tech in soccer-themed scrubs walked by, squeezed Laura's shoulder, and murmured condolences before leaving us alone again.

"Do you work here?" I asked. "Everyone seems to know you."

"CJ has epilepsy. We're here a lot for tests and doctor's visits, so we've gotten to know people. Hospitals are kind of like small towns, aren't they?"

"Especially when they're *in* small towns," I muttered.

"It's so sudden," she said. "I mean, my dad had heart problems, but they weren't life-threatening. He even applied for a drug trial last year, and he wasn't sick enough to qualify. Ironic, isn't it?"

Ironic, but not unheard of. Besides, I was concerned about last night, not last year. "How did he get to the hospital? I'm surprised he drove himself in with a heart attack."

"He thought he had the flu. He'd been feeling poorly for a few days and finally decided to come in. I offered to drive him, but he didn't want me to leave CJ alone so late at night."

"Ms. Madigan?" A tall, silver-haired man in a doctor's coat and burgundy silk bow tie approached. Behind him stood a blonde woman in a boxy navy suit, eyeing us curiously. "I missed you upstairs. I'm Alexander Hardy, the cardiologist who treated your father. I wanted to give you my condolences in person."

"Thank you," she replied, stumbling over the words. "It's . . . a shock."

"I want you to know that we used every available means to resuscitate your father, but the damage to his heart was severe and irreversible. There was nothing we could do." He turned to me. "Are you a friend of the family?"

"This is Frankie Stapleton," Laura said, before I could introduce myself. "She's the one who found my dad outside. She's helping me get . . . closure."

His eyebrows lifted. "That's very kind of you."

I shrugged, unsure how to respond. Instead, I directed my words toward the woman behind him. "I didn't catch your name. Are you on the cardiac team?"

"Ashley?" Hardy frowned. "Of course not. She's—"

"Ashley Ritter, Pharmagen Biomedical," she said, stepping forward to shake my hand. "I'm the project manager for the Cardiodyne trial."

"Yes," Hardy said with a forced laugh. Clearly, he didn't like being interrupted. "She's a regular Girl Friday. Knows her way around a spreadsheet *and* a coffeemaker."

The dismissal was blatant. I met Ashley's gaze, saw the flash of anger there, quickly replaced by a pained smile. I'd been in her position a thousand times when I was starting out, dismissed as a pretty young thing instead of treated like a colleague. Countless surgeons had sent me to get coffee while they "practiced real medicine."

They were still waiting for their cappuccinos.

"Would you like to join us?" Laura asked, breaking the awkward silence. "I had some questions . . ."

"We're on our way to a meeting." Hardy said regretfully. He withdrew a business card from his chest pocket and set it on the table, the gesture stiff and fumbling. "Contact my secretary, and we can set up an appointment, if you'd like. Again, my condolences."

He strode away without another word, beckoning for Ashley to follow. She hurried after him, glancing back at us with a frown.

I shook my head. If Ashley wanted respect from Hardy—or anyone else—she needed to start demanding it. But I had bigger concerns right now. "Laura, I'm happy to answer any questions I can, but I wasn't your dad's nurse. I can't explain any of his treatment."

"I know, but you spent time with him. Did he seem like he was in a lot of pain? Or scared? Did he say anything?"

"He mentioned CJ," I said. The truth would only make her grief more raw; rather than lie, I sidestepped her other questions and asked one of my own. "Were they close?"

"Best buddies," she said wistfully. "They were always going fishing or working on a project around the house. My dad is—" She caught herself, closed her eyes, and tried again. "He was a handyman—a real jack-of-all-trades. Plumbing, electrical, house painting, carpentry. You name it, he did it. CJ loved working with him, especially since his own father is barely around."

"You're divorced?"

"We've been separated for almost three years," she said. "But I can't afford a lawyer on top of CJ's medical bills, and Jimmy's more interested in gambling chips than chipping in. Money's been so tight that my father had started paying for CJ's new medication. He said it was the least he could do to help." Her voice broke on the words.

Just wanted to help, Clem had said.

"He sounds like he was a great guy."

"He really was." She wiped her eyes, seeming to gather up the shreds of her composure. "Anyway, I wanted to thank you. It would have been worse, thinking that he'd died out there, all alone. I would have wondered if the doctors could have saved him. At least I don't have to wonder now."

I knew the danger of second-guessing yourself, of imagining how things *could* have been. Of thinking a different choice might have saved a life that had been lost. In a hospital, it was a staggeringly heavy responsibility. You could either learn to carry it or be crushed by it. I'd seen plenty of nurses burned out for exactly that reason, and I'd seen plenty of patients' families paralyzed by it.

I was glad I'd been able to give Laura some measure of comfort alongside her answers. But for me, our conversation had only raised more questions.

FIVE

On impulse, I gave Laura my number, telling her to call if she wanted to talk further. Clem's death had left me feeling oddly unsettled. It was as if my blue polyblend scrubs were a kind of armor, and treating a patient without them, away from my own hospital, had stripped me of my usual defenses.

I headed up to the maternity ward, where Charlie insisted I go home. "You couldn't nurse a teddy bear, you're so wiped out."

I wanted to point out that this was fine advice from someone who, a day before, had begged for my help. But Rowan was stable, Riley was starting to go stir-crazy, and my mother was looking frazzled.

"Come back after dinner," Matt suggested, handing over my backpack and steering me toward the door. "We'll put you on diaper duty."

"But . . ."

"Aren't you the one who loves the night shift?" Charlie asked, dragging her eyes away from Rowan to wrinkle her nose at my appearance. "Seriously, Frankie. You're a wreck. Go home."

Going home meant enduring an interrogation about failed engagements and my failure, thus far, to provide my fair share of grandchildren. I wondered if Rowan's arrival would buy me a reprieve. Probably not. But my thoughts were starting to blur from fatigue, and even the simple act of scrubbing my hands seemed unmanageable.

"You'll call me if anything changes?"

She nodded. It was good to see my sister bouncing back to her usual no-nonsense self, even if she was sporting a variety of IV bags. Worry was etched at the corners of her eyes and mouth, but she'd lost the panicked, desperate look that she'd worn when I arrived. "Tell Mom to stop at the store and get the weekend's totals, will you?"

"Focus on Rowan," I said. "Forget about the store."

"Some of us don't have that luxury," she snapped. Matt touched her shoulder, and she pinched the bridge of her nose. "Sorry. Can you give Mom the message, please? It's not like I'm asking you to take over."

"No problem." She was even more exhausted than I was, I reminded myself. Stressed beyond belief. The store had always been a bone of contention between us—Charlie blamed me for leaving her to run it alone, and I was hurt that she'd rather see me miserable behind the counter than doing what I loved.

I'd thought coming home now might have healed that wound, but a single visit couldn't repair a decade-old rift. I forced a smile, blew a kiss to Rowan through the isolette, and made my escape.

My car was still in the ER lot. I kept my head down as I walked through the waiting room, not wanting to chance another encounter with Dr. Costello. One glimpse of me through the ER doors, and he'd be calling what little I'd seen of hospital security.

I couldn't get Clem out of my head. I replayed every moment since I'd arrived at Stillwater Gen, unable to shake the feeling that I was missing something. Plenty of things in medicine were inexplicable—miraculous recoveries, freak accidents, long shots that paid off, and sure things that didn't. Maybe Clem had been more ill than he'd told Laura. Maybe he'd been bad about taking his medicine or started an all-bacon-and-butter diet. Maybe he'd given up. Nothing was more fatal than a loss of hope. But I thought about his "World's Best Grandpa" hat, and the fact he'd used what little breath he had to talk about CJ, and "giving up" didn't fit.

I didn't notice the person in front of me until I'd slammed into a broad, dark-blue chest. I yelped, stumbling backward, and someone gripped my arms to steady me.

"Geez, Frankie. Am I that forgettable?"

I closed my eyes. I knew the voice, low and amused, and it wasn't forgettable. Not even close. Not even when I'd tried, and I'd tried very, very hard over the last twelve years.

I opened my eyes, looked up (and up, and up, because the owner of the navy-blue chest was a solid foot taller than me), and saw exactly what I expected. What I'd expected since the minute I'd crossed the city limits.

Noah MacLean.

Ex-fiancé number one.

"Sorry," I croaked. "I was . . . somewhere else. It's good to see you, Noah."

Like a puppy who'd grown into his feet, my high school boyfriend had grown into his looks. The face that had been swoon-worthy at eighteen had lost its softness, the dark-blond hair cut military short instead of straggling over his collar. The scar over his right eyebrow, a memento from a stray baseball sophomore year, added character, as did the faint beginnings of lines around his moss-green eyes.

"You, too. Saw you last night, actually."

For the first time, I noticed the badge on his pocket and the gun at his hip. "You're a cop?"

"Sheriff's deputy." He let go of me, and my arm tingled where he'd held it. "We were spread pretty thin last night, thanks to the bus crash. I rode along and helped transport some of the kids."

I flashed back to the girl with the pom-pom, the tug of familiarity when I'd heard the paramedics' chatter.

"That was you? Why didn't you say something?"

He grinned, the broad smile throwing me off-balance. "I figured you'd heard enough from Costello. Somebody told me Charlie's here?"

"Yeah. She had a little girl this morning." I couldn't help smiling, and his own grin matched it. But I didn't want to talk about Charlie. "Do you know Costello?"

His brow furrowed. "Sure. I know most of the ER staff."

"What about the patients? Did you know Clem Jensen?"

"Doesn't ring a bell. Who is he?"

"The heart attack I found. The one Costello was so angry about. He died this morning."

"Aw, crap. That's a tough break, Frankie."

I waved the words away. "Could you look into him?"

He drew back. "You want me to run a background check on your patient?"

When Noah put it like *that*, it sounded . . . sneaky, not to mention presumptuous. The last time we'd spoken, I'd thrown his ring—and his promises—back in his face. Now twelve years later, I was asking a favor? Coming home had scrambled my brain.

"He seemed like a nice guy, and now he's dead. It doesn't seem right." I rubbed the back of my neck, trying to work out the kinks. "I guess I wanted some closure. Never mind. It was stupid of me to ask."

"Not stupid. I can't run an official background check for no reason, but I can ask around. You know how Stillwater is—somebody must have known him."

"Thanks," I said, marveling at his nonchalance. Was this Noah's way of making amends? More likely, it was his way of saying I was forgiven for my part. In light of all the hurt I'd caused—Noah, Peter, my family—a little forgiveness felt nice.

"You're welcome." He paused. "You look good, Frankie. City life agrees with you."

I wasn't sure how to respond. "You, too" seemed too flirtatious; agreeing seemed vain. Rather than parse out the right answer, I asked, "Did you figure out what caused the crash?"

"Bus driver was new. They were coming back from a game in Silver Lake, took a turn too fast, overcorrected, and collided with the second bus. Remember that hairpin curve over by the quarry?"

The quarry, where all the kids used to swim on hot summer days. And nights.

I fiddled with my watch. "I remember."

He smiled, slow and easy, and I knew he remembered, too. Finally, he said, "It'll take me some time to find out about your patient. How long you home for?"

"Not long," I said, flustered. "I . . . Charlie needed me, and I had some vacation, and . . . here I am." I took a deep breath and willed myself to stop babbling. "I'm not sticking around. In fact, I should go now. Good to see you, Noah. Deputy MacLean."

"Always zero to sixty with you, isn't it?" I couldn't tell if his tone was amused or mocking. "Then you slam on the brakes."

Ah. That explained the whiplash.

★   ★   ★

Downtown Stillwater was as quaint as ever. Late on a Sunday afternoon, pedestrians milled about the sidewalks and the grassy town square. Kids chased each other around the white gazebo while their parents looked on. Some of the storefronts had changed, but most were filled, and all boasted picturesque autumn displays of pumpkins and dried corn. The sandy-orange brick village hall watched over it all, a chalkboard sign announcing coffee with the mayor next Wednesday. And anchoring the northeast corner of the square was the family business I'd run from, twelve years ago.

The sign in front of the two-story clapboard building hadn't changed, dark blue with white letters: Stapleton and Sons Hardware, Est. 1873. The windows displays were cheery and inviting: rakes and mums, firewood and cast-iron pans, and red wool blankets. When I was little, the displays had been covered with dust, stubbornly utilitarian: a ladder, some cans of paint, teetering boxes of drywall screws. After my dad had died, my mom threw herself into keeping the store afloat. She quickly realized that if Stapleton and Sons was going to survive, we needed to do more than sell hand tools and two-penny nails and other bits of home improvement. We needed to sell the *idea* of home.

Despite the steady flow of pedestrians, not enough of them were entering the store, I noted. Especially not on a Sunday afternoon. Charlie might have a reason to worry after all.

As I craned my neck to peer in the windows, a bundle of orange fur shot across the street. I hit the brakes just in time to avoid flattening whatever it was. The creature disappeared down the alley, and I set off again, heart pounding.

Five minutes later, I was home.

The saltbox Cape Cod I'd grown up in hadn't changed, either. Red brick, green shutters, carefully tended beds of marigolds in the yard, and window boxes full of vibrant, shaggy mums.

My key chain held only three keys: apartment, car, bike lock. Simple, light, uncomplicated. And at the present moment, inconvenient. I was locked out.

Before I could knock, the door swung open. "What took you so long?" my mother asked. "We got here ages ago."

I slipped inside, keeping my face averted. "I ran into someone."

"Who?"

"Nobody," I said. "An old friend."

An old friend I'd need to see again if I truly wanted more information on Clem. The realization didn't bother me as much it should have.

My mother tapped her foot. "Well, which is it? Nobody or somebody?"

I ignored the question. "Charlie wanted you to pick up the weekend totals from the store before your next visit. Where's Riley?"

"In back with her soccer ball, as usual. So we can talk." She settled her arms across her chest.

"I know." I toed off my gym shoes and threw myself onto the couch, anticipating the same lecture I got every time I set foot in this house. "I'm never going to find someone. I'm never going to be happy. I'm going to die alone and bitter and miserable."

Had Noah found someone? I hadn't thought to check for a wedding ring, not that I had any reason to—or any right, for that matter.

"That's not what I was going to say," Mom began.

I cut her off, temper mounting as I straightened. "I'll give you the first one. But I am happy. I'm not alone—I have friends and a career and a very busy, fulfilling life. I'm not bitter, and I wasn't miserable until we started having this conversation. What I *am* is exhausted."

She eyed me, spine stiff. "Are you finished with your speech?"

My shoulders sagged, exhaustion compounded by guilt. "Yes."

"Good. What I wanted to say is that I am very grateful that you came home. We all are. I hoped that you would consider staying, at least for a while."

"Mom . . ."

"Since you're so happy with your busy, fulfilling life, however, I won't waste my breath." She stalked back into the kitchen, calling over her shoulder, "Your bed's made up. I suggest you use it."

Thirty-four years old and I'd been sent to my room.

★   ★   ★

The tidy brick house, like the business, had been in our family for generations. Following in my parents' footsteps, Matt and Charlie had lived in the apartment above the store for a few years, moving back in after Riley came along. Squeezing three generations under one roof required a game of musical bedrooms—my mom took over the guest bedroom on the first floor, while upstairs Matt and Charlie took my parents' old room, and the room I'd once shared with Charlie had become Riley's. Cozy, my mother called it, but we all knew she meant cramped.

I slogged my way upstairs, every step an effort, and stumbled toward the tiny guest room I usually stayed in. Barely big enough for a twin bed and a nightstand, it was the only spot in the house I was guaranteed privacy. But when the door swung open, the bed was gone, replaced by a crib and a rocking chair. I slumped, backpack sliding to my feet, and gave serious consideration to curling up on the pink-and-green braided rug.

"You can have the top bunk, if you want," Riley said from behind me.

"The top . . ."

"The top bunk." She towed me down the hall and threw open her door. "See?"

Purple. That's what I saw. Purple everywhere, simultaneously deep and bright, so intense my eyes vibrated. A few spots were taken up with posters of the U.S. Women's Soccer Team, or adorable puppies, but the color was inescapable. It was like walking into a giant African violet. The green-and-white rag rug covering the wooden floor only heightened the effect. In the corner was my old bunk bed, the one Charlie and I had slept on until I left for college, the purple polka-dot comforters made up with military precision.

"You redecorated." My backpack hit the floor with a thud.

"Mom said I could pick any color I wanted!"

"That was . . . nice . . . of her," I managed.

"You can have the top bunk," Riley repeated, her little face pinched with anxiety. "If you want. It's my favorite, but Grandma says you're the guest, so you get to pick."

"Bottom," I said automatically and climbed in. "But . . ."

Her eyes lit with glee. "This is the best, Aunt Frankie. It'll be like a sleepover every single night!"

I looked around at the violently violet walls, then up at the shining face of my new roommate.

"Fantastic," I said, and fell asleep.

Riley, I discovered a few hours later, snored. She stopped when I jostled the mattress, but the damage was done. If I were home, I'd be midway through a shift by now, and my body wouldn't let me fall back asleep.

Moonlight filtered through the leaves outside my window, casting shifting patterns across the hardwood floor. A moment later, Riley resumed snoring. I groaned, threw back the polka-dotted comforter, and headed downstairs.

To my surprise, the kitchen light was already on. My mother sat at the table, a cup of tea at her elbow, her latest book club selection in front of her.

"What are you doing up?" I glanced at the wall clock—a chicken in the middle and eggs marking the hours. My mother collected poultry, for reasons she'd never explained, and the collection had taken on a life of its own: tea towels, sugar dishes, mugs, spoon rests, and some truly awful art projects that looked like Riley's handiwork. Every time I came home, more had hatched, and the effect of all those beady eyes and sharp beaks was unsettling. I turned my back on the assorted birds and focused on her. "It's after midnight."

She shrugged. "I don't need much sleep these days."

I nodded and searched the pantry for cereal.

"I saved you some food," she said, going to the fridge and pulling out a plastic-wrapped plate. "Riley was worried when you missed dinner. Chicken casserole."

"My days and nights are switched, that's all. She could have woken me up."

"You needed the rest," she replied, popping the food in the microwave and handing me a napkin embroidered with a malevolent-looking hen. "I was hoping it would improve your disposition."

Sinister birds aside, I did feel better. "I'm sorry I snapped."

She patted her hair. "I know. Now eat."

I thought about saying more—there's something about a warmly lit kitchen in the middle of the night that invites conversation—but instead, I shifted to safer ground. "How's Charlie?"

"She's doing well. Rowan had a good evening, and Matt came home around ten. I'm sure she would appreciate it if you were there when the doctor came by in the morning."

"I'll be there," I promised.

"Good. Now I'm going to bed."

She'd stayed up to check on me, I realized. The book, the sleeplessness . . . they were excuses, and I should have seen through them immediately.

"Thanks for the dinner, Mom. It's really good."

She smiled and set about locking up, making sure the porch light was on and opening the kitchen door so she could secure the screen. "What on earth? Get out of here!"

I sprang up. "Who's there?"

"Not who," she said and pointed to the back steps. "*What.*"

Sitting in the circle of porch light sat a tangle of orange and white fur, green eyes glowing. It spotted me and yowled fiercely. My mom jumped back and snatched up the broom. "That thing sounds like a demon. It *looks* like one, too."

"It's a cat," I replied. "I think."

A familiar cat, actually. It looked like the creature who'd darted in front of my car as I drove home. The one I'd nearly flattened.

"Well, it's not coming in," she said. "I can see the fleas from here."

The cat stared at her balefully, then nudged something toward the door.

"Ugh! Francesca, what . . ."

I squinted. "It's a mouse. Or maybe a vole."

She handed me the broom, then stalked away, calling, "Whatever it is, get rid of it. And send that thing away before you lock up."

"Did you follow me home?" I asked when I stepped outside. The cat stared at me, unblinking. "I hate to break it to you, but stalkers are not generally looked upon with favor."

I swept up the mouse—not a vole, on closer inspection—and headed to the trashcan to dispose of the corpse. The cat trailed after me, protesting at the theft of his plaything. Backlit by the porch light, I could see hints of its scrawny body beneath the thickly matted fur. I reached out, hoping to get a sense of exactly how malnourished the creature was, but he hissed and took a swipe at me.

"Fine," I said, snatching my hand back. "Suit yourself."

But I couldn't help putting a spoonful of chicken casserole on a saucer and leaving it on the porch before I locked up and went back to bed.

SIX

The next morning dawned clear and crisp, the sky pink with sunrise as I headed to the hospital. Doctors tend to round early, and I was eager to hear how Rowan was progressing. Even a single day—or night, as Clem had shown—could change everything. I shook off the melancholy that threatened, determined to stay positive in front of Charlie.

The doctor was pleased with Rowan's progress—she was doing so well, he wanted to start her tube feedings earlier than expected. Charlie's relief shone in her eyes. "Stapleton girl," she murmured as she reached through the isolette to stroke Rowan's tiny hand.

"Stapleton girl," I agreed. "Tough as nails."

Shortly after the doctor left, however, Garima appeared outside the NICU. A frown was etched between her eyebrows, and a security guard stood behind her, looking profoundly uncomfortable.

"Be right back," I told Charlie, who nodded and kept singing to Rowan. I joined Garima outside. "What's wrong?"

"The vice-president wants to see you," she said and glared at the guard. "But this gentleman won't say why."

Now security showed up. "Let me guess. Paul Costello's still mad?"

The guard lifted his hands in apology. "Mr. Strack told me to bring Miss Stapleton down, ma'am. He didn't say anything else."

"Do you want me to come along?" Garima asked me.

"Am I in that much trouble?"

"I doubt Walter Strack would summon you to his office solely to introduce himself. He's too busy trying to sell this place to the highest bidder to interact with patients or their families."

My hands turned clammy, but I pasted on a smile, aware of Charlie watching us through the window. "I'm sure it's fine."

As it turned out, my meeting with Walter Strack, vice-president of Stillwater General, was anything but fine.

Strack was a bland-looking man in his fifties, sandy hair starting to recede along the temples, jawline soft and sagging above an expensive-looking tie. After a brisk introduction and an insincere query about Charlie's health, he sat down at his sleek glass-and-chrome desk, adjusted his tie, and proceeded to ruin my life.

"Clement Jensen's death was obviously a tragic event, Miss Stapleton, despite the best efforts of my staff to prevent it. As you know, sometimes these matters are out of our hands." He sighed heavily. When he spoke again, the regret in his voice had hardened into something far less compassionate. "Unfortunately, while I am confident that my staff acted appropriately, your actions—your *unsanctioned* actions—have opened us up to a lawsuit."

"A lawsuit?" Laura didn't strike me as the type. "His daughter wouldn't sue. She wanted answers, not cash."

"Not Mrs. Madigan. Her husband . . ." He consulted the paperwork. "James."

"Jimmy? They're not together. He's barely in the picture!"

"Whether he is 'in the picture' or not is irrelevant. Mr. Madigan has the right to file suit, as he is married to the next-of-kin. He informed us of his plans this morning." Strack looked like he'd smelled something rancid. "He even, quite thoughtfully, came prepared with a settlement offer."

Jimmy's more interested in gambling chips than chipping in, Laura had said. "That's a little fast, don't you think? He's trying to bluff you into a big payout. He doesn't have grounds for a suit."

"He absolutely does, thanks to you."

I straightened, making my tone as coldly official as his. "With all due respect, Mr. Strack, my actions were well within the standard of care. Giving a patient nitro is a doctor-approved protocol at every hospital I've ever worked at." Normally, nurses aren't authorized to dispense medication without a doctor's orders. But most hospitals had standing orders, or protocols, written by staff physicians. These protocols were like blanket prescriptions, allowing nurses to automatically dispense certain medications in specific, time-sensitive situations. I'd followed Chicago Memorial's protocol to the letter.

"You aren't authorized to work in this hospital. You have no idea what our protocols are."

"It was an emergency situation! If anything, I gave Clem a fighting chance. I'm certainly not responsible for his death."

"It was reckless." He tapped the report in front of him with a stubby finger. Paul Costello's words, no doubt, and they carried far more weight than mine. Clearly, he was blaming me for Clem's death—but why? Was he angry that I'd showed him up in the ER, or was it something more insidious? Had he missed something? Was he worried the hospital would blame him for the delay in treatment? Was it pride, or an attempt to shift the blame?

Strack continued. "According to this, you didn't run an EKG. You didn't even ask for help."

"There was nobody around to ask," I protested. "Everyone was inside dealing with the bus accident."

"You should have tried harder." He leaned forward. "And you should have stayed out of Mr. Jensen's room. You had no legitimate reason to be there. Who's to say you didn't 'help' him to an early grave?"

I froze. Even the whisper of a malfeasance charge—deliberately committing harm against a patient—could end a career. This wasn't just bluster or idle threats or careless talk. This was trouble. Deliberate and dangerous, coming at me with the force of an F-5 tornado.

My own thoughts whirled as I tried to make sense of it. Amid the chaos, the missing piece—the source of the unease plaguing me since I'd first met Clem—finally surfaced in my mind. His reluctance to enter the ER. The way he'd gripped my sleeve, insistent. The desperate gasp of his words, wasting precious breath when he had none to spare. *"Not . . . accident."*

Clem wasn't talking about the bus accident. He was talking about his heart.

Which sounded crazy, but no crazier than the idea that I had killed Clem, as Strack was suggesting.

Before I could say anything, Strack continued. "Do you know what I think happened, Miss Stapleton? I think you wanted to save the day. You grew up in Stillwater, if I understand correctly."

"Yes," I said, keeping careful hold of my temper. If I told Strack Clem had been murdered, he'd think I was trying to throw suspicion on someone else. Paul Costello, for example. He'd twist my words and use them to ruin me. "How is that relevant?"

"I think you wanted to show us how it's done in the city. You wanted to be greeted as a hometown hero, but you took it too far. Now a man is dead, and you could cost this hospital millions."

So much for holding my temper—or my tongue. "Which one bothers you more?" I asked. "Because I know which one worries me. Clem's death *was* a tragedy, but I don't think it was unavoidable. I definitely don't think it was my fault."

"Well, we'll see what the state licensing board says."

I drew back. "Excuse me?"

He smiled, lips compressing into a thin, cold line. "I'm not sure how they handle things in Chicago, Miss Stapleton, but here at Stillwater General, it is standard procedure to launch an investigation any time a patient dies within twenty-four hours of admission."

"Of course," I said through frozen lips.

"If it turns out your actions contributed to Mr. Jensen's death in the slightest, not only will I personally file a complaint with the Department of Professional Regulation, I'll have you charged with manslaughter. At the very least, Miss Stapleton, you will never practice nursing again."

SEVEN

Strack's words hit me like a lightning strike, leaving me stunned and speechless in my chair.

Which was better than leaping across the desk and strangling him with his stupid silk tie. Considering he'd just accused me of killing a patient, homicide—even justifiable homicide—wasn't in my best interest.

Nurses are good at compartmentalization. It's how we keep from breaking down at the tragedies we face daily, so we can prevent the next one. So I locked away my outrage and stalked out before Strack could utter another word. An orderly and a patient both drew back in alarm as I approached the elevator, and I forced my expression to smooth out. By the time I reached the maternity ward, I looked like my usual pleasant self.

Or so I thought.

"What's wrong?" said Charlie, the moment I entered the NICU. Rowan was snuggled up against her chest, a gauzy blanket covering them both.

"Nothing," I said, and tried to change the subject. "They started you on kangaroo care already? That's great."

Studies had shown that preemies responded well to skin-on-skin contact with their parents—it helped them regulate their breathing, gain weight, and maintain their body temp. Once a baby was deemed stable, most NICUs encouraged as much kangaroo care as possible, adjusting the monitors' cords to allow for maximum bonding time.

Charlie allowed herself a brief smile before saying, "If nothing's wrong, why was security looking for you?"

"Parking permit," I said breezily, brushing my hair out of my face. "Had to move my car."

Rowan shifted slightly, and Charlie patted her back, eyes narrowed at me over the baby's downy head.

"Really?" she replied. Her voice turned light and crooning. "Did you know your Aunt Frankie has a tell, Rowan? She does. Aunt Frankie twirls her hair whenever she lies. Ever since we were little."

I dropped my hand and scowled, but Charlie continued. "She's lucky Grandma didn't figure it out when she was sixteen and sneaking out of her room at night. When you're bigger, you'll be able to beat her at poker, and we won't have to pay for college."

"Hey Rowan," I called, matching her tone. "Did you know your mama's a know-it-all?"

She smiled. "Which is why my kids won't be sneaking out in the middle of the night."

I thought about Riley, with her stubborn little face and her quick mind. She'd be more than a match for Charlie, if she wasn't already. "You keep telling yourself that."

But Riley came by her stubborn streak honestly. "What's going on, Frankie?"

The last thing Charlie needed was another crisis; her attention needed to stay on Rowan and her own recovery. This was my problem to deal with. No doubt she felt the same about whatever was happening at the store, and the knowledge that she was harboring secrets of her own eased my conscience slightly. To keep my hands busy, I crossed to the sink and began scrubbing in. "I was parked in a tow zone, so I had to move the car. That's it."

"Without your keys? Your bag's right here."

I closed my eyes briefly, my stomach doing the same jolt and plummet it always had when I got caught doing something wrong. I hadn't felt it in more than a decade.

I sighed and chose my words carefully. "There was a guy. In the parking lot."

"Today?"

"No. The night I came home. He was having a heart attack, but the ER staff was busy dealing with an accident, so I helped out." Anticipating her question, I said, "The hospital administration wanted to go over some of the details with me, so they sent a security guard rather than page me."

Charlie frowned. "Is he okay?"

I hesitated. "He died this morning."

"Oh, Frankie. I'm sorry."

I pinched the bridge of my nose. The temptation was to tell her everything was okay, that I was fine, that this sort of thing happened all the time. But it *wasn't* okay, not by a long shot. A man was dead, and I was being blamed, and my instincts were screaming at me that something was very, very wrong inside Stillwater Gen.

I looked at my newborn niece, wires and tubes trailing from under the blanket where she snuggled; and I looked at my little sister, worry lines carved deeper into her forehead than they should be, and I wondered if even a locked ward and intensive monitoring could keep them safe.

It would have to. Rowan needed treatment, and this was the only place she could get it.

"Is there a lot of paperwork, when a patient dies?" Charlie's question brought me back to myself.

"There's always paperwork," I replied, and tried to smile. It was the truest fact of hospital life—everything required paperwork, electronic or hard copy. Everything was documented, down to the last bandage.

My smile turned genuine. Somewhere within the pages of Clem's chart lay proof of my innocence—and someone else's guilt. All I had to do was follow the paper trail back to the killer.

★ ★ ★

I stayed with Rowan and Charlie until after lunch, mulling over how I could get my hands on Clem's chart again. Strack certainly wasn't going to hand it over. Despite my insistence that Laura wasn't behind the lawsuit, it was possible that she blamed me for Clem's death now that she'd had time to process it. I considered asking Garima, but what would an obstetrician need with an elderly man's chart?

"Earth to Frankie," Charlie said. "You still thinking about the patient? The one who died?"

I hesitated. "Kind of."

"Go home," she ordered. "Riley will be coming home from school soon. You can help her with her homework."

"I thought Mom was watching her."

"She is. But it'll get your mind off your patient, and it would make Riley feel good to have some special aunt time, too."

"I don't want to leave you alone," I said, spurred on by something more fearful than sisterly devotion.

She gestured to the nurse working nearby. "Someone checks on us every fifteen minutes. More often, if I sneeze or change position. Besides, Matt's done with classes for today, so he's on his way."

"I can stay till he gets here."

"We're fine. This way Mom can run by the store before she visits."

Quit worrying about the store, I wanted to say. But that was well-covered ground, and I didn't want to spoil the mood—Charlie would only reply, as always, that *someone* had to, the implication being that I didn't worry enough. Judging from the frown lines bracketing her mouth, there was plenty to worry about. Confronting her would only make it worse, so instead I went for the casual approach.

"How's business, anyway?"

"Fine," she said shortly, arms tightening around Rowan.

"Was it a good summer?"

"I said it was fine."

True—but she hadn't meant it. I wasn't the only Stapleton with a tell, and right now Charlie was rubbing her wrist, the same one she'd broken falling off the swings when she was eleven.

Summer was the busy season, with do-it-yourselfers flooding the aisles and making return trips for "one more piece," families looking to buy Dad the perfect tool or new grill for Father's Day, and lawn-obsessed retirees looking for the latest weapon in the war against crabgrass. A lousy summer meant a tight winter, especially with hospital bills piling up. The store had weathered lean years before, but I'd never seen Charlie this tense about it.

Then again, I'd made it crystal-clear I wasn't interested in the store. Why should she confide in me now?

"How about I bring Riley over after dinner?" I asked, deliberately bright. "She's missing you."

Charlie's expression softened. "I'm missing her."

"Sounds like a plan." A plan that dovetailed nicely with my own: avoiding Walter Strack. He didn't seem like the type of administrator who stayed past five, and I'd already seen how lax evening security was at the hospital. I suspected that my presence at Stillwater General wasn't particularly welcome, which is why I'd stayed huddled in the NICU, sniffing Rowan's delicious baby scent all day. Out of sight, out of mind—I hoped.

I stood and stretched, easing the soreness in my back. My muscles were unaccustomed to sitting for so long, but pacing the NICU made Charlie—and everyone else— nervous. I brushed a kiss over Rowan's tiny head. "Back after dinner, then."

"Bring me dessert," she called.

Garima caught me by the elevators. "Sorry! I meant to catch you earlier, but we had twins and then a full schedule at the office. I heard about Strack. Do you want to get coffee?"

"Wish I could—I'm taking care of Riley this afternoon, then bringing her over for a visit with Charlie."

She considered, then shrugged. "What about later tonight? We can go to Crossroads."

"Is that place still around?"

She nodded. "I know it's not a fancy Chicago cocktail bar . . ."

Like the ones I'd gone to with Peter. No, Crossroads was a bar on the outskirts of town, run-down, wood-paneled, with peanut shells on the floor and animal heads on the walls. In Wicker Park, it would have been considered the height of irony, an excuse to charge ten dollars for a can of beer. In Stillwater, it was a place to grab a cheap drink and shoot a round of pool.

"Sounds perfect," I said, just as her phone buzzed.

"Nine o'clock?" she asked, frowning at the text. "I need to run. And Frankie . . . you need a lawyer."

*　　*　　*

On my way out, I checked the hospital directory. Alexander Hardy, the doctor who'd treated Clem, had an office in one of the sleek new buildings on the perimeter of the hospital. He'd offered to talk to Laura—maybe I could convince him to help me find out what had gone wrong.

I crossed the manicured grounds, marveling at how Stillwater Gen had grown. There was nothing else like it for a hundred miles; you'd have to cross state lines to find the nearest comparable hospital. If Garima was right, and the board was looking to sell, they were in an excellent position.

Dr. Hardy was with a patient, according to his receptionist, so I settled in with a year's worth of women's magazines, each promising to transform my home, my career, my relationships, and my diet in twenty-one days. In the last seventy-two hours, I'd had enough transformation to last me a lifetime, however, and I tossed the magazines aside.

Then again, hadn't I wanted a change? A chance to get out of town and get myself together? Figure out what I really wanted? Stillwater wouldn't have been my first choice—or even my fiftieth—but it wasn't exactly boring. Once I found Clem's killer and got Charlie back on her feet, I could go back to Chicago and my old life . . . if I wanted it.

Assuming, of course, I didn't lose my license.

Garima's words came back to me. Like most nurses, I had a union rep—but that was through my own hospital, not Stillwater Gen. I had no idea if they would fight for me in this situation, and it seemed unfair they should have to. Whether I'd violated hospital protocol or not, I'd been trying to save a man's life. Someone else was responsible for the taking of it.

The hospital wouldn't report me until they'd completed their investigation, but it was obvious Strack had made up his mind about who was responsible for Clem's death. If I wanted the truth, I'd have to find the killer myself.

"Miss Stapleton?"

Alexander Hardy stood in the doorway of the main office. As before, he was wearing a bow tie and French-cuff shirt under his doctor's coat, his spare, angular height reminding me of a whooping crane.

"Call me Frankie," I said, approaching him with my hand extended. We shook, his skin surprisingly clammy. As discreetly as possible, I wiped my palm on my jeans. "I was hoping I could talk to you about Clem Jensen."

"Oh?" His eyebrows lifted and he gestured toward his office, tucked at the end of the hall. It was decorated in English manor wannabe, all dark wood and rich leather furniture, the walls covered in brocade wallpaper and oil paintings of fox hunts. A cut-glass decanter of amber liquid and matching tumblers rested on an ornate sideboard, while built-in bookshelves held an array of medical journals and several back issues of *Wine Spectator*. Suddenly, my holey jeans and fleece jacket made me feel painfully underdressed.

"I was wondering if you could tell me a little more about his case." I gave him my most winning smile, the one I usually reserved for Peter's endless work parties and fundraisers. My VIP smile, he'd named it one night after a bottle of very expensive champagne. "Or even . . . if you could let me see his chart?"

"That would be a violation of privacy laws," he said, settling himself behind the desk. "Which I suspect you already know. As I said before, we did everything we could to resuscitate Mr. Jensen, but there was simply too much damage to his heart."

I chose my words carefully, not wanting to throw Marcus under the bus. "According to his daughter, Clem was managing his heart condition. Considering the medication he was supposedly taking, it seems strange he would throw a clot."

"Supposedly?" He said, as if the suggestion was a personal affront. "Are you implying he wasn't taking his medication?"

"I'm not implying anything. I'm asking if you noticed anything strange about his blood work."

"Discussing Mr. Jensen's case with you would be unethical," he said shortly. "Furthermore, I doubt the hospital would appreciate me interfering in an active investigation."

My VIP smile dropped away. "I didn't do anything wrong."

His expression cleared, and he reached across the desk to pat my hand, the gesture dripping with condescension. "Then the investigation will prove exactly that, my dear. Is that all? My schedule is really quite full."

I sank back in my chair, racking my brain for another angle. "Laura Madigan said her father had applied to your drug trial but didn't get in."

"Confidentiality seems to be a concept you struggle with," Hardy said dryly.

"I'm not asking about Clem. Laura already filled me in. But you can tell me about the drug, can't you?"

He studied me.

"It's not confidential," I added. "Everyone at the hospital knows about it, and you'll have to publish the results of the trial before you can get final FDA approval. What's the harm?"

"None, I suppose," he said after a moment. "Cardiodyne is a new class of drug; it improves cardiac cells' susceptibility to electrical impulses from the nervous system, addressing an area of chronic heart failure that's been previously ignored."

"And Clem wasn't sick enough to make the trial?" Before Hardy could respond, I waved my hand. "I know, I know. Privacy laws. Where are you at in the approval process?"

"We're in the final stages; Pharmagen should bring it to market within the next year. It has the potential to save many lives."

"Too bad it couldn't help Clem," I said softly. "Thank you for your time, Dr. Hardy."

"You're welcome," he said, escorting me to the door. "Forgive me for asking, but were you close to Mr. Jensen? I'd been led to believe you'd only just met."

I lifted my hands and then let them fall to my sides. "I found him. I feel responsible—but not for his death, no matter what Paul Costello thinks."

He frowned. "Paul?"

"He's the one pushing for this investigation, isn't he? He's been out for blood since the minute I brought Clem into his emergency room."

"I see. Perhaps it's best you give him a wide berth, then. Paul Costello is not someone to be crossed, Miss Stapleton."

"Yeah, well . . . neither am I."

★   ★   ★

I pulled into the driveway in time to spot Riley and my mother walking home from school. When had my mother gotten so *small*? Her gait was slower than I remembered. Could the few blocks to Stillwater Elementary have worn her out? Riley was trailing behind, scuffing through piles of leaves, oversized backpack threatening to topple her over. When Mom caught sight of me, she quickened her pace, gesturing for Riley to keep up.

"How's your sister? And Rowan?" she asked. She sounded short of breath, and her hands trembled for a moment before she thrust them in the pockets of her wool coat.

"They're both good," I said. "So I thought I'd come see my favorite second grader."

I'd pitched my voice loud enough to carry, and a grin spread over Riley's face.

"Want to play soccer, Aunt Frankie?" she called.

"Homework," my mother said firmly. "Someone has a spelling test."

"On Friday! That's four whole days," Riley protested.

"Which means you'll have plenty of time to practice." She pointed toward the front door, and Riley resumed trudging toward the steps. "Snack, then homework."

Before I could protest, my mother held up a hand and said, "Wait for it."

A moment later, we heard Riley's squeal of delight, and her head popped back into view. "Ranger cookies!" she cried, clutching one in each fist.

"You still make those?" I asked. Ranger cookies were my mom's go-to comfort food—chocolate chips, oatmeal, coconut, and cornflakes, crispy outside and cake-like inside. My own stomach rumbled at the memory.

"They're Riley's favorite," she said.

"Good taste," I said. "I told Charlie we'd swing by after dinner, but she was wondering if you could check in on the store before then."

Mom made a noise that sounded like agreement but didn't explain the request.

"Is there a big order coming in? You just picked up the receipts on Sunday, right? She can't have done that much business on a Monday."

She leaned against the wrought-iron porch railing. "Francesca, quit prying."

"I'm not prying."

"Oh?" She raised her eyebrows.

"Charlie seemed worried, that's all. Is the store in trouble?"

"Did Charlotte say it was?" she returned.

"She said it was fine."

She marched into the house, calling over her shoulder, "There you go, then. It's your sister's store now, and if she wanted to tell you more, she would."

"So there *is* something to tell."

"Quit prying," she muttered again, as Riley appeared with cookies on a plate and a glass of milk.

"These are for you, Aunt Frankie. Grandma always says these were your favorites when you were little."

"Still are," I said, settled in at the kitchen table to help with homework.

"Hey, Riley," I said, once we'd made our way through spelling and multiplication. "Is there a kid named CJ at your school?"

"CJ Madigan," she said promptly. "He's in my class. He's sick a lot."

"That's too bad. Is he nice?"

Riley considered this. "I guess. For a boy. He wasn't in school today, because his grandpa died."

"I heard."

"I bet he's sad," she mused. "He liked his grandpa. They went fishing a lot, out at his grandpa's cabin. Once, CJ brought a fish they caught together to show-and-share.

They mounted it on a board so it still looked alive. It was pretty cool."

"Sounds like it." I shuddered. Chickens in the kitchen were bad enough. Taxidermy fish would give me nightmares. "Let's crank through the rest of this homework. What's the capital of Alabama?"

While I quizzed Riley, my mom popped lasagna in the oven and ran over to the store for her mystery errand.

"Can I *please* play soccer now?" Riley moaned when we'd finished.

I put my head down at the table and waved toward the backyard.

She escaped, and moments later came the rhythmic thunk of a soccer ball against the garage door.

"That's a ridiculous amount of homework," I said when my mom returned, screen door slapping behind her. "I didn't even have that much in high school."

"Never mind the homework," my mother said, fuming. "You *killed* a man?"

I lifted my head. "Nice to know the rumor mill still runs full-steam."

"It's all over the store," she said. "Three separate people stopped me to get the details. Georgina Melville says the Baptist church has already put together a prayer chain for your victim. Helen Barker says the Methodists are starting one for you."

I let my forehead drop back to the oak tabletop.

"Francesca Stapleton."

"I didn't kill anyone, Mom. I do not kill people."

"Clem Jensen was a customer! As if business weren't already—"

"Wait. You knew Clem?" A handyman, Laura had said. It made sense that he'd have an account at the store. "What was he like?"

"Nice enough, I suppose. He paid his bills on time."

"Did he have any enemies?"

"What kind of question is that, especially from the person who—"

"Mom. I did. Not. Kill. Clem. I found him in the parking lot, gave him first aid, then brought him into the ER. He was alive the last time I saw him."

"Then what happened? He up and died?"

"Something like that. Do you know anything else about him?"

She shook her head. "He wasn't from Stillwater. His billing address was in Dover Creek, on the west side of the river."

"You looked it up?" At least I knew where I got my prying from. "Anything else you can tell me?"

"What's to tell? It's not as if I'm in the store as often these days. Charlotte would know more." She glared. "Not that you're going to mention it to her. Not a word."

"Not a word about what?" said Riley, popping back in.

"Nothing," my mother said. "Wash up for dinner."

"Nobody tells me anything," Riley grumbled, and stalked off.

"I'm serious, Francesca. I don't want Charlotte getting upset over something like this."

"Something like her sister being a killer?"

"You said he was alive!"

"He was—but if you're hearing it, Charlie will, too. People talk."

"I'm aware," she said dryly. "This wouldn't have happened if you'd gone straight upstairs to see your sister."

"I went upstairs as soon as I was done. Besides, Charlie wasn't in crisis—she was checking inventory reports when I came in."

"You didn't know that," she said. "You decided a stranger's life was more important than your sister's. Than your niece's."

I threw up my hands. "I spent fifteen minutes, tops, in the ER. If I'd left Clem alone, he would have died."

"He died anyway."

"Well, he shouldn't have," I snapped, and my mother stopped to give me a quick, searching glance before returning to dinner preparations.

"Helen said his family is suing you?"

Breathing deeply, I reined in my temper. "Not me. The hospital. And it's not his family; it's his son-in-law."

"I don't know what the world's coming to these days," she sniffed. "People sue at the drop of a hat, don't they? And poor Clem's not even buried yet."

She had a point. Clem died on a Sunday morning, and by lunchtime Monday, Jimmy Madigan was suing. How had he moved so quickly? It seemed impossible he could have found a lawyer and put together a settlement proposal in twenty-four hours.

Unless he'd known Clem's death was coming.

I needed to talk to Laura—to find out more about Jimmy, and Clem, and exactly how much bad blood was between the two. I wished I'd gotten Laura's number instead of just giving her mine.

Then again, I was having drinks with Stillwater's equivalent of social media.

"Do you know Laura Madigan? She's a librarian, I think?"

"Yes, of course. She runs the children's department. Riley participated in the summer reading program this year, so we saw quite a bit of her. She was Clem's daughter, wasn't she? I should bring her a casserole."

"A casserole?"

"Food's more useful than flowers," my mother said, with the assurance of someone who'd been there. "Especially when you have children to feed. Speaking of, it's time for dinner."

The meal passed pleasantly enough, though it was a constant battle between my mother's insistence on etiquette and the ravenous appetite of a soccer-crazed eight-year-old. I could see why Charlie had asked me to run interference—Riley and my mom had a knack for pushing each other's buttons, and Matt wasn't there to referee.

Finally, the meal was over, the kitchen cleaned, and we'd arrived at the hospital in my mother's massive Buick. I checked my watch—6:20, which meant the shift change hadn't happened yet. Exactly as I'd hoped.

"You two go on ahead," I said.

"You're not coming?" Riley asked.

"I need to stretch my legs." It was true. I'd spent most of my day sitting in the NICU or at the kitchen table—at work, I was typically running from one crisis to another. All that pent-up energy was making me restless, and Clem's death had made me even more so. "I'll be in soon."

My mother's mouth tightened, and she slipped an arm over Riley's shoulders. "You carry the cookies."

I waited until they'd gone inside, then circled the staff parking lot. Strack, I noticed, had a reserved space, complete with his name. He seemed like the sort to lord his position over lesser mortals, but at least the spot was empty, so it was probably safe for me to go inside. I kept to my loop as the streetlights flickered on and cars began filtering in, the new shift coming to take over.

The wind was picking up and the temperature was dropping quickly. I turned up the collar of my vest and stuffed my hands into my pockets as a navy Prius pulled in at the far end of the row. A moment later, the driver unfolded himself from the car, his bald head and massive shoulders forming a distinctive silhouette. I grinned in triumph.

"Marcus! Hey, wait up!"

He squinted at me. "Frankie? Anyone ever tell you nice girls don't lurk in dark parking lots?"

"Haven't you heard? I'm not very nice."

He grinned, his teeth bright white against his dark skin. "Oh, I've heard. Strack and Costello want your head on a platter. I shouldn't be talking to you."

"And yet you are."

"What can I say? I'm a rebel. Hold these."

He handed me a stainless steel travel mug and a reusable glass water bottle.

"Nice to see you're staying hydrated. And caffeinated."

"Tools of the trade," he said, ducking back into the car and emerging with a Superman lunchbox.

I raised my eyebrows, and he patted it affectionately. "Birthday present from my wife. Now," he said, "I know you aren't hanging out here just to steal my turkey club. What's going on?"

"Clem Jensen. I want to see his chart—and the post-mortem." He opened his mouth to protest, but I rushed on. "Strack's trying to get my license revoked. I need to prove I had nothing to do with Clem's death."

"It's a formality," Marcus protested. "Once they realize they won't find anything, Strack will leave you alone."

"I don't think so," I said, handing him his mug. "Strack's not just going after my license. He's looking for criminal charges, too."

Marcus drew back. "That's messed up."

"I know. Which is why I need to see Clem's files."

"They won't tell you anything new. And if Strack finds out, I could lose my job. You know how hard it would be to find another one with that kind of mark on my record? I've got a family to support." He shook his head. "I'm sorry, Frankie. I'd help you if I could, but . . ."

I swallowed. I hadn't meant to confide my suspicions to anyone yet, but Marcus had a point. If I was going to ask him to risk his job, he had a right to know why. And he deserved to know that, if my suspicions were correct, he hadn't lost a patient—Clem's life had been *taken*.

"Something's off," I said. "Everything about Clem's death feels weird to me."

Marcus said nothing.

"You know I'm right," I said. "You felt it too, didn't you? That ice in your gut and on the back of your neck. He shouldn't have thrown a clot, not with the meds he was taking. And once he was admitted and stabilized, he shouldn't have crashed. Not so quickly, not from respiratory arrest, considering he was admitted with an MI."

"It happens," he said weakly.

"It shouldn't have. Clem told me his heart attack wasn't an accident. It was the first thing he said to me, but I didn't understand what he meant. Please, Marcus. I know it's your job on the line, but it's mine, too. It's my whole life. And Clem's life. I already asked Hardy, but he won't help me, and I'm running out of options."

Marcus's huge hands tightened on his coffee mug. He opened his mouth to speak, closed it again, and then stared at his shoes. "Strack's on the warpath, Frankie. He's already called me in for questioning once, and he's been real clear we're not done. If I got caught helping you . . . or even talking to you . . ."

He trailed off. A car door slammed a few rows away, and he jerked, checking to see who it was. "I'm sorry," he said again. "I can't risk it."

EIGHT

"Who was that man?" my mom asked as soon as we returned from the hospital. She'd sent Riley upstairs, which should have been my signal to disappear as well.

"What man?" I dug in the rooster-shaped cookie jar, avoiding her eyes.

"The one in the parking lot. You were waiting for him. I spotted you from the window. Are you seeing him?"

I spun to face her. "I've been home for three days, Mom. I've spent almost every minute with Charlie, Riley, or you. When would I have the time to meet somebody?"

"Anything is possible with you," she said, and it didn't sound like a compliment. "I wouldn't have said you had time to get caught up in Clem's death, either. What's his name?"

"Who?" I asked, and started unloading the dishwasher.

"The man you were meeting. Clandestinely."

"He's one of the cardiac care nurses. I had some questions for him about Clem."

She made a noise of disapproval. Then: "Is he single?"

"Married."

"Oh." She paused. "Happily married?"

I stared at her, then turned my attention back to the silverware. "His wife packed his lunch, so I'm going to say yes."

"Hmm. He might have single friends," she said hopefully.

"I won't be here long enough to find out."

Her shoulders sagged, but she rallied. "Long distance relationships can work."

I groaned. "I'm not interested in a relationship right now. With anyone."

"Because Peter broke your heart?" She covered my hand with hers.

I drew away and kept my voice light as I reached for a towel. "Because he didn't."

"I noticed he's called you several times. Have you considered reaching out to him?"

"Not even once." In fact, I hadn't felt the urge to check in with anyone in Chicago—not just Peter, but my friends and coworkers too. I felt a brief jolt of panic at how easily I'd left behind my old life.

I hefted a stack of plates into the cabinet. "Right now, I'm more interested in finding out why Clem Jensen died. Is there anything else you can tell me about him?"

"Not really. I don't spend much time at the store these days, you know. He was a steady customer. I don't remember any complaints about his work." She hung her egg-patterned dishtowel on the drying rack and added, "Isn't this your girls' night with Garima? I'll finish up here. You get ready."

I went upstairs and surveyed the clothes I'd jammed into my backpack. Nothing I'd packed qualified for a girls' night, but Crossroads didn't have much of a dress code to begin with. Still, I switched into a coral-colored sweater and frowned at my reflection.

Clem had been paying for CJ's medication, and cutting-edge drugs didn't come cheap. How was he managing?

"Are you going back out there?" Riley asked, wrapped in a fuzzy purple bathrobe. Her hair hung in wet ropes down her back, and she seemed oblivious to the puddle forming around her.

"Back out where? To the hospital?" I rubbed styling cream into my hair and tried to shape it into something more like curls than steel wool. "I'm going to Crossroads with a friend."

"Did you already go there?"

"A long time ago. Why the interest in dive bars, kid?"

"Grandma said you needed to get back out there," she said nonchalantly, examining a tube of lipstick. "Can I wear this?"

"Not until you're twenty." I plucked it out of her hands. "What else did Grandma say?"

"I don't know. She was talking on the phone. She thinks you're getting a maid."

I turned. "A maid?"

She nodded eagerly. "Because you're old."

"I'm thirty-four, Riley. That's not—oh. Did Grandma say I'm an old maid?"

"She says you're getting to *be* one. But I said you're a nurse, and nurses have more fun than maids."

"We do," I assured her.

"Riley," my mother said from the doorway, "don't gossip. And don't repeat stories you don't understand."

I smiled sweetly. "I think she understood perfectly, Mom. How do I look—you know—for an old maid?"

"Very nice," she said, folding her hands in front of her and giving me a dour look. "Pity you're wasting it on the crowd at Crossroads. Do you have a key?"

I shook my head, and she waved her hand. "Get mine out of my purse. Put them back when you get home."

"Thanks," I said, as a horn sounded outside. "That's Garima—don't wait up. Us old maids tend to stay out pretty late."

★　　★　　★

Not only was Crossroads still standing, it was exactly as it had always been: loud, messy, welcoming, and full. Garima and I edged through the crowd watching ESPN to a back booth. I sat where I could see the room, marveling at how little everything had changed.

"So," Garima said, after she'd ordered a glass of the house wine, "have you gotten that lawyer yet?"

"I was hoping to handle it myself," I muttered.

"That's what got you into this mess," she said. "And what have you got to show for it? A malfeasance investigation and a back injury. You're smarter than this, Frankie."

She had a point. From the moment I'd tried to bring Clem inside on my own, I'd done nothing but hurt myself—literally and figuratively.

"You're right," I said, chastened. "I'll call Chicago Memorial tomorrow, get in contact with my union rep."

"I'm glad to hear it," she replied. "Even a report to the Office of Professional Regulation is going to make your life difficult, you know. Once a complaint is filed . . ."

"I know," I said. Depending on the complaint, the OPR could temporarily suspend my license, and that mark would stay on my permanent record. "Strack knows it, too. He's the one who should be coming under fire," I said, my temper gathering steam. "The ER didn't have enough staff on duty during a multivictim trauma, and that's the administration's fault, not mine."

We paused to order a pizza after the waitress brought our drinks. When she left, Garima said, "It's all about the money. Strack is pushing to sell the hospital, and we're a far less attractive investment if we're fending off a wrongful death suit. If he can shift the blame to you, the hospital won't have to pay out nearly as much, which will make potential buyers very happy. Once the deal goes through, he'll negotiate a lucrative new position for himself, I'm sure."

"He's going to destroy my career to line his own pockets?"

"Absolutely," Garima said. "Plenty of people use Stillwater General as a stepping stone. We get a lot of doctors and administrators who stay long enough to pad their resume, then head somewhere with more prestige and more money. Not many people are here for the long haul."

Myself included. "What about you?"

She smiled. "My family is here. Besides, I've worked hard to build a great department. I'm not willing to hand that over to someone else so I can have a bigger office."

I took a long swallow of mediocre beer, considering her words. "What about Paul Costello? Is he looking for greener pastures?"

She shook her head. "He and Meg moved here after his wife died. It seems unlikely he'd want to uproot her again."

An ugly suspicion bloomed in me. "What if he's responsible? What if he screwed up—gave the wrong order, or missed something in the initial diagnosis? Could he be using me as a scapegoat?"

"It's possible," Garima said slowly. "Do you really think Clem's death was suspicious?"

"According to his daughter, his heart problems weren't severe—he was managing it through medication. And yet his blood work looked way, way off when he was admitted."

Garima stopped in the middle of blotting grease from her pizza. "I'm not going to ask how you saw his test results."

"Best not to," I agreed. "The point is, he shouldn't have had a heart attack, but he did. And he shouldn't have died . . . but he did. I can't help thinking there's more to the story."

"Maybe," she said. "But you're going to have a tough time getting it. Strack's made it clear nobody should be talking to you. There was a memo."

"You're talking to me."

"I'm not great with memos," she said airily. "I'm too busy delivering babies to read them. Besides, they can't suspend me unless they want to lose their level-three NICU designation."

"Nice," I said.

She smiled. "Now, since I've given you the inside scoop on the hospital, give *me* the inside scoop on the surgeon."

"No scoop," I said. "The surgeon called it off right before I came out here."

"Why?"

I finished my beer before answering. "Because I didn't want to marry him."

"Which seems reasonable. Except . . . why were you engaged to someone you didn't want to marry?"

"That," I said, "is an excellent question."

"He's not your first, is he?"

I choked slightly. "Come again?"

"Weren't you and Noah MacLean engaged? At the end of senior year, right? Everyone said he popped the question on prom night."

Reflexively, I brushed my opposite thumb over my ring finger. "We were just kids."

"What happened?"

"I wanted to leave Stillwater. He wanted to stay." I shrugged. "Hard to do both."

It was as simple as that. And infinitely more complicated. I'd known, even then, that I had to leave Stillwater. My father's death had taught me that nobody's future was guaranteed, so you had to make the most of every single moment. Drink in the world in great, noisy gulps and treat your days like one giant adventure, because you might not get another chance.

At seventeen, Noah—hot-headed, smart-mouthed, and sweeter than most people realized—had felt the same way. He'd encouraged me to go away to college, to see the world, to break free of Stillwater. But as my horizons expanded, it became harder to return every Christmas, harder still to pass the summers behind the counter of the hardware store when there were so many other places to see. Gradually, boredom turned to resentment—of the store, of my family, of Stillwater itself. That's when I knew I had to leave for good.

At the same time that I realized I couldn't stay, Noah had realized he couldn't leave. There'd been no money for school, so he worked at a local garage, taking the occasional night class at the community college and watching over his brothers and sisters when his parents couldn't—or wouldn't. Once his dad took off, nothing in the world could have convinced him to abandon those kids.

An impasse, then, broken into jagged pieces on a late-summer afternoon, when I'd told him I wasn't coming back, and he'd told me he wasn't leaving, and neither of us displayed much compassion for the other. I'd fled, leaving behind my chip of an engagement ring and some vital piece of my heart I'd spent the next few years training myself not to miss.

"I see," Garima said softly. "And that's got nothing to do with the surgeon, right?"

"Nothing," I said firmly. "I need another beer. Want a refill?"

She gestured to the barely touched wine glass in front of her. "I'm set."

I made my way up to the bar, which was packed solid. Our waitress stood at the end of the counter, back to the railing, holding her tray like a shield. In front of her was a weedy-looking man, unshaven, his hair slicked back and his flannel shirt limp and grubby in the dim bar lighting.

"Enough, Jimmy," I heard her say. "I'm working."

"And I'm buying," he said with a smirk.

She shoved past him. "Not from me."

"Come on, darlin'. Play nice and I'll leave a big tip."

"Thought you were broke, Madigan," called the bartender. "You finally get a job?"

Jimmy Madigan. I froze, unable to stop staring. Laura's husband. No wonder she wanted a divorce—I couldn't imagine what she'd seen in him to begin with. They seemed not just mismatched but from two entirely different species.

"I'm not gonna need one," he replied. "Big payout coming my way real soon."

"You say that every time you head over to the riverboat," said the bartender. "Hasn't happened yet."

"Not the boat," Jimmy said. "Didn't you hear? My wife's old man died."

"Clem?" The bartender shook his head. "That's a damn shame."

Jimmy snorted. "Not for me. Couldn't wait till he kicked off, the way he was always interfering. A man's marriage is his own business. I warned him to stay out of it."

Had he, now? Interesting—I'd assumed there was bad blood between the two men, but this sounded like more than animosity. This sounded like a motive. Even though my skin was crawling, I edged closer.

"What was there to stay out of?" the waitress scoffed. "She dumped you."

"She didn't appreciate what she had," Jimmy said, turning a ferocious scowl on her. "Now that Daddy's not taking care of her, she'll come home. Especially after the hospital pays up."

"For what?" she shot back.

"A settlement. That's what they call it, so I don't sue for . . ." He put his hand over his heart. "Emotional distress."

The bartender turned toward me, clearly disgusted. "Help you, sweetheart?"

I jolted. "Oh. Um . . ."

Jimmy turned to focus on me, his eyes traveling lazily over my body. Up close, his complexion was sallow, skin drawn tightly over sharp cheekbones and jaw. In a kinder face, it would have been striking, but Jimmy just looked . . . hungry. "Put it on my tab," he ordered the bartender and sidled over.

"Haven't seen you here before." He smelled of cigarettes and stale beer. I shifted away, but he followed, deliberately crowding me.

"Just visiting," I said coolly, and turned to the waitress. "We're ready for the check."

"Sorry about that," she replied. She ripped our bill off the order pad and held it out.

Jimmy plucked it from her hand, held it out of my reach. "Night's just starting. Why don't you stay? We can get to know each other better."

He trailed a finger along my arm, and instinct kicked in.

Nobody's ever happy to come to the ER; some people, in fact, are downright uncooperative. And while nurses like Marcus, roughly the size of Mount Rushmore, can easily restrain patients, I lack the height—and muscle mass—to stop a raging meth addict through sheer force. Instead, I've developed other techniques.

Grabbing his wrist, I twisted, fast and hard, far enough to transfer the force up to his shoulder. Not enough to break anything, of course, but I applied enough torque to make his face go white. He dropped to his knees, swearing a blue streak.

The room stilled.

"Thanks, but I know everything I need to."

From behind me, Garima whispered, so low only I could hear it, "Don't give Strack more ammunition."

With a sigh, I let go. Jimmy scrambled up, color flooding his face, spewing obscenities.

Garima pulled out her wallet, but the bartender waved her away. "No charge, ladies. Thanks for the show."

"Our pleasure," she said and hustled me out of Crossroads.

★ ★ ★

"Jimmy wanted Clem dead," I said as we drove home. "You heard him. He wanted Laura back, and he was always looking for a chance to make a buck."

"You think he killed Clem so he could sue the hospital? That seems a little complicated for a guy like Jimmy. He doesn't strike me as the criminal mastermind type."

"Maybe he wasn't thinking about a lawsuit," I admitted. "But he might have been hoping there was a life insurance policy or some kind of inheritance."

Garima glanced at me, then returned her attention to the road. "An hour ago you were talking medical error. Now you think it's murder?"

"I don't know what to think," I said. "Which is why I want to see the postmortem."

"Strack isn't going to give it to you," she said. "Why not go to the police? I'm sure Noah would listen to you."

He might, but listening and believing were two different things. I'd squandered Noah's belief in me twelve years ago, and I doubted it would be easily replenished.

"What would I say? I have a gut feeling? Jimmy Madigan was running his mouth at a bar? I need some kind of proof. If I can't get it from Clem's chart, where am I going to find it?"

We drove through the deserted town square, antique streetlights glowing warmly along the empty sidewalks. Most of Stillwater went to bed early, especially on a weeknight. As we passed the darkened windows of Stapleton and Sons, I wondered again what Charlie wasn't saying and if the books would tell a different story altogether.

And then it hit me.

Medical records weren't the only paper trail Clem had left. "Stop the car!"

Garima, ever-unflappable, coasted to the curb. "What's wrong?"

"Clem was a handyman," I said. "My mom said he was a wholesale customer, so we must have records about his account."

"How does that help you?"

"His account balance should give me an idea of how his business is doing—if he has a lot of clients, if he's paying his bills on time. If Clem's making good money, Jimmy has a better motive."

"You could also ask his daughter," Garima said, in the same no-nonsense tone she had taken with Charlie. "If she's his next-of-kin, she can probably get his bank records."

"I met Laura yesterday," I said. "If I ask for her father's bank records, she'll think I'm a lunatic, at best. Plus, she's grieving—I don't want to tell her it was murder until I know for sure."

"Fair point," Garima said. "Do you want me to go in with you?"

"Nah. I'll be fine," I said, climbing out of the car.

"How will you get home?"

"Walk," I said. "It's not so bad from here. I did it all the time when I was a kid."

"It's late," she pointed out. "Are you sure that's safe?"

"It's Stillwater," I replied. "Thanks for the girls' night."

"Anytime," she said. "Be careful, Nancy Drew."

I snorted and waved as she drove off.

The night was cool and clear as I made my way toward the back parking lot. My mom's key ring was jam-packed, but it was easy to pick out the one I needed. The store's oversized brass key was the same one we'd had when I was a kid.

I fitted the key into the lock and gave it the usual tug and twist. I heard the familiar thud of the deadbolt, the screech of the door as I pushed it open, and then . . . nothing.

That wasn't right. I should have heard the alarm, a shrill beeping that lasted until someone punched in the security code. If the code wasn't entered in sixty seconds, the alarm company alerted the police.

Had Charlie upgraded to a silent alarm? I dashed to the control panel, in the back of the store. The last thing I needed was Stillwater's finest arriving on the scene, lights ablaze. I'd never live it down.

The control panel was the same one we'd had growing up, but the digital display wasn't requesting a code or counting down, the way it used to. Instead, it blinked a steady, repeating message: "System offline. Call manufacturer for reinstatement."

I hadn't heard an alarm because there *was* no alarm. Charlie had let the contract lapse. Stillwater Gen wasn't the only place lacking in security.

Annoyed, I turned to survey the room and found myself frozen. I was alone in the family store for the first time since I was a teenager.

It smelled exactly the same. The faintly dusty scent of machine oil and lumber and metal, the lingering aroma of coffee, the funky, almost vegetal odor of rope, contrasting with the sharpness of freshly mixed paint. I forced myself to take a halting step toward the back counter, fumbling in the semidarkness. My fingers brushed against the varnished wood, and suddenly, I was six years old and seated atop the counter, practicing my spelling and stuffing my cheeks with powdered sugar–covered doughnut holes while my father debated the merits of hex-screws versus Phillips with a customer, his laugh filling the room. He reached out to tug my pigtail, and I caught a whiff of his aftershave—bay rum, familiar and dear.

I blinked, and the memory vanished.

Alone again.

I hadn't given much thought to the matter when I was a kid, but now the full weight of nearly a century and a half pressed down on me. Stapletons had run this store since shortly after Stillwater was founded in the late 1800s. The oak counter under my hand was the same that had been here back then; generation after generation of my ancestors had stood behind it—and everything we sold.

I had turned my back on all of it.

Twelve years ago, I'd told myself I was chasing a dream, leaving Stillwater for a bigger, better life. Now I wondered if I'd also been running away from both memory and responsibility. What did it say about me, that I'd stayed gone for so long? Nothing flattering.

I wandered the worn wooden floor, not bothering to turn on the lights. Even now, I knew every inch of the store by heart, and each one held memories.

Stapleton and Sons was originally a single building—seven aisles wide, stocking everything from hammers to drawer pulls to paint thinner, the merchandise crammed all the way to the ceiling. Up front was a single register and seasonal goods. Over the years, the store had expanded, taking over what had once been a five-and-dime next door. The second room held construction materials—plumbing equipment, drywall, lumber, and the like, as well as bigger merchandise—lawnmowers and grills in the summer, and snowblowers and salt in the winter. But the real action happened at the back counter. This was where we took care of special orders and wholesale customers, people who needed pipe or lumber or a chimney's worth of brick. The regulars viewed it as a sort of social club. Metal stools were tucked under the massive oak slab, so they could settle in and discuss a project at length; a special few even kept their own coffee mug hanging from the pegboard along the back wall.

Clem would have spent time here, with the other contractors, and it struck me that Charlie must have known him. I wondered how hard she'd take the news of his death. Charlie was a practical sort of person; normally I wouldn't have expected hysterics. But her state of mind right now was anything but normal.

Either way, she'd have information on him in the office.

The floorboards creaked beneath my feet as I made my way to the staircase, situated between the main room and the addition. My mom had argued for linoleum when I was a kid, but my dad had insisted on keeping the original wood. History was more important than convenience, he'd said. I was glad to see Charlie agreed, though the floor could use a fresh coat of stain—the center of each aisle was worn down to bare wood. She'd fixed up the front windows, but everything else remained where it had always been. If I cared to look, I'd find extra stock in the basement, current orders in a wire bin behind the counter, and old files upstairs.

Out of habit, I skipped over the noisy fourth stair and used the key to unlock the second-floor apartment. Cozy and bright, it had been the original Stapleton home, back in 1873. Over the years it had been a bachelor pad, a newlywed love nest, and a mother-in-law's suite. Unlike Matt and Charlie, I'd never lived in the apartment—though in high school, there had been plenty of nights I'd snuck out and met Noah here.

Since he and I were both still alive, I assumed my mother had never found out.

Now the apartment served as office space. I flicked on the lights and trailed through the rooms, getting reacquainted. The kitchen held industrial quantities of coffee supplies and a few snacks. One bedroom was stuffed to the gills with papers and filing cabinets, while the other held toys and an ancient twin bed. A scarred wooden table sat in the middle of the living room, a laser printer on the floor nearby. The sight of all those invoices and the old printing calculator sent me back in time to the nights when my mom would bring dinner from home and we'd eat from paper plates on the floor while she did the books. Charlie and I would fall asleep, curled up like puppies, until it was time to go home—but this tiny, slant-roofed apartment felt like home too.

I sat down at the table and began sorting through papers. The stack of orders was depressingly short—and the stack of bills alarmingly long. Guilt twinged in my gut. Charlie had made it clear that this wasn't my business, quite literally. Yet here I was, pawing through the books as if I had a right to inspect what I'd walked away from.

I don't know how long I examined the papers on the table. None of them related to Clem, but I couldn't look away. Business was down. Accounts weren't paying their bills. The weekend sales had dropped off to the point that Charlie was covering weekends herself, and they were down to two other employees—one of which was Uncle Marshall.

I frowned. We'd always had employees, and we'd treated them well. But Uncle Marshall didn't seem to be pulling a paycheck.

I wasn't sure *Charlie* was drawing a paycheck.

I pushed the papers away. Prying again, and this time for no reason other than sheer nosiness. This wasn't what I'd come for. None of the papers looked like they related to Clem, so I moved to the bedroom and started rifling through the filing cabinets. The drawers shrieked, metal on metal, as I pulled them out, and I shuddered.

In the silence that followed came the long, low groan of the fourth stair.

I froze.

Old houses settle and creak. Like people, their bones grow noisy as they age, no matter how well kept they are. But this wasn't the typical noise of a house settling.

Someone was here.

I hadn't locked the door behind me.

Stupid, stupid, stupid. My name was all over the hospital now, thanks to Strack and the lawsuit. In a town like Stillwater, it wouldn't be hard to track me down—everyone knew where my mom lived. But to find me at the store, at this time of night, meant I'd been followed.

Jimmy.

Whether he had killed Clem or not, I'd humiliated him at Crossroads. He could have easily tailed Garima's car and seen me enter. Completely alone and easy prey.

Not so easy, though. He should have realized that when I wrenched his arm.

My temper surged, along with the impulse to teach Jimmy the lesson he'd failed to grasp the first time we tangled. But as I looked around for a weapon, finding nothing but a stapler, reason crept in. My phone was downstairs, out of reach. No doubt Jimmy was better armed, and I already suspected he was capable of murder. As much as I hated to admit it, flight was a better choice than fight, at least for now.

Stapler in hand, I slipped into the bathroom and locked the door behind me. Above the toilet was a small window overlooking the flat roof next door. It wouldn't be my first time sneaking out this way.

The window was unlocked. I made a mental note to talk with Charlie about the store's lack of security, then slid the sash up. The swollen frame emitted a squeal of protest, and I went still, certain the intruder had heard it.

Nothing but stealthy footsteps.

I popped out the screen, climbed onto the toilet lid, and . . .

"Sheriff's department! Come on out."

I groaned. So much for avoiding attention.

"Out. Now. Hands where I can see them."

"Noah?"

A beat.

"Frankie?"

Definitely Noah. I wobbled on my makeshift perch and jumped to the floor, cracking my elbow on the side of the sink. "Ow!"

"Frankie!" The knob rattled in the frame, and then there was the thud of flesh hitting wood. "Are you okay? Is there someone . . ."

"It's just me." I fumbled with the lock and wrenched the door open.

Noah, gun drawn, stood inches away.

"What are you doing here?" I asked, gaping at him.

He holstered the gun and studied me. "Someone called in suspicious activity—no car in the lot, and someone moving around upstairs. I was close, and when I got here the back door was open."

"That was me," I said, rubbing my elbow.

"I can see that." He paused, peering over my shoulder. "Climbing out the window?"

"Like riding a bike," I said. "You never forget how."

He chuckled. "What are *you* doing here?"

I paused. "Paperwork."

"Thought the business was Charlie's thing." The words echoed the last fight we'd ever had. *There's no reason for me to stay. The business is Charlie's thing, not mine.* As if Noah was no reason at all.

When I could keep my voice even, I said, "Charlie's got her hands full right now. You know, with the newborn?"

Noah's radio crackled, requesting his status. "Hold on," he said, and turned to speak with the dispatcher. Then he shifted, putting his full attention on me again, and I felt myself flush despite the cold night air pouring through the window.

"So," he said, "urgent hardware business. At midnight on a Monday."

I wrestled the sash down while I answered. "Turns out that patient of mine—Clem Jensen—was a customer. I wanted to look at his account." To deflect more questions, I asked one of my own. "Have you found out anything, by the way?"

"Not yet," he said. "Why are you so interested? Seems like you'd be the last person to get involved with the good citizens of Stillwater."

The barb stung, but I didn't want him to see it. I brushed past him into the living room. "I don't like losing patients."

"Especially when you're being blamed," he said, following me.

"You heard?" Not a surprise, but the urge to defend myself was stronger than I'd expected. It wasn't just outrage or my reputation. Clearly, Noah's opinion of me hadn't changed since our breakup. Selfish, he'd called me back then. Thoughtless and self-absorbed. The words had been spoken in anger, and in hindsight, I could see there was more than a little truth to them. But for him to look at me now and see a failure—a negligent, incompetent failure—was more than I could bear.

It struck me that he might have heard an entirely different account. He might have heard Strack's version of the story. He might even believe it.

"Clem shouldn't have died," I blurted, needing him to hear my side of the story. "I want to figure out why he did."

He waved a hand at a paper-covered table. "You think the answer is in a bunch of invoices?"

He didn't sound suspicious, only skeptical. There'd been a time when I could size up Noah's moods with barely a glance, but I was out of practice. I scrutinized him, trying to understand the angle of his eyebrows and the curve of his mouth, the way he held himself still and watchful under my gaze, like he knew what I was doing and was returning the favor.

"When you investigate a crime, do you always know where the evidence is?" I asked eventually.

"If I'm lucky, sure. Most crimes aren't that complicated. It's a lot of chasing, but you usually know where you're going. Nothing wrong with straightforward, Frankie." Despite his earlier irritation, his gaze had softened.

"Not always, right? Sometimes you have to . . . poke around. See where things lead."

Now his lips hitched into a reluctant smile. "Something like that."

"Well, medicine's the same way. There are a lot of factors that come into play when you treat a patient—history and environment and personality and biology. The more information we have, the better we can treat someone. The more I know about Clem, the better the chance I can understand why he died."

"He died because his heart stopped working."

"His lungs, actually. I think there's more to it than that. I think it was deliberate."

"Murder?" he asked. "Who would kill Clem Jensen?"

"His son-in-law, for starters." I explained about my run-in with Jimmy at Crossroads, and Noah held out a hand, palm up.

"Don't tell me any more," he said. "Jimmy could file a complaint, you know. I'd rather not arrest you for assault."

"He was harassing me! It was self-defense."

"I'm sure it was. Jimmy Madigan tends to think he can punch above his weight, and it never ends well for him." He allowed himself a small grin. "He just didn't realize who he was messing with."

"How very sexist of him," I said.

"The guy's all talk, Frankie. To open an investigation, we need proof."

"Which is why I'm here." I held up a sheaf of papers as an example.

He glanced around the room, crammed with files and invoices. "Big job. Want some help?"

"Aren't you on patrol?"

"Technically, I'm off duty," he said after a pause. "I was heading home when the call came in. I was nearby, so I took it."

"Not *that* nearby," I said without thinking.

His brow furrowed in confusion, and then his eyes shuttered. "I moved."

I could have kicked myself. Did I really believe he would have stayed in his childhood home? Noah had lived on the south side of town, in a neighborhood of tiny, run-down cottages next to the train tracks. His dad was a nasty drunk—mean, when he was around, which wasn't very often—and his mother was . . . tired. Worn down, scared, helpless, and more than willing to let Noah take on the task of raising his younger siblings. Once Noah's father abandoned the family, any thoughts Noah had of escaping Stillwater were abandoned too, leaving us in an impossible situation.

I considered asking how his brothers and sisters were faring now but decided against it. Our past was painful enough; poking at the sorest spots seemed unnecessarily cruel. It was obvious he'd moved out—and up, no doubt.

If Noah had moved out, he might also have moved on.

My gaze drifted to his left hand. No ring. Which didn't necessarily mean anything, I reminded myself, ignoring the flutter somewhere behind my sternum.

"Don't you need to get home?" I asked, hoping it sounded nonchalant.

"Nope." He didn't elaborate further.

"By all means, then." I led the way into the bedroom, grateful that it looked more like a hoarder's paradise than an actual bedroom. It was cluttered with castoff family furniture in various states of disrepair, and boxes of files were stacked on every surface.

Noah whistled, long and low. "We could be here till dawn."

"You don't have to help," I said quickly. "I can manage."

"I don't mind. Besides—wouldn't be the first time we stayed here all night." He lifted an eyebrow. "You have a curfew?"

I felt my cheeks heat, remembering the other times we'd stayed here. "I'm a little old for a curfew."

"Lila might disagree."

He was probably right.

"The invoices are filed by date, not name," I said, opening a box and tilting it toward him. "We'll have to go through and find them individually."

"How far back are we going?" he asked, pulling the cardboard lid off the nearest box.

I considered. "Two years should be enough."

"Got it," he said.

We worked side by side, making a central pile of Clem's invoices. Each had his name and address printed at the top. The silence between us felt comfortable, until we reached for a box simultaneously. Noah's fingertips brushed the back of my hand, and we both drew back as if scalded.

The mood grew tense. Finally, he cleared his throat and said, "How's living with Lila again?"

I made a face, and he laughed, the charge in the air dissipating. "That bad?"

"Not really," I admitted. "I'm bunking in with Riley. It's definitely a short-term situation."

He nodded slowly. "When do you go back to Chicago?"

Unlike the first time he asked, I kept my voice light. Effortless, even, as if I wasn't wondering what he'd make of my answer. "I haven't decided yet. I've got some vacation time saved up, and I want to make sure Charlie's back on her feet before I leave."

"Don't you have a wedding to plan?"

I went cold. "A wedding?"

"Lila hasn't been shy about telling people. A surgeon, huh?"

Apparently, my mother hadn't deemed the *end* of my engagement quite as newsworthy as the beginning.

"Noah . . ." My hand went to my necklace, where I'd kept Peter's ring, and I tried to summon the words to tell him the truth.

Before I could continue, he spoke, his voice rough and gentle at the same time.

"It's okay, Frankie. Is he a good guy, at least?"

I swallowed and nodded. Peter *was* a good guy. He just wasn't my fiancé. Rather than admit it—to let Noah see how I'd failed yet again, how I'd hurt someone I claimed to love yet again—I kept quiet.

With any luck, I'd be back in Chicago before the truth came out.

"I'm happy for you," he said. "Really."

I nodded again and lifted the pile of invoices we'd found. "This is plenty, don't you think?"

"If you say so," Noah said, obviously relieved to be talking about something else. "What are you looking for?"

I studied the flimsy carbon copy. "How much business he was doing. Laura said he'd been paying for her son's epilepsy medications, and that can't have been cheap."

"Wouldn't her insurance cover it?"

"Laura said she couldn't afford to pay for the meds *and* a divorce lawyer, so it doesn't sound like it. Even with insurance, people can still spend tons of money on prescriptions. It's kind of a racket."

I'd seen it countless times: people with chronic conditions who couldn't afford to pay for the latest drugs, so they'd given up entirely—which only made them more sick. Most of the time, there was an older drug that was nearly as effective and hundreds of dollars cheaper. But there was less incentive to prescribe it or a generic version when the doctors were getting all sorts of "bonuses" from the drug companies—conferences and samples and dinners and gifts. Not all doctors were like that, and most would prescribe something less expensive if the patient asked—but even a handful was too many.

I scanned the invoices, trying to estimate how much Clem would charge customers, how much he'd clear. "He's doing steady business, but he's definitely not getting rich. How's he affording those medications?"

Noah shrugged. "Could have sold some property or inherited. Won the lottery or hit a big jackpot at the casino. Maybe he plays the stock market."

"He didn't seem like the Wall Street type," I said, thinking back to his worn T-shirt and droopy mustache. "I guess anything's possible."

"Possible, yes. Likely, no." He scrubbed a hand through his hair, kept his voice kind. "It doesn't seem like there's a lot to investigate here. The guy had a heart attack and died. In the hospital. I know you feel a connection, and I know the hospital's trying to pin this on you. But you're reaching."

"What about CJ's medication? That doesn't seem weird to you?"

"That a grandfather would spend his last cent helping his grandson? Not really. Your mom would do the same for Charlie's kids, right?" He took my hand in his, calluses rasping against my palm, his thumb brushing the place where my engagement ring should have been. "I'll keep asking around about Clem. But we're not opening an official investigation unless you have something else to tell me."

As far as I was concerned, Jimmy was still my prime suspect, with motives ranging from money to bitter revenge. There were plenty of other things I wanted to share—the truth about Peter, my worries about the store—but I couldn't bring myself to tell him any of it, not when he didn't believe me about Clem.

"There's nothing else," I said stiffly, tugging my hand free.

His eyebrows lifted. "You're sure?"

I smoothed my hair, hoping it would settle my composure. It would be so easy to confide in Noah again. Standing in this familiar room, after all this time, it was as if past and present were overlapping, the distinctions fading. The Noah before me looked suddenly younger, earnest and endearing, and I felt alarmingly vulnerable.

"A thousand percent," I said, lying through my teeth.

"Glad to hear it," he said. "Funny, don't you think?"

"What's that?" I scooped up the invoices and shoved them into my bag, planning to study them when I could actually focus.

He reached forward and tugged at the lock of hair I'd been twisting around my finger. "The way people don't change. Not really."

"People change," I protested. "I have."

"Mmn-hmn. Do me a favor, Frankie. Stay away from the casino."

"Why? You think Clem might have been in over his head?" It was an angle I hadn't considered.

"No," he said, voice lazy and amused. "But you still can't bluff."

NINE

Despite what you've read, warm milk will not put you to sleep. True, it contains tryptophan, same as a Thanksgiving turkey, and tryptophan can induce drowsiness. But you'd need to eat six pounds of turkey—or drink four gallons of warm milk—to truly knock yourself out.

Which didn't stop me from tiptoeing into the kitchen, heating up a mug of 2 percent, and sprinkling it with nutmeg, hoping the quiet childhood ritual would soothe me. My body hadn't adjusted to a daytime schedule yet. It longed to be back in the ER, with its bright lights and constant motion and spiking adrenaline.

I pulled my phone from my purse and dialed a number I knew would answer.

"Chicago Memorial Hospital, Emergency Department."

"Mindy! It's Frankie! How's it going?"

There was a pause. In the background, I could hear the usual noise of the ER—the shouts of patients and the measured replies of doctors, sirens and loudspeakers and monitor beeps. But Mindy's voice lifted above it all.

"Peter dumped you?"

I'd known it was coming, but the question stung regardless.

"He did."

"Does he have another piece?"

"Another—no, Min, he doesn't."

"Well, we're giving everyone in Peds the cold shoulder until he comes groveling."

I took a sip of tepid milk. Gross. "I appreciate the sentiment, but it's not necessary."

"Aw, listen to you, putting on the brave face. Maybe he just needs some time. Guys get cold feet, you know. He'll change his mind."

"He's not going to change his mind."

"You don't know that," Mindy said. "Look at Kate Middleton. Prince William dumped her, and what did she do? She went out and showed him what he was missing. Next thing you know, she's got a big old rock on her finger and the wedding of the century. Learn from Princess Kate, Frankie. Make sure when you show up next shift that you're looking fabulous."

"I'm telling you, it's fine. More than fine. He was right to break it off."

There was a burst of noise in the background, some new patient rolling in. Mindy shouted to someone, then returned. "He was right? You're okay with it?"

"I am," I assured her. "Better we figured it out now, rather than after the wedding."

"Think about the alimony," she moaned. "You'd never have to work again."

I didn't mention that was already a possibility.

"So if you're not calling to get the scoop, what's up? How's life in the sticks? Dying of boredom yet?"

"You'd be surprised," I said. "I was wondering if you had the number of our union rep."

"Is he trying to get you fired?" she asked, outrage back in full force.

"Peter? No!" I trotted out my carefully prepared story—I wasn't ready to tell anyone at work about Strack's threats. Even though I was confident I'd done the right thing, I didn't want the news to get back to my bosses. The threat of an official complaint would chip away at my professional reputation—the one thing I had going for me right now. "My sister had the baby, and I need to stay longer than expected to help her out. I was going to apply for family leave—not much, just a few weeks—and I was hoping they could help me with the paperwork."

Another pause, as Mindy responded to someone's question, her voice muffled. Then, "You need to contact Human Resources, not the union."

"Sure," I said with a weak laugh. "Sure. Might as well get me both, though. Just to be on the safe side."

There was silence, and the squawk of a radio in the background. "Whoops," Mindy said. "I'll text it to you, okay? We've got two GSWs coming in."

"Sure," I said, wishing I was there to help, "Mindy—"

She'd dropped the phone with a clatter. I listened for a while, hearing the familiar shouts and sounds of the ER buzzing with the two gunshot victims' arrival. It was functioning perfectly well without me, and the knowledge made me feel lonelier than ever.

TEN

Charlie was in the middle of changing Rowan's diaper when I arrived at the hospital the next morning.

"Want to help?"

"I plead Auntie privilege," I said. "Looks like you have it under control."

"Come on," she teased. "A dirty diaper should be nothing compared to what you see at work."

This was true. Nurses deal with every bodily fluid imaginable, and it's never as neat and tidy as it looks on TV.

"I'm off the clock," I said and threw myself into the rocking chair.

"Did Riley get off to school okay this morning?"

"She did. I packed her lunch."

"You?" Her eyebrows lifted. "She's picky about her lunch, Frankie."

"I noticed. She really eats peanut butter and banana sandwiches? With bacon? Can I start calling her Tiny Elvis?"

"Every day for the last two years." She finished diapering Rowan and grudgingly passed her to me, mindful of the tubes and monitor leads trailing from beneath the blanket.

"Well, if it's good enough for The King . . ." I said. Rowan pursed her lips and squeaked softly. "How are you, short stack? They treating you okay in here? Making friends?"

"She can make friends when she's older," Charlie said firmly. "When can we go home?"

"Rowan's got a few more weeks, minimum, like the doctor told you. We need to fatten her up. This really is the best place for her, Charlie."

She sighed. "I know. What about me?"

"Ask Garima," I said. "I'd guess a few more days. Your blood pressure isn't totally stable, and you've got plenty of healing to do from the surgery. Most people would like the break, you know."

"I'm not most people," she said. "I need to get back to the store."

"You said it was fine," I reminded her, knowing full well that Stapleton and Sons was far from fine, hoping she'd finally open up.

She tucked the blanket around Rowan more securely, avoiding my eyes. "It is."

Ah. So that's how it was going to be. She must have sensed my skepticism, because she added, "I don't like being away from Riley, either. And I want to sleep in my own bed."

"Join the club," I muttered. Then, "I could help, you know. If something was wrong."

She scoffed. "Sure. Don't you have enough going on already?"

"What's that supposed to mean?" I said, trying to sound insulted instead of guilty. Matt had warned me that Charlie had radar, but the last thing I wanted was to cause her more stress.

"Mom keeps texting me to ask how you're doing."

"She's freaking out because Peter and I split up."

"That's what I figured," Charlie replied. "At first. But you're obviously worried about something, and I don't think it's the engagement. You've barely mentioned Peter, not even to trash-talk him. You wanted to end it, didn't you?"

I didn't deny it. I didn't need to.

"Dr. K won't tell me anything, either. I've heard the nurses talking about you, but every time I try to listen in, they change the subject."

"Rude to eavesdrop," I singsonged. If prying was my besetting sin, eavesdropping was Charlie's. From the time she was a little kid, she wanted to be in on all the adult conversations. Handy at Christmastime, but now it was a problem.

She shrugged, completely unabashed. "It's about that patient, isn't it? The one who died? You're involved somehow."

"I didn't do anything wrong," I assured her, but I couldn't quite tell if she believed me. Fair enough; I didn't believe her about the store. Sad, though, that neither one of us trusted the other enough to confide in. A single visit wasn't enough time to mend that break, and I felt a pang of regret. "I'm handling it. There's nothing to worry about."

She shook her head. "Don't you get it? I worry about everything."

"You don't need to worry about this."

"Good." She met my eyes squarely. "We have enough trouble as it is, Frankie. Don't bring us any more."

Before I could reply, she looked past me, face brightening. A moment later, Matt ambled in, looking like a giant amid the delicate equipment of the NICU. "How are all the Stapleton girls today?" he asked.

"Good," we chorused, but Matt frowned as he washed his hands, clearly picking up on the tension between us. That was the thing about families—they knew when something was off, even when they couldn't put a name to it. I was willing to bet Laura knew more than she realized about Clem's death.

"I'll let you three have some family time," I said, handing Rowan over to Matt. "I need to make a phone call."

A quick call to directory assistance gave me Laura's number. She sounded surprised to hear from me but not displeased, which I took as good sign.

"How are you doing?" I asked. "How is CJ?"

"I'm coping," she said warily. "We both are. I assume you heard about the lawsuit."

"News travels," I said, settling into a far corner of the cafeteria and blowing on my scalding-hot coffee. I hoped Stillwater Gen had a decent burn unit.

"I didn't want Jimmy to file the suit," she said defensively. "I had no idea he was even planning it."

"I know." I didn't want Laura see me as the enemy—especially when the *real* enemy was still out there. "It didn't seem like something you'd do."

My position in the cafeteria gave me an excellent view of the entrance. I watched as Walter Strack, Dr. Hardy, and Ashley Ritter came in and ordered their food to go. The conversation was animated, brief snippets drifting toward me, phrases like "control group" and "overseas markets" and "approval process." No doubt Cardiodyne would give the hospital's reputation quite a boost when it won FDA approval. That kind of prestige could be a lucrative bargaining chip for Strack when negotiating a sale. Would it be enough to offset a lawsuit, though?

"Do you think the hospital was negligent?" I asked Laura.

Across the room, Ashley caught my eye and smiled briefly before refocusing on Strack. He waved away her attempts to pay, said something I couldn't catch, and then laughed. After a beat, Ashley joined in.

Laura was quiet for a long time, mulling over the question. "I don't think so. He had heart problems, and his diet was terrible. The only exercise he got was fishing. I kept telling him the medication could only do so much, but . . ." She trailed off, sounding defeated.

"You're sure he was taking his medication?" I asked gently.

"Every day. I nagged him constantly. I should have spent more time enjoying him and less time nagging."

"You were taking care of him." I pressed myself farther into the corner as Strack's group stopped to dose their coffees with cream and sugar. Thankfully they were too busy chatting to notice me. A moment later, they'd left again. "That's a good thing."

She exhaled shakily. "I guess so. But looking back . . . I'm glad I had that last phone call with him, at least."

I'd forgotten that Laura had talked to Clem after his surgery. "What did you talk about?"

Her voice grew thick and wistful. "We didn't have long. He was so tired, and weak from the surgery. I wanted to come to the hospital right away, but he wouldn't let me. He didn't think it was safe to leave CJ home alone. I told him I could call a friend to stay with CJ, but he was adamant. He didn't want me anywhere near Stillwater Gen."

I straightened. "Were those his exact words?"

She paused. "I think so. He could be so stubborn. I stayed home, and the next thing I knew, the hospital was calling to say he was gone."

"When did Jimmy tell you he was filing the lawsuit?"

"Monday morning," Laura said, practically spitting the words. "I haven't spoken to him in months, and the next thing I know, he was on my front porch at the crack of dawn, telling me not to talk to anyone from the hospital, that he'd found a way to make some cash and he'd split it with me. I don't *want* the money. It won't bring my father back, and I don't want to spend the next year dealing with lawyers and court dates when I should be helping my son grieve."

Amid the rush of sympathy, I latched onto one fact, the thing Laura *hadn't* said. "You didn't tell Jimmy about your dad?"

"Why would I? He spends every penny he makes, and I don't have a dime to spare for him—so he's not interested in us. God forbid he was ever interested in his son."

The base of my spine prickled, the same ominous feeling I'd had before. "How do you think he heard about Clem?"

"Same as anything else in this town," she said. "We grow gossip right alongside the corn and beans."

I tried to smile at the familiar joke, glad Laura couldn't see my true expression. Even Stillwater's rumor mill didn't work that fast. Clem had died late Sunday morning; a day later, Jimmy was in Strack's office threatening to sue. Either Jimmy had an inside source at the hospital or he'd known Clem was going to die.

The question was, should I tell Laura? She had a right to know that her ex was a murderer, but as Noah had pointed out—twice—I had no proof. It would be easy for her to dismiss my accusations as an attempt to clear my own name. Worse, what if I was wrong and this was all an accident? Laura was already devastated. For once in my life, I decided to proceed with caution.

Now was as good a time to start as any. "You mentioned that your dad was covering CJ's medication. What was he taking?"

"Apracetim. It's new—he's only been taking it for the last six months or so, but it's made such a difference—he's going weeks between seizures now."

"Was it expensive? I know new medicines are usually pricey."

"It was. My insurance didn't even cover it," she said, confirming what I'd told Noah. "Dad's business was booming, so he insisted on paying for it."

I thought back over the invoices I'd seen. If Clem's business was booming, he wasn't buying his supplies at Stapleton and Sons. His account had shown a steady stream of orders for the last year, not a sudden spike of jobs.

"Dad's business," she said, voice trembling. "I guess I have to add that to the list, don't I?"

"The list?"

"Of people I need to tell. The funeral home, the bank, now his customers . . . I didn't expect there would be so much paperwork, but there are stacks and stacks in his living room. I don't know how I'm going to get through all of it."

An idea struck me, followed by a sharp stab of guilt.

"I could help," I offered. "Your dad was a customer of ours; we have all his invoices." Which was true. They were sitting in my backpack. "We could go over them together, and I could help you notify his customers."

Technically, I wasn't lying. And it was for a good cause. If I could figure out where Clem's newfound riches were coming from, I might also find proof that Jimmy was after them.

"I couldn't ask you to do that," she protested weakly.

I let Laura mull it over while I glanced around the cafeteria. Ashley had left her purse by the coffee station. Returning it would give me the perfect chance to ask about the hospital's investigation. It was obvious she was close to both Strack and Hardy, so chances were good she knew something—and she might be grateful enough to share.

I made my way toward across the cafeteria, saying, "You're not asking, I'm offering. I can't hang around the hospital all the time—Charlie's never been good at sharing, so I barely get to hold my niece. When I'm home, my mom grills me about finding a husband. You'd actually be helping me out."

"Really? You're sure?"

I scooped up Ashley's buttery leather tote. It was big enough that I could probably fit Rowan inside, but heavier than it looked. I slung it over my shoulder, saying, "I'm absolutely sure, Laura. Why don't you bring CJ over for dinner tomorrow night? My mom always makes enough to feed an army, and he can play with Riley while we go over your dad's paperwork."

"That would be wonderful," she said, and the relief in her voice almost made me forget that I had an ulterior motive. "But all his files are at his cabin. Would it be okay if we drove over and sorted through them together? I haven't been to his place since . . ."

"No problem," I assured her. "We'll have dinner, and my mom can watch Riley and CJ while we go out to your dad's. How's six thirty sound?"

We arranged the details, and I hung up, ready to track down Ashley.

Who was standing two feet away from me, cheeks flaming.

"Hey," I said, slipping her bag off my shoulder and holding it out awkwardly, like I'd been caught stealing. "I was about to come looking for you."

"Isn't that always the way? Just when I think those guys are taking me seriously, I flake out." She shook her head. "I'd better get back before they decide I'm only good for making coffee. Thanks, Frankie."

"You're welcome." Before I could ask her about Strack's investigation, she'd already spun away and headed out, heels clicking on the linoleum. I'd missed my chance.

All the more reason to make my visit with Laura count. Now I just had to tell my mom we were expecting company.

ELEVEN

As I was heading back to Charlie's room, I spotted Meg Costello sitting near the cafeteria doors, drawing furiously on a few scattered papers.

"Hey, Meg," I said, and her head snapped up, eyes wide. "May I join you?"

"I guess." Hastily, she shoved her papers into her messenger bag.

"Awesome," I said, sitting in the chair opposite her and tucking my feet under me. "I hope your dad wasn't too hard on you Saturday night. He knows you were only helping me out, doesn't he?"

She nodded. A set of colored pencils sat on the table between us, and she scooped them up hurriedly, depositing them alongside her papers. Her gaze flickered to my backpack. "You got your bag back?"

"Oh, were you the one who left it at the nurse's station?" I'd wondered how it had gotten from the parking lot to a locked floor.

Meg held up the ID badge around her neck. "I have a key card, so I can deliver flowers and stuff. But I didn't know which room you were in."

"Well, thanks. You're a lifesaver."

A smile ghosted her face, then faded. It transformed her, if only for an instant—but it was long enough for me to see that Meg Costello was a pretty girl, when she didn't look miserable. Her honey-colored hair was held back with a headband, revealing deep-set hazel eyes behind the thick glasses.

"What are you working on?" I tilted my head, got a glimpse of the paper poking out of her bag. "Comic book?"

She tugged it closer, her round cheeks blushing scarlet. "Graphic novel."

"Cool."

But she didn't look like it was cool. Her eyes stayed downcast, her shoulders hunched, clearly mortified. "Meg, lots of people read comic books."

"Graphic novels," she repeated, then paused. "Don't tell my dad."

Understanding clicked into place. "Let me guess: God's Gift to Emergency Medicine doesn't approve?"

Her mouth trembled. "It's not going to get me into Harvard."

"Do you want to go to Harvard?" She didn't answer. "I see. Your dad wants you to go to Harvard."

"He says I could be a surgeon," she said. "He thinks I have the hands for it."

I studied her hands, noticing the pencil smudges down the side and ink stains on her fingertips. "Looks like you have the hands for drawing," I said lightly.

She shrugged again.

"I won't tell him. But Meg . . . if your dad is so crazy about Harvard, he should apply. They're your hands. They should be doing what makes *you* happy. Nobody else. It's your future, sweetie."

"Quite a statement from someone with no future to speak of," Paul Costello said from behind me.

"Dr. Costello," I said, twisting around to face him. "What a . . . surprise."

"I told you to get out of my ER," he snapped.

"Good thing this isn't the ER," I replied. I leaned back in my seat, propped my feet on a nearby chair, and took a leisurely sip of my coffee.

"Meg," he said, biting off the words. "You're about to miss your shift. Go on."

Silently, she picked up her bag. The pile of papers slid out, spilling dozens of sketches across the floor. Meg bent to gather them up, but Costello beat her to it. "What's this?"

"Nothing," she said quickly.

He flipped through them with a scowl. "Another comic book?"

"They're called graphic novels," I cut in, but Costello ignored me.

"You have a B in physics. You should be focused on pulling up your grade, not drawing cartoons." He tossed the stack on the table.

"But . . ."

"We'll talk about it at dinner," he said curtly. "Right now, you need to check in at the volunteer desk. Go," he barked, and she fled, leaving her sketches behind.

He watched her go, his own shoulders slumping for an instant. Then he rounded on me. "Is this what you do for fun, Stapleton? Stick your nose where it doesn't belong? Leave my kid alone."

"She's a good artist," I said, glancing at Meg's drawings. "You shouldn't be so hard on her."

"Do you have children?"

I nearly spit out my coffee. "God, no."

"Then don't tell me how to raise mine. You might have a decent handle on emergency medicine, but you have no idea what it's like to be a parent."

True, but I knew what it was like to be the kid who wanted to choose her own path. I knew how much it hurt when your family tried to block the way. I opened my mouth to tell him so, but he spoke over me. "It's time for you to go."

"Is that why you went whining to Strack about me?" I gave him a withering look. "I didn't think you were the type to have administration fight your battles."

He stiffened. Nice to know I'd touched a nerve. "Walter Strack came to me with a complaint, not the other way around. You think I have time to waste on hospital politics? I'm too busy saving lives."

"You didn't do so hot with Clem Jensen, did you?"

"Jensen wasn't my fault." His scowl deepened. "We got him to the cardiac cath lab in under ten minutes, which was something, considering how hard he was fighting us."

Startled, I asked, "Clem tried to decline treatment?"

He eyed me with disdain. "What, you don't get paranoid patients in the city? He was in and out of consciousness, totally delirious. We gave him a dose of lorazepam and he settled down."

He was right, actually. It was common for patients, especially those in a lot of pain, to become delusional. They often accused people—staff, family members, total strangers—of trying to kill them. But in Clem's case, it no longer seemed like paranoia. It seemed like a perfectly rational fear.

"And you didn't notice anything strange about the case? His meds or any of his symptoms?"

"Maybe you didn't notice because you were too preoccupied grandstanding, but we were a little busy Saturday night. There was nothing off about the guy. We stabilized him, got him to the cath lab, and they transferred him up to the cardiac ICU. End of story."

"Then why are you trying to pin his death on me?"

"Are you deaf? Strack came to me, Stapleton. Not the other way around. I don't give a damn what they decide, as long as it keeps you out of my ER—and away from my daughter."

He gathered up Meg's sketches with surprising care, considering how dismissive of them he'd been earlier. Then with a final, ice-blue glare, he stalked off.

For a moment, I stood bewildered, clutching a cold cup of coffee. All along, I'd assumed Costello was behind the hospital investigation. Who else would have a reason to ruin my reputation and my career?

Someone who thought I was a threat. Who was afraid of what Clem might have told me, who needed to discredit me in order to protect themselves?

Clem's killer.

* * *

"Nice of you to stand up for Meg," Marcus said, falling into step with me as I walked toward the elevator. "Poor kid needs somebody on her side."

"Were you there? I didn't see you." Hard to believe I'd miss someone as massive as Marcus.

He shook his head. "I was in the hallway. But voices carry—especially Costello's, when he's on a rampage."

"Great. As if I wasn't already notorious."

"You aren't the first nurse Costello's yelled at, and you won't be the last. Nobody's going to hold it against you."

"Strack will." I tried to gather my thoughts. "Costello says he wasn't the one who complained about me to Strack. Do you buy that?"

He considered it, ushering me inside the elevator. "Costello thinks he's king of the ER. The man's convinced he doesn't answer to anybody, including the administration. He'd assume he dealt with you, and that was the end of it."

As much as I hated to admit it, that did sound more like Costello's style—abrasive arrogance, not slithering behind the scenes. "If that's the case, where's Strack getting his information? Someone complained about me. He even knew that I'd been in Clem's room on Saturday night. He mentioned it the first time he called me into his office."

"Wasn't me," Marcus said, pressing the buttons for our respective floors. "Strack was there when I talked to Legal, and he already knew you were in the room. He asked me about it."

"I wasn't accusing you," I assured him. "Did you see Costello on the floor that night?"

Marcus shook his head. "He never leaves the ER when he's on duty. Besides, every doctor on call that night was downstairs, helping with the bus crash. Cardiac was a ghost town. I didn't even realize you'd left."

I chuckled. "It's a good thing you came in to wake me. If I'd missed Charlie's C-section, Strack would be the least of my problems."

"What are you talking about?" Marcus said. "I didn't wake you up."

"Well, somebody did, and I owe them." I paused. "I can't really blame them for telling Strack, either. They were looking out for their patient."

"Mr. Jensen was my patient," Marcus said slowly. The elevator doors opened, but he made no move to leave. "We've got fourteen beds, and everybody has their own cases, unless there's a code. Nobody else worked with him that night. I would have seen it in the chart."

The elevator doors began to slide shut, but I mashed the "door open" button and stared at him. "Someone came in that room while I was sleeping. The door woke me, and I heard footsteps. I even asked about Clem's medications."

"You didn't ask me anything," he said. "And I was the only staff member in the room that night. I checked his vitals five minutes before you showed up. The next time I went in, you were gone."

"Then who woke me up?"

Marcus scowled. "Someone who wasn't supposed to be there."

TWELVE

Clem's mystery visitor continued to gnaw at me. I'd been a foot away from the killer. If I'd been a little more alert, I could have identified him. I could have saved Clem's life—a second time. The instincts I relied on so heavily had let me down.

Unfortunately, I had plenty of time to mull over where I'd gone wrong. As soon as I'd mentioned having Laura and her son for dinner, my mother went into party-prep mode—which is how I'd ended up covering the store the next morning, while my mother arranged everything for the impromptu party that night.

"I haven't done this in more than ten years," I pointed out as I poured a travel mug of coffee.

"It's like riding a bike," my mom said, trying to smooth down my hair. "You never forget. You might even enjoy it."

Before I could tell her how unlikely that was, she added, "And it will be good for people to see you out and about. Show them you have a clean conscience."

"I *do* have a clean conscience." As regarded Clem, at least. My engagement was a different matter entirely.

"Even better," she said and shoved me out the door.

Which is how I found myself behind the back counter of Stapleton and Sons, exactly as I'd never wanted.

My mom was right, at least in one respect. Not much had changed. The contractors were surprised to see me behind the counter, but when I asked them about Clem, they had little to say. "Kept to himself lately," one of them told me. "Seemed happy enough, though."

Once the early morning rush was out of the way, I settled into the familiar rhythms: restocking shelves, answering the occasional phone call. But just as Charlie's books had shown, business was slow. I tried chalking it up as a typical weekday, but if the dearth of customers was typical, Charlie was really in trouble. The bell over the front door jingled, and I practically leapt over the counter in greeting.

"Marcus?" His bulk took up the entire aisle, shoulders brushing against a display of paint chips.

"I need a rake." He looked around furtively and headed toward the back counter.

"Sure. They're in the next room." I pointed, adding, "Left hand side, by the garden supplies."

He ignored me and continued to the back counter. "Sounds good."

"You want me to choose a rake for you?"

He frowned. "Or a hammer. Better make it a hammer."

"Okay." I grabbed a standard twenty-inch hammer from the hand tools aisle before joining him. "They do different things, you know. They're not interchangeable."

He gave me a wry smile. "You're good people, Frankie. The way you tried to help Mr. Jensen. The way you stuck up for Meg Costello. Not everyone would."

"Thanks."

"There was someone else in Mr. Jensen's room that night," he said, pulling out his wallet.

"There was," I agreed, a cautious hope taking root inside me.

"Doesn't smell right, does it? Especially now they're trying to pin his death on you."

I shook my head, counted back his change.

He weighed the coins and bills resting in his massive palm. Then he shrugged and pulled a sheaf of papers from inside his coat. "Here you go."

"Clem's chart?" I said hoarsely. "You said . . ."

"He was my patient. Can't just let it go."

I clutched the papers. "Marcus—"

"I can't do much else," he warned. "Probably best if we aren't seen talking again, especially not at the hospital. Hope this gives you a start, anyway."

"It's more than a start," I said. "It's huge. Thank you."

"Glad we didn't go with the rake." He picked up the bag with the hammer and grinned widely. "I've got two days off. Wouldn't want to spend them doing yard work."

★   ★   ★

Charlie's loss of customers was my gain. I spent the rest of the morning going over Clem's chart: a minutely detailed record of every test and procedure he'd undergone, every reading of his vitals, every medication he'd taken during his brief stay at the hospital. I flipped to the last page and felt a rush of gratitude—Marcus had even managed to get me a copy of Clem's postmortem report.

The findings were consistent with what I'd been told. Clem had gone into respiratory arrest, then cardiac failure. Essentially, his lungs had stopped working, and the lack of oxygen had triggered a second, fatal heart attack.

The medical examiner, however, hadn't explained why he'd gone into respiratory arrest. In his opinion, the cause of death was consistent with Clem's general health and history of heart trouble—his lungs had likely been damaged during the heart attack and couldn't bear up under the strain. Multiple organ dysfunction, they called it.

Most of the time, medical examiners find what they're looking for; they're confirming a cause of death, and it's human nature to see what they expect. In a case like Clem's, for example, the ME expected he would find cardiac failure, so he did. The fact that Clem was supposed to be medicating for those exact problems didn't faze him. He assumed, as Marcus had, that his blood work showed noncompliance, regardless of Laura's insistence otherwise.

Nobody looked for answers to questions they didn't think of. Nobody looked for clues to a murder that hadn't happened.

Except me.

I tried to think it through logically. Noah had wanted proof. Was this enough?

I had Clem's declaration that his heart attack wasn't an accident—but the hospital would argue he was delusional, which is why Costello had given him the lorazepam.

I had blood work that showed he wasn't taking his meds, despite Laura's insistence otherwise, which bolstered Strack's case.

I had the report on Clem's surgery: Dr. Hardy and his team had successfully busted the clot and inserted a stent. According to the ME, Clem's primary cause of death was respiratory arrest—the heart attack was secondary.

I rubbed the back of my neck, reading through the report again, trying to figure out what was bothering me. The cardiac team had responded swiftly: Marcus had called a code within seconds of the alarms sounding, and the crash team responded instantaneously. Yet it had been too late. Clem's vitals had plummeted too quickly for their efforts to make any real difference.

He'd been gone before they got there.

"Excuse me?"

I glanced up, shoving the papers behind the counter. A frazzled young woman, baby on her hip and circles under her eyes, stood before me.

"Sorry! I didn't hear the bell. Can I help you?"

"I hope so. My basement's flooding."

"Oh," I groaned. "That's the worst. Did the sump pump fail?"

Because Stillwater was located on the river, every house with a basement also had a sump pump—designed to carry water to the street instead of allowing it to flood the basement. The woman nodded. "We just replaced it last summer."

My heart sank. "With one of ours?"

The last thing Charlie needed was to be held liable for a flooded basement or to develop a reputation for shoddy merchandise.

She shook her head, her cheeks turning pink. "The HouseMasters out on the interstate."

I hadn't realized there was a HouseMasters—a big-box hardware store—anywhere nearby. Suddenly Charlie's books made a lot more sense.

"What did your plumber say?"

"We're looking for a new plumber," she said. "But I don't understand what happened. It was a new pump. I've heard it run. Why wouldn't it work?"

"Well, it's new, so it probably wasn't the battery. I would guess there's something wrong with the sensor switch. If that's not triggered, the pump won't kick in, and you won't know it's flooded until you see the standing water."

"I'm seeing plenty of it now," she muttered. "Any recommendations for a plumber?"

"Sure," I said. As always, we kept a red binder underneath the register with a list of trusted contractors and service people. It was not a particularly long list, but I noticed Clem's name was on there, in my mom's small, precise script.

That was all the character reference I needed.

"Here you go," I said, handing her a piece of paper with several plumbers' numbers on it. "Let me know when you're ready to order that pump—we'll remind the plumber to make sure the sensor's calibrated properly."

The words reverberated in my head, tolling like a bell. As soon as she left, I snatched up Clem's chart again.

A cardiac patient—especially one just out of surgery—would be under continuous monitoring. Remote telemetry, we called it. A real-time readout of his pulse, respiration, and heart rhythms were sent to a wall of monitors at the nurses' station. If his vitals dropped, alarms would sound both in the room and at the main desk, alerting the crash team.

But you could lower the threshold, set the monitors not to trigger an alarm until a patient's vitals were dangerously low. The killer could have recalibrated Clem's monitors, buying themselves time and privacy.

Even so, most monitors had a failsafe—a built-in minimum that would trigger the alarm, even if the settings were tampered with. The alarm should have sounded, giving Marcus and his team enough time to respond.

Assuming, that is, they'd heard the alarm. It was possible to turn off the sound on a monitor, no matter what the readings were. We did it all the time for terminal patients who were gradually slipping away, so that the noise wouldn't intrude upon a grieving family's last moments together. You could turn it off at the nurse's station as well. It would be easy to overlook, especially in the chaos of a shift change.

Vitals dropped off a cliff, no warning, Marcus had said. It would have seemed so, to the team: Clem been fine during a vitals check, twenty minutes before; by the time the alarms sounded, his respiration and heart rate had bottomed out. But when I checked the records more closely, zeroing in on those twenty minutes, it didn't look like a jagged falling off of air and blood. Clem had sunk, quickly and smoothly, like a stone dropped into deep water.

I studied Clem's pulse ox measurements—the amount of oxygen in his bloodstream. Seven minutes before the alarm sounded, his numbers started falling. Even the efforts of the crash team hadn't reversed them. My throat grew tight at the realization.

The ME was partially right. Clem had suffered respiratory failure, but not a sudden one. It had taken long, agonizing minutes. Had he realized what was happening as he suffocated to death? I hoped, for his sake, that he'd lost consciousness first, that he hadn't been afraid or in pain. I hoped the killer had granted him that small mercy.

Because there *was* a killer. There was no longer any doubt in my mind that Clem had been murdered. Now I needed to figure out how. Tampering with the monitors had hidden the crime, but the killer would have needed a way to cut off Clem's air. Marcus would have noticed if Clem's O_2 line had been tampered with, and a pillow over Clem's face would have been noted in the postmortem.

Which left drugs.

Plenty of poisons could cause organ failure, but the medical examiner would only screen for poison if he'd thought Clem's death was suspicious—which he hadn't. At this point, the only way to check would be to perform a second, more thorough, autopsy. And the ME would only do that if someone—the police or the family—requested it.

All I had to do was figure out a way to ask Laura.

THIRTEEN

Telling someone their father was murdered is a poor way to start off dinner conversation. You can't exactly introduce the topic while asking a guest to pass the green beans. Even dessert won't soften the blow. So even though I wanted, desperately, to tell Laura the truth about her father's death, I forced myself to make small talk while we ate.

Riley and CJ regarded each other warily until they found common ground in their hatred of the hot lunch program. When he wasn't bemoaning the rubbery rectangles that passed as school pizza, CJ was quiet. He was a small-boned kid with thin, pale cheeks and neatly combed brown hair. Already soft-spoken, he had a habit of lapsing into silence, dark-brown eyes straying to the framed picture of Charlie and me, perched on the railing of Stapleton and Son's front porch, my dad standing behind us with his arms wrapped around our shoulders. Thinking of Clem, no doubt.

"My grandma made brownies," I overheard Riley confide as they carried their plates to the kitchen. "I helped. They're extra chocolate-y."

"I don't have a grandma," CJ said. "I don't have a grandpa anymore, either. He died."

"My grandpa died too, but it was a long time ago. I wasn't even born. Was yours fun?"

"Yeah," he said. "He taught me how to fish. He even taught me how to get the guts out, and get the scales off, after you caught one."

If he'd hoped to gross Riley out, he'd told the wrong girl. "Coooool," she said, eyes widening. Pride swelled within me.

"I insist," my mother said from the dining room. "I made too much, and there's barely room in the refrigerator."

"But—" Laura protested. "I'm sure you could—"

"Take the lasagna," my mother said firmly, and Laura must have recognized the futility of arguing. Mom had planned to send them home with food all along, and I was beginning to suspect she was sneakier than I'd realized.

"Thank you," Laura said eventually. "And you're sure you don't mind watching CJ?"

"Of course," she replied. "He'll be good company for Riley. Go on," she said, shooing us out the door.

"Your family seems nice," Laura said as we drove along the dark rural roads. Clem lived on the other side of the Illinois River, on the outskirts of Dover Creek, a town too small to properly be called a town.

"They can be," I said and instantly felt ashamed, complaining about my mom when Laura was going to bury her father soon. "It feels strange to be living at home again."

"I bet," Laura smiled. "Where are you sleeping?"

I made a face. "I'm bunking with Riley. She snores, but it's only a temporary arrangement."

She nodded and mercifully didn't ask about how long I was staying.

"I'm surprised your mom lives with your sister and her family."

I shrugged. "We grew up in that house, so my mom was already living there. I don't know how they make it work, but they do."

"It's nice," she said. "My dad's lived alone since my mom died. I called him every morning, and he stopped by to play with CJ most days, too. But Jimmy would never have let him live with us."

"How long did you say it was since you and he split up?"

"Three years," she said. "He's in and out. He'll go weeks without seeing CJ, sometimes more. I wish he'd move away permanently, but he's like one of those bad pennies, always turning up."

Cornfields flashed by the car, endless rows of dried stalks like a gaunt, ghostly forest, leaves shifting with the restless wind.

"Does Jimmy have a criminal record?" I tried not to sound too eager, but Jimmy was the closest thing I had to a suspect.

She slowed to turn onto the road that ran alongside the river. In the moonlight, the current churned, dark and glinting. "I don't know. I try to have as little to do with him as possible."

"Sounds like a good policy."

"I really appreciate this," Laura said softly. "CJ doesn't even want to go to the house. He said it makes him too sad. It makes *me* too sad."

"I'm glad I can help." Guilt wormed its way through my stomach, making me regret the lasagna I'd eaten.

We rode in silence the rest of the way, bumping down increasingly uneven, increasingly dark roads, until she turned down a dirt path. A moment later, the headlights lit on a tidy-looking cabin tucked in a clearing. A homemade wooden swing hung suspended from the branch of a massive oak tree, creaking gently, and the tires crunched on the gravel drive. Laura parked in a patch of grass beside a small barn.

"This is adorable," I said, looking around. The clearing gave way to prairie grasses, and beyond that was forest, far enough away so that the trees didn't feel like they were looming over you. The wide expanse of sky was breathtaking, the constellations vivid and fresh. Overhead, the nearly full moon hung cool and luminous, casting crisp shadows and silhouettes. I breathed deeply. "It's like a fairytale."

"It was a summer cabin, but he winterized it himself," she said, pride and affection mingling in her voice. "He wanted something close to the river so he could fish. I worried about how remote it was, but we had such fun here."

I wondered if Laura saw memories instead of shadows as she gazed around the darkened clearing. I hoped, for her sake, that they were good ones. She led the way up the painted steps and through the screen porch, then into the unlocked cottage, reaching unerringly for the light switch.

Inside was a disaster. It looked like someone had ransacked the house, and I reached for my phone, ready to dial 9-1-1. But Laura's demeanor, tense yet unsurprised, suggested it was the usual state of things.

"He gave up cigars about a year ago," she said, inhaling deeply. "Still smells like them, though."

She led the way through the stacks of newspapers and magazines, past half-assembled blenders and lamps and a fireplace with cold ashes piled in the grate. She gestured to the couch in front of the fireplace. "My dad's office."

"Not a big fan of filing, I see." Papers—invoices, manuals, brochures, notes, receipts—lay in untidy heaps across what I assumed was a coffee table.

"I think it's why I became a librarian," she said, smiling. "My rebellious phase involved putting things in alphabetical order."

"We're going to need to go through all of that." My voice betrayed my dismay.

She nodded. "If it's too much . . ."

"I'm happy to help," I told her, omitting the real reason. "For now, let's concentrate on finding open invoices. Everything else we can either burn or put aside for later."

Two hours later, the fire blazed merrily as we threw junk mail and old brochures into the flames. The table in front of us was nearly clear, and a pile of papers, sizable but tidy, sat on the sofa between us.

"Is this the last of it? Would he have kept anything in a workshop, maybe?"

"He only kept fishing stuff and tools in the barn, and the second bedroom was CJ's, for their overnights." Tears welled up, and she covered her eyes. "I'm sorry. Coming in here and handling all his stuff seems so final, but I still can't believe he's gone. It doesn't seem real."

"That's totally natural," I said. "You don't need to apologize."

"I should be past it by now," she said. "There are stages of grief, aren't there? Denial's one of the first. I shouldn't be looking around and expecting to see him."

My heart twisted. "Laura, my dad died when I was CJ's age. Even now, when I go home, I expect to wake up and find him making pancakes and burning the bacon. I'm angry when I see he's not there, and it's been twenty-six years." Which might explain some part of why I came home so rarely, but I pushed the thought away. "Grief isn't a straight line, it's a spiral. You're going to pass through those stages again and again, for the rest of your life. But as long as you're moving up on the spiral instead of down . . ."

I trailed off, and she gave me a watery smile. "Thanks, Frankie. I don't know why you're being so nice to me, but I appreciate it."

Now, I told myself. Tell her now. But the force of her grief stopped me. Better to wait until I had more answers than questions. "Laura . . ."

"I'm going to fix some tea," she said and pushed herself off the couch. "Want some?"

What I really wanted was to find Clem's medication. It would have been the easiest way to poison him, assuming it was a slow-acting drug, and it would explain why his blood work was off. Not to mention, it would be a lot easier to convince Noah that Clem had been murdered if I could hand him a bottle of poison instead of a chart I wasn't supposed to have.

"Sure," I said. "Okay if I use the restroom?"

"Of course," she called back.

Instead of the tiny bathroom, clearly visible from where I was sitting, I slipped into Clem's bedroom, keeping my footsteps light. It was as messy as the rest of the house. Nudging a mound of dirty laundry aside, I scanned the top of the dresser for pill bottles. Nothing but a framed picture of a much-younger Clem with a woman who must have been Laura's mom, countless school and candid pictures of CJ, and what must have been Laura's senior graduation picture, complete with the requisite head-tilt and demurely folded hands. A few of Clem's fishing conquests were mounted on the walls, and I avoided their glassy gaze as examined the nightstand next to the unmade bed. One of the fish burst into song, warbling about taking him to the river, and I jumped back, hand over my heart.

"Are you okay?" Laura called.

"Yeah, just a wrong turn." I glared at the plastic fish and made my escape.

The bathroom was barely big enough to fit me. If I stood in the center of the room, I could touch opposite walls simply by lifting my arms. I couldn't imagine how Clem had managed it. I flushed the toilet and ran the water as if washing my hands, hoping the noise would cover my inspection of the medicine cabinet.

Clem was a man of simple hygiene. Toothbrush, toothpaste, safety razor, and shaving cream. A comb and a can of spray deodorant. A box of cotton swabs and a bottle of aspirin. But that was it. I gently shut the cabinet door, turned off the water, and pondered. Clem's meds had to be in the kitchen. I needed to get Laura out of the way.

"Let me help," I said, popping into the kitchen. "You shouldn't be waiting on me."

"I'll have to sell this place," she said miserably. "He worked so hard to fix it up, and CJ loves it here, but . . ."

I took the tea kettle out of her unresisting hands and set it on the stove. "You could move in, couldn't you?"

She blinked, as if she'd never considered the idea. "I don't know. Maybe."

"Laura," I said gently. "Do you know who inherits? Did your dad have a will?"

She shrugged. "A basic one. Everything goes to me."

I rummaged for mugs in the cupboard, keeping an eye out for pill bottles. "What about your husband?"

"Jimmy? He doesn't get anything." There was no smugness in her words, only relief.

"Can he claim your inheritance as joint property? Ask for half in the divorce?"

"I suppose. I'd need to ask a lawyer, but it's not like I can afford one." She paused and handed me the box of plain black tea bags. "Unless I sold this place."

Clem's bank account wasn't carrying much of a balance, but riverfront land with a restored cottage would bring a nice chunk of change. We'd also found a small life insurance policy in the piles of paperwork. Plenty of motive for Jimmy to get rid of his father-in-law, especially if he thought Laura would be divorcing him soon.

"Go sit by the fire," I ordered as the kettle began whistling. Laura obeyed gratefully. Once she was in the other room, I began my search, calling out, "Do you want sugar? The milk has probably gone bad."

"No, thanks."

Nothing yet. I tugged on cabinets and drawers, trying to sound as if I was looking for snacks. "You should eat something."

"I just ate," Laura pointed out.

I kept searching. Nothing, nothing, nothing, and then . . . "Bingo." Inside the battered metal breadbox stood a collection of orange plastic pill bottles.

"What's bingo?" Laura asked from behind me.

I jumped and turned to face her. "Toast," I said, improvising. "Toast is a good consoling food. Let me fix you some."

"I'm not hungry."

"When was the last time you ate?"

"Dinner at your house. A few hours ago." She frowned. "Is everything okay? You seem tense."

"Just worried about you," I assured her.

Outside, a branch snapped, loud as a gunshot. Laura whipped around. "What was that?"

While her back was turned, I snatched up the pill bottles and tucked them in my vest pocket. "Wildlife?"

"I don't *hear* any wildlife," she said. She was right. The sound of crickets and rustling birds had stopped, the surrounding forest holding its breath. I followed suit.

Laura crossed the living room with slow, cautious steps, and I realized how visible we must be through the large picture windows, lamplit against the darkness outside. For the second time that night, I pulled out my phone, ready to call the police. My other hand reached for the chef's knife resting on the counter.

"Hello?" Laura called, stepping onto the screen porch before I could stop her. "Is someone there?"

The silence held, deep and impenetrable. There was a quick shuffling sound, as if someone was crunching through leaves, and I tightened my grip on the knife. Before I could tell Laura to come back inside, she darted forward and slapped at the porch wall.

The clearing outside lit up like a football field—floodlights crisscrossed the yard, bringing everything into halogen-lit sharpness.

Laura's shoulders relaxed. "Come see," she said. I joined her, still gripping the knife, and she pointed to a pile of firewood. The bushy ringed tail of a raccoon disappeared behind it.

I set the knife down and pressed my hand to my chest. "Time to go, don't you think?"

"Definitely," she said, tucking her hair behind her ears with shaking hands. "We can come back if we need anything else. During the day."

We locked up the cabin, double-checking every door and window, and headed to the car. Before climbing inside, I paused to listen again. There was nothing to hear but the murmur of the river and the whisper of leaves, the faint rustling of animals through prairie grass. If there was something else out there—something big enough to make a branch snap—it was either long-gone or very, very good at hiding.

"Do you think we got everything we needed?" Laura asked as we drove away.

My hand drifted to my pocket, where Clem's medication was nestled. "I hope so."

I locked the door and kept my gaze fixed on the side mirror until we were safely back in town.

Later that night, I lay on my bottom bunk and listened to Riley's snores. One arm dangled over the edge of her mattress, poking out through the guardrail, swaying gently.

My gut told me a stray raccoon hadn't been the only one lurking outside the cabin. It didn't take a genius to figure out that the only person who'd make that kind of trek was the person who'd murdered Clem. But why? To scare us, or worse? Was there something in the cabin the killer hadn't wanted us to find? I'd examined the pills I'd swiped, but unfortunately, none of them were marked with a skull and crossbones. I'd need to look them up online or, better yet, find someone to help identify them.

In the meantime, Laura and I had compiled a list of Clem's customers. I was hoping one of them would be able to explain where Clem had gotten the money to pay for CJ's medicine. Every detective story I'd ever read said to follow the money, and that's what I intended to do. So far, all the trails led back to Jimmy Madigan. A little more proof, and I'd be able to clear my name *and* get justice for Clem.

A few feet away, the window rattled. I went still.

The noise came again—tiny raps scattering across the glass. As if someone was throwing gravel.

Riley snorted and rolled over. I slid out of bed and crept to the window, peering through the curtains to the yard below.

And there, in a bed of fading marigolds, stood Noah MacLean.

FOURTEEN

Noah looked up at me, grin spreading across his face, eyes crinkling, and in the moonlight, it was easy to imagine I had fallen back in time.

How many nights had he come to my window, just like this? More than he should have, fewer than I would have liked. The window squeaked once as I lifted the sash and carefully popped out the screen.

Some things you never lose the knack of.

"What are you doing?" I hissed, leaning out to get a better view of him. He was clearly off-duty, sporting well-worn jeans and a chamois-colored work shirt, thumbs hooked in belt loops.

"You wanted information about Jensen, didn't you?"

I checked my watch. "At one in the morning?"

"Figured you'd be up. Don't you work nights?"

"I'm not working."

"You were up, though."

I couldn't deny it.

"Come on down, Frankie," he cajoled, mischief in his voice.

"What about my mom?" I said reflexively, hearing echoes of my seventeen-year-old self. I shook my head. "Nevermind. Hold on."

I tugged my fleece over my head and clambered out the window, lowering it again so the draft wouldn't wake Riley. The trick to sneaking out of my house was that, instead of climbing—or dropping—down to the yard, it was better to climb *up*, grab hold of the Japanese maple that soared alongside the house, and make your way down the tree. Less scrabbling against the brick, easier on the fingertips, and when my mom sawed off the limb directly across from my bedroom window, much sneakier. I took the same path now, but what had seemed like a daring climb as a teenager paled in comparison to some of the ascents I'd completed in the last few years. Even so, my heart was racing, my hands so slick I wished for a bag of chalk.

I landed softly on the grass a few feet away from Noah, who'd reached out an arm to steady me. Unnecessary, but I didn't shake him off. I curled my bare toes in the chilly grass.

"You could have used the door," he said mildly.

"What's the fun of that?" I kept my voice low and glanced up at my darkened window, but the purple-striped curtains didn't even twitch.

"Just like old times," he said, and I lifted a brow. "Okay, fine. This time, we're only talking."

"Good," I said, and led the way to the backyard. My mom's cutting garden swayed gently in the night breeze. This late in the season, most of the flowers were spent, but the sunflowers and hydrangeas were holding on, the blooms ghostly in the moonlight. Riley's swing set stood nearby, and I settled myself on the tire swing. Wordlessly, Noah spun it around, and I lost myself in the dizziness for a moment. When it slowed, I looked up at him. "What did you find out about Clem?"

His expression darkened. "Hi, Noah. How was your night, Noah? Thanks so much for poking around on my behalf, Noah."

I sighed. "Hello, and how was your night, and thanks for doing this."

"Hello to you, too. My night was productive." He gave the swing a gentle push. "And you're welcome."

"I appreciate it," I said. "I really do. What did you dig up?"

"Clem Jensen was a jack of all trades. He was the guy you hired when you had a bunch of little jobs you wanted taken care of in one go, or when your contractor bailed halfway through, or you needed some routine maintenance. Putting in storm windows or removing window air conditioners, cleaning out the gutters every fall or rototilling the vegetable garden every March."

That fit with the records we'd found at his house—a few big, monthly accounts, but mostly it was an assortment of small- to medium-sized jobs. None of them were regular, but taken together, it was enough to make a living.

"Was he good at it?"

"Seems like it. Had a reputation for doing the job right, not charging an arm and a leg. He did a stint in Vietnam, so he spent some time down at the VFW. Otherwise he mostly kept to himself or spent time with his daughter and grandson. He was pretty crazy about them, I guess—his wife died about ten years back, so they're all he had.

Everyone I talked to said Clem was a pretty good guy. Not a lot of close friends, but he'll be missed."

Good to know, I mused, but nothing earth-shattering. "Anything else? Had he been acting strangely lately?"

He squinted at me. "Funny you should ask. Seems your friend Clem had turned into quite the dreamer in the last few months."

"Oh?"

"Used to be, all he could talk about was the grandson, but in the last few months, it was all about making plans for the future. Taking a big fishing trip out west, getting rid of the son-in-law."

"Getting rid of? He wanted to kill Jimmy?"

"He never came out and said that. He kept hinting that things were going to change, that his ship had finally come in. Said he'd finally hit the jackpot."

"He was gambling?" I hadn't seen so much as a matchbook from the casinos at the cabin, but maybe that was because he'd given up his cigars.

Noah frowned. "That's what I figured, but according to his friends at the VFW, Clem wasn't a gambling man. His wife thought it was a sin, and his daughter thought it was a waste. Even when he went to the casinos, he never did more than play the nickel slots and hit the buffet."

So Clem's windfall was still a mystery. Annoyed with myself for landing back at square one, I said, "Shouldn't you be reading this from a little notepad? Cops love their little notepads."

"Maybe if this was an official investigation. Since it's a favor for a friend, I decided to be a little less formal." He paused, then leaned forward and plucked a maple leaf from my hair, and held it out to me like a flower.

I took it from him, careful that our fingertips didn't touch.

"Are we friends now, Frankie?"

I ran my thumb along the veins of the leaf. "I guess so? If you want to be."

He didn't say anything for a long time. Then, "I get it now, why you had to leave. I shouldn't have tried to guilt you into staying."

I swallowed hard. "No more wrong than me trying to guilt you into coming with me. It was a long time ago, Noah. We were kids. We didn't know any better."

"And now we're friends," he said, eyes fixed on mine, steady and warm despite the shadows.

"Friends," I agreed, and told myself that was exactly as it should be.

"So let me ask you, as a friend . . . why are you looking into Jensen's death?"

"You sure this isn't the deputy asking?"

"The friend who happens to be a deputy. I know the hospital is trying to pin this on you, but they're grasping at straws—they won't find anything. And don't give me some song and dance about getting to know your patient—you're worried about Jensen's financials, which has nothing to do with his heart."

"Maybe," I said, and decided to take a chance on Noah. "Maybe not. I think Jimmy Madigan killed Clem."

"That's a big accusation," he said, folding his arms and shifting firmly into deputy mode.

"You've met the guy. He's a total dirtbag, he blames Clem for the breakup of his marriage, and he's always looking to make a buck. If Laura inherits Clem's estate, Jimmy could claim it as joint property, since they're not officially divorced. That's how he's able to sue the hospital too. So he actually gets paid twice—once through the inheritance, and once through the lawsuit. Do you know how much money the hospital could settle for? He could have a million reasons to kill Clem. Literally."

"That doesn't prove Jensen was murdered. Just because you've got a body and a suspect doesn't mean you have a crime, Frankie. I know you're trying to save your job, but running around accusing people of murder—even a jerk like Jimmy Madigan—isn't going to help you."

"You think I'm doing this for myself?" I stood, fists balled at my sides. The night air was sharp, but I was so angry I no longer felt the cold. "Clem was murdered."

"Not according to anyone at Stillwater Gen," he said. "I talked to the medical examiner, off the record, and he says there's nothing suspicious about Clem's death."

"He didn't look hard enough."

"Right. He doesn't know how to do his job, but you do? Are you going to do my job, too?"

"That's not—"

"Just because I'm not a city cop doesn't mean I'm an idiot," he said. His jaw hardened. "You want to talk motive? You've got a pretty good one."

I gaped at him, but he pushed on.

"Not to kill Clem. Nobody thinks you're a murderer, but you're pretty damn desperate to clear your name. We declare Jensen's death a homicide, and you're off the hook, aren't you? You'll go back to your real life and forget about Stillwater for another ten years."

He wasn't entirely wrong. I'd planned to stay until Rowan was safely home, then go back to Chicago. Ten years seemed like a stretch, though. "This isn't about me. It's about Clem, and his family, and the fact that a killer is walking around your town this very minute."

"Then find me some proof," he said. "I want to believe you. But . . ."

"But you don't."

He didn't argue.

"Fine," I snapped. "You want me to gift-wrap it for you, too?"

I started back across the yard, but Noah caught up to me in a few easy strides, grabbing hold of my arm.

"Frankie, wait. Can you . . ." He scrubbed his free hand through his hair, a gesture of sheer frustration. "Promise me you'll be careful."

"Of what? According to you, Clem died of natural causes. You want me to watch my diet?"

He bristled. "On the off-chance you're right, whoever killed Clem Jensen thinks they've gotten away with it. If they think you're on to them, they'd have a motive to kill you, too."

I wrenched away, too angry to acknowledge he might be right. "Thanks for asking around."

Without another word, I scrambled up the tree and back inside the house, not bothering to check if Noah was still there. Carefully, I slid the window down, drew the curtains, and turned toward my bed.

And stifled a shriek as Riley popped upright, training her flashlight on my face.

"Whatcha doin', Aunt Frankie?"

FIFTEEN

"Riley!" I threw my arm over my eyes, trying to block the blinding rays of the flashlight. "You're supposed to be asleep."

"Were you sneaking out?"

"No!" I whispered. She cocked her head, eyebrow lifted in pitch-perfect imitation of Skeptical Charlie, so I clarified. "I was sneaking *in*."

"But first you snuck out." She jumped down, landing on the floor with a thud. For a scrawny kid, she certainly sounded like an elephant. She shoved the curtains open and played the flashlight across the yard. "Who were you talking to?"

"Shhhh. You're going to wake up your dad. Or Grandma."

"Grandma takes her hearing aid out at night," Riley said smugly. "Sometimes she doesn't even wear it during the day."

I did not want to ask how Riley was making use of that information. "Fine. The point is, you need to get back in bed."

"You were talking to *a boy*."

"Riley . . ."

"Is he your boyfriend? Grandma said you were getting married, but Mom said you're not old enough. Then Grandma said you *weren't* getting married."

"I'm older than your mom," I pointed out, stung.

Riley shrugged and peered out the window, angling her body to view the street.

"There's a police car driving away," she said with a gasp. "Were you talking to the police? Are you going to jail?"

I gathered up my patience and my frayed nerves and smoothed the temper from my voice. "I have a . . . friend . . . who is a police officer. I had asked him a question, and he came over to give me the answer."

"Why didn't he knock?"

"Because it's late," I said. "He assumed everyone was sleeping. Which they're supposed to be."

"Why didn't he call?"

I blinked. "He didn't have my phone number, I guess."

"What was the question?" Slowly, she made her way back up the bunk bed ladder. Her long john pajamas were festooned with glow-in-the-dark stars.

"Boring stuff," I said. "Don't worry about it."

"Was it about CJ's grandpa?"

I paused. "Yeah."

"Grandma told one of my teachers that you didn't kill CJ's grandpa. She sounded pretty mad."

Nice to know my mom was using her powers for good. "She's right."

"I know. You're really, really good. That's what you said. Grandma said so, too."

"Well, there you go." I eyed the clock. It was nearly two AM. If Charlie found out I'd kept Riley up this late, Clem wouldn't be the only dead body in town.

Riley pulled the covers up to her chin and stared up at the ceiling. "CJ's supersad. His grandpa sounded cool. They did a lot of fun stuff together."

"Yeah, like what?"

"They built a boat. They take it fishing, and sometimes they even eat the fish for dinner. CJ gets to cut the scales off and everything."

"That does sound cool."

She turned to face me, head propped on her hand. "CJ said his grandpa took him out for breakfast all the time. I don't get to go out for breakfast, like, *ever.* It's always toast. Or oatmeal."

Considering Riley's propensity for wearing her meals, eating in was probably a smart call on Charlie's part. Charlie, who said I wasn't old enough to get married. A tiny bit of revenge seemed appropriate. "You know what? I'll take you."

"Can we get sausage biscuits? CJ said his grandpa loved sausage biscuits. Mom won't let me have one, though. She says they're heart attacks on a plate."

"They are," I said. "Here's the deal. I'll take you for sausage biscuits—this weekend—but only if you keep quiet about . . ." I waved at the window. "You know."

She looked insulted. "I wasn't going to tattle."

"Sausage biscuits it is, then. Go to sleep, Riley."

"Okay." She snuggled in under the covers and clutched a threadbare stuffed rabbit. "How old do I have to be before I can sneak out too?"

"Forty. Goodnight, Riley."

"Goodnight, Aunt Frankie."

A moment later, her face reappeared, upside down, inches from mine. Her braids dangled toward the floor. "Is he cute?"

"Who?"

"The police officer."

"Goodnight, Riley."

She disappeared again, and the bunk bed squeaked as she settled herself in. "Hey, Aunt Frankie?"

"What?"

"If you didn't kill CJ's grandpa, who did?"

"I don't know. But I'm going to find out."

SIXTEEN

"Morning, Frankie," Matt said when I stumbled, bleary-eyed, into the kitchen the next morning. He was standing at the stove, pancakes sizzling on the griddle. Riley, sticky and cheerful, waved at me from the table. "Coffee's ready—help yourself."

I did, breathing in the rich scent along with burnt bacon and maple syrup, the familiar smells and sounds transporting me back. My father's pancake tradition had been on Sundays, when he opened the store later and we could have a leisurely breakfast together. But everything else was heartbreakingly familiar and such a surprise that I had no time to guard against the stab of grief.

"No class today?" I asked Matt while fixing my coffee with the same focus I used during emergency surgery.

"Not until this afternoon," he replied.

"Pancake day!" Riley cheered.

I drained the rest of my coffee and refilled the mug.

"Late night?" Matt asked mildly.

"Not really," I said, and Riley giggled. I shot her a dirty look and mouthed "sausage biscuit."

She quieted immediately.

Matt glanced back and forth between us as he deposited a fresh stack of pancakes on the table. Riley offered me the plate, but I held up a hand, memory stealing my appetite. "I'll stick with coffee."

"Are you going to see Mommy today?" Riley asked me. "Can you ask her when she's coming home?"

"Will do."

"I haven't really had a chance to thank you," Matt said, pouring out the last of the batter, a sizzle rising up. "I know you weren't thrilled about coming home, but it means a lot to all of us. Especially Charlie."

When I didn't respond, he grinned and added, "Even if she hasn't mentioned it herself. Have things changed a lot?"

I hadn't really spent a lot of time with Matt; he and Charlie had married after I'd left town, so our interactions had tended toward distant-but-pleasant. I knew he taught American Lit at the community college, along with basic composition and creative writing. He helped out at the store as needed, but he was no handyman—Charlie took care of most home repairs. And I knew he was utterly devoted to his family, which left me feeling like even more of an outsider.

"Less than you'd expect."

"I didn't realize you and Noah had reconnected," he said off-handedly.

"Noah MacLean?" I darted a glance at Riley. "We didn't . . . we're not . . . how do you two know each other?"

"He audited one of my classes a few years back. We've been friends ever since." Matt studied me for a moment. "I take it Charlie hasn't mentioned that either."

"Charlie hasn't mentioned a lot of things," I muttered.

"Riley, go wash up. Time to get ready for school," Matt said, not taking his eyes off me. When she was out of earshot, he continued. "Sorry. I assumed you knew we were friends with Noah."

"Not a problem," I assured him. "It was a long time ago, and we've both moved on."

He nodded, but his expression was thoughtful.

"I'm more interested in what's happening at the store," I said. "My mom won't tell me, and Charlie insists everything is fine, but we both know that's not true."

Matt began scrubbing the ancient cast-iron griddle with water and a handful of table salt, just as we always had. "That's a conversation you should have with Charlie."

"Oh, I will," I assured him.

* * *

Garima was finishing rounds as I entered the maternity ward later that morning. "Charlie's already in the NICU," she said. "Heads-up—she's in a mood."

"Perfect," I said. "So am I."

Garima grinned, then sobered. "By the way, Strack's secretary said he'll wrap up your investigation by next week. He expects they'll have enough to file an official complaint with the state board."

"That's ridiculous," I said. "Why the rush job?"

"They've found a buyer for the hospital," she said. "But apparently, the company is leery of entering into negotiations while there's a lawsuit pending. Strack wants this resolved so they can move forward."

"Nice to see he holds the truth in such high regard." I shook my head. "I'd better go calm Charlie down."

"I'm sure the staff will thank you," she replied. "Dinner tonight? At the diner?"

I nodded and made my way over to the NICU. The nurse buzzed me in, and I made my way to the sinks in back. Charlie looked better today. She was wearing a hospital gown and a navy cardigan with leather patches at the elbows, so oversized I assumed it was Matt's. Her hair was tied back in a neat braid, and her brown eyes were bright—with energy or anger or both.

Probably both.

"What were you doing in the store?" she asked.

I ignored her while I scrubbed in, then headed directly to Rowan's isolette. "Good morning, Rowan! Looking good without that CPAP machine, girlfriend."

It was true. Without the mask, Rowan's face was completely visible. Even the miniature cannula she wore for oxygen didn't obscure her tiny features, and I was surprised to see how expressive she was, pursing her lips and wrinkling her nose. She was even opening her eyes now, gray-blue and watchful.

"I thought your people slept all the time," I told her, sticking out my tongue and raising my eyebrows in a look of mock surprise. Rowan stared as if I was the most fascinating person on the planet.

"Shows how much you know," Charlie said. "Don't you spend time with babies at work?"

"Not really. I mean, people bring infants to the ER, but they're usually full term, and we have specialized nurses for them. They're better at starting IVs and other procedures. I feel like some sort of giant next to them."

"A giant?" Charlie snorted. "You wish."

"You're one to talk. What have you got on me, an inch?"

"Inch and a half," she replied loftily.

The tension had lessened, and I reached in to take Rowan's hand. "You ready to discuss the store without throwing a tantrum?"

"I wasn't throwing a tantrum," she said. "Mom had no business asking you to take a shift."

"It was her business for twenty-odd years," I pointed out. "It's not like I'm incompetent."

"No, just disinterested."

"Why are you so bent out of shape?" I turned to face her. "I helped out for one day."

"I don't need your help." There was an ugly twist to the "your" that set my own temper blazing. Even so, mindful of Rowan's tiny fist clutching my pinky, I kept my voice neutral.

"You need somebody's help," I said. "You're hemorrhaging customers."

"Some days are slow," she protested. "It happens."

"Every day is slow," I replied. "Is HouseMasters the problem, or is something else going on?"

"We're managing." The rocking chair squeaked as she picked up speed.

"You can't even afford a working security system. When's the last time you took a paycheck?"

The minute the words left my lips, I regretted it.

"Have you been going through my books?" Her cheeks paled, then heated, and her voice was a low, furious whisper. "How dare you? That is my business, Frankie. Mine. You didn't want it, remember? What right do you have to interfere?"

Before I could snap a reply, Rowan stirred, squeaking as if she sensed the tension. I took a long, slow breath, my defensiveness vanishing.

"None," I said softly. "I wanted to help."

"You can't," she shot back. "It's not something you can patch up and send home. It's not some patient you can hand off at the end of a shift. You can't just waltz into town, save the business, and waltz out again. It doesn't work that way."

"There's got to be something I can do."

"Well, there's not," she said, tears filling her eyes. "I wasn't even going to tell you."

I reached for the nearby tissue box with my free hand and passed it over. "Why not?"

She blew her nose instead of responding.

"Okay, fine. I get why you might not want to ask for my help." The knowledge stung. "But why on earth would you keep it a secret?"

She toyed with the end of her braid, not meeting my eyes. Finally, she mumbled, "I didn't want you to think I was a failure."

"Charlie . . ." I paused. I hadn't said a word to Charlie about the hospital's investigation, only partly because she needed to focus on Rowan. I hadn't wanted to admit that I had made a mistake, that I might lose my license, that I had failed to save Clem. I'd masked my fear with action and bravado. How could I blame my little sister for doing the same thing?

"You're not a failure," I said firmly. "Even if the store goes under . . ."

Even if the business failed, it didn't mean Charlie had failed—there was more to her life than a building full of paint cans and power tools. If only I felt so certain about my own situation.

"I am *not* going to be the one who loses the store," she said, voice cracking. "One hundred and fifty years, it's lasted. It's our legacy."

I shook my head. "Come here, you idiot."

Slowly, she joined me next to the isolette.

"Look at your daughter," I said. "Look at that tiny little fighter. Think about Riley for a minute—how smart she is, how tough. The store isn't your legacy, Charlie. These girls are."

Charlie reached inside and smoothed Rowan's cowlick with shaking fingers. "I know. But I wanted to pass the store on to them."

I sighed. "You will. For now, let me worry about it. Rowan needs you more than the store does."

Charlie nodded, dashed away the tears building on her lashes. "You'd do that?"

I squeezed her hand. "Just because I don't want to run the store doesn't mean I don't know how. I'll handle Stapleton and Sons. You handle Rowan."

"Frankie," she called as I was leaving, "what's your legacy?"

I pondered for a moment and thought about Clem. About the patients I'd treated over the last twelve years.

The lives I'd saved and the lives I hadn't, and the knowledge that, every single time, I'd done all I could. It was satisfying, no doubt, and in a way, my work rippled out into the world when my patients returned to their lives, their families, their own work.

But at the end of the day, was it enough? I'd picked up and left Chicago at a moment's notice, but my absence hadn't created a vacuum. Someone else had taken my shifts, and the ER carried on. There was nobody in my apartment waiting for me to come home, not even a houseplant or a goldfish. The freedom I'd worked so hard to achieve suddenly seemed a little hollow.

My job was my life's work, yes—but maybe it wasn't supposed to be my whole life.

"Still figuring that out," I said. And I would. Right after I found Clem's killer.

SEVENTEEN

No matter what Noah thought, I had a suspect with a clear motive. Now I needed to show Jimmy had had the means—and the opportunity—to kill Clem.

After I left Charlie and Rowan, I headed to the hospital pharmacy, tucked into a back corner of the basement. Inconvenient, but also out of sight from prying eyes. I'd moved Clem's medication into one of my mom's old pillboxes—the plastic kind with a separate compartment for each day of the week. The last thing I needed was for someone at the hospital to catch me with prescriptions I wasn't authorized to have, and anonymity seemed like the best preventative.

I strolled up to the dispensing window and peered around, but nobody was in sight. I rang the bell and waited, pasting on a sunny smile.

A moment later, the pharmacist appeared: a dour-looking man wearing thick, black-framed glasses and a spotless lab coat. His salt-and-pepper hair was ruthlessly gelled into place. "Can I help you?"

"I hope so," I said, checking his nametag, "Nestor. I was wondering if I could ask you some questions about my dad's medication."

"Oh?" He adjusted his glasses. "Was the prescription filled here?"

"I'm not sure." I slid the pillbox across the counter. "He was admitted for chest pain, and they wanted to know what heart medications he was taking, but this is all I could find at his house. I was hoping you could tell me what they are."

His eyes flicked over the box, then back to me. "The nurses should be able to help. I'm in the middle of preparing some solutions that require my full attention."

Of course the nurses could have helped. I could have looked up the drugs online too, if I'd used the computer at the store. But the discrepancy between Clem's medications and his blood work were the closest thing I had to proof. Independent verification would make it harder for Noah to dismiss me.

"If the nurses got it wrong, it could be really terrible. You're an expert, and this is kind of a life-and-death situation. You're really the only one I trust to help." Crocodile tears were not in my skill set, but I widened my eyes and gave him a tremulous smile.

If Nestor the pharmacist actually believed me, I was going to consider heading over to the casinos and trying my hand at poker.

"Well," he said grudgingly, smoothing down his lab coat. "I suppose it wouldn't take too long."

He held out his hand for the box and I passed it over, gushing my thanks.

He disappeared into the back and came back a moment later with a stainless steel tray and a pair of tweezers.

"Let's see what we have," he mused, opening the first compartment. Using the tweezers, he removed each pill and placed it in a neat line. He did the same with the remaining days, placing each new pill directly underneath its duplicate, nudging them delicately until they were symmetrical, with precisely the same amount of space between them.

"Hmm." He reached for a light, as well as a magnifier. "Heart problems, you say?"

I nodded. "Blood pressure, cholesterol, the usual."

"Standard prescriptions for heart problems are warfarin and benazepril," he said. He consulted his computer, no doubt calling up the same drug manual I used at work. I waited, holding onto the counter to keep from drumming my fingers.

"But these aren't those," he said after a moment. "This dosage of warfarin, for example, should be a flat-faced, tan oval."

"Isn't that tan?" I leaned in.

"Not quite. And I'd say it's more of a circle than an oval." He used the tweezers to flip each pill over, bending so close his nose nearly brushed the steel pan. "The indicator code has been worn away."

I'd noticed that, too. The numbers and letters etched into tablet's surface were barely legible. "Do you think someone filed them off?"

He glanced at me, frowning. "What would possess someone to do such a thing?"

"So it's accidental?"

"It could have happened when he transferred the pills to this container. Or it might been mishandled at the dispensary." His gaze sharpened. "He didn't fill that prescription here, did he?"

"Oh, no," I said. "Some chain pharmacy."

He sniffed. "That's something, anyway. If one of my clerks was this sloppy, I'd fire them immediately."

"You're the head pharmacist? I had a feeling. You're really good at this."

He preened. "This is Thrombinase. One of Pharmagen's, I think. It's used to increase platelets in the bloodstream, which *promotes* clotting. No cardiologist would ever prescribe this for a patient with heart disease. Perhaps you misunderstood his condition?"

"It seems that way," I said. "What about this one?"

He bent over the table, inspecting the pinkish-brown triangle. "This looks very similar to benazepril, but . . ." He turned back to the computer. "Yes. It's actually an over-the-counter vitamin K supplement. Harmless for most people, but it's certainly wouldn't help someone with a heart condition."

He straightened and began transferring the pills back into the container, his movements precise and meticulous. "I'm afraid your father hasn't been telling you the truth about his health. You should let the nurses know what he's really taking, so they can treat him accordingly."

"Oh, I will definitely let people know," I said grimly.

He passed me the box and tugged at his shirtcuffs. "If that's all . . ."

"Yes, thank you." Then I paused, a memory surfacing. "Actually—one other question. Do you stock Apracetim?"

"We don't keep it here regularly," he said. "But we can order it from the manufacturer. Does your father have epilepsy as well?"

"No, no," I assured him. "My friend needs it for her son, and she wants to comparison shop."

"There's not much point. It's new enough that it will be expensive regardless of where she gets it."

"I'll make sure to tell her. Thank you so much for your time."

I made my way back upstairs, gripping the pillbox so tightly my knuckles turned white.

Laura wasn't wrong about Clem, but neither was Marcus. Clem *had* been taking medication . . . just not the right ones. Without the warfarin, he would have been far more likely to throw a clot, causing a heart attack. And both Thrombinase and vitamin K would have made him even *more* prone to clotting.

Someone had tampered with his medication—someone with access to the cabin and knowledge of Clem's routine. But they'd also need a working knowledge of pharmacology, and I couldn't quite picture Jimmy having that kind of expertise.

The rest of it fit so neatly—Jimmy might not be welcome at Clem's cabin, but he'd certainly know where it was. I'd already seen that Clem wasn't the type to lock his door. Since Jimmy wasn't working, he would have had plenty of time to wait until Clem had left for a job, then let himself in and swap the medications. It explained how he would have heard about Clem's death so quickly—he'd been *waiting* for it. When the initial heart attack hadn't killed him, he'd gone to the hospital to finish the job.

It wasn't without risk, but Laura had said Jimmy was a gambler. He'd bet on his own weaselly brand of intelligence and the hospital's desperation to avoid bad press, and now he thought he'd won.

He hadn't counted on a wild card: me.

EIGHTEEN

Evidence stowed in my bag, I made my way to Strack's office, my outrage growing with every step. Jimmy might have triggered Clem's heart attack by swapping out his medication, but something else had stopped his lungs. I needed to find out what it was, and the only way to do that was to order an autopsy—assuming Clem hadn't already been embalmed.

The secretary glanced up, startled, as I strode in.

"Clem Jensen," I said. "Has his body been released to the family?"

She blinked. "I don't believe so, but you'd have to check with Mr. Strack."

I jerked a thumb at Strack's door. "Is he in?"

"He's in a meeting."

"That's okay," I said, striding past her. "This won't take long."

Strack, Hardy, and Ashley looked up as I barged into the sleek glass-and-chrome office, all of them sporting identical expressions of dismay.

"Miss Stapleton," Strack said, standing as I approached. "We're in the middle of a meeting."

"Right, right. The Cardiodyne trial. Gotta make Stillwater Gen look nice and shiny for your buyer."

He straightened his tie and tried to look offended. "Cardiodyne holds great promise, and Stillwater General is proud to be at the forefront . . ."

"Save it for the staff newsletter," I snapped. Ashley looked wounded, like she was a puppy I'd recently kicked. "Has Clem Jensen's body been released to the family?"

He stiffened. "I'm not at liberty to disclose that information."

"That's a no, then." A wave of relief overtook me. No doubt, the legal department was unwilling to release Clem's body while they were facing a lawsuit. There was still time.

"Have you ordered an autopsy yet?" I hadn't seen it in the chart, but I wanted to be sure.

Hardy's brow lowered. Next to him, Ashley seemed to shrink back, as if she wanted to disappear from the conversation completely.

"Autopsies are very stressful for the family," Strack hedged. "It's not as if the cause of death is in question."

"I disagree," I said. "You don't know what killed Clem Jensen. How about you, Dr. Hardy? Any theories?"

"My report was completed and passed along to all the necessary parties," he said coolly. "If I'm required to make further statements, whether for the lawsuit or your licensing hearing, I'll be happy to do so. But not before then. Certainly not to you."

I cocked my head to the side. "You told Laura Madigan her father's death was unavoidable. That's a statement. Are you saying you lied to the patient's next of kin?"

"You're a nurse," Hardy said with a shrug. "You've never lied to a patient's family in order to ease their pain?"

"No, actually. I haven't. Interesting that you don't seem to think Laura Madigan deserves the truth. I'll make sure to tell her lawyer."

Not that Laura *had* a lawyer, of course, but even the hint of a threat had Strack turning a mottled shade of puce.

"We're done here, Miss Stapleton," Strack said, taking me by the elbow. "Any further communication should occur through our attorneys."

"You don't want to do an autopsy," I said, jerking away. "You'd rather pay off Jimmy Madigan than let this drag out because it might interfere with a potential sale. How do you think the people in this town are going to respond when they find out you care more about lining your own pocket than finding out the truth behind Clem Jensen's death? What if it wasn't a heart attack? What if it was malpractice, or medical error, or murder? Word gets out and you can kiss any shot at a sale good-bye."

"That sounds very much like slander," Hardy pointed out. "People who spread those kinds of rumors could be sued for defamation."

"Not if it's true," I said. "I have to think that the FDA is going to think twice about approving a drug when one of the trial's organizers is under investigation, too."

"Our test results speak for themselves," Ashley said, her voice colder than the Illinois River in February. So much for female solidarity.

"Shifting blame won't help you, Miss Stapleton," said Strack. His left eyelid was twitching, I noted with satisfaction. "You engaged in professional misconduct by treating Mr. Jensen without our authorization. I'm confident that the state board will agree, regardless of anything an autopsy might find."

"You'd better be sure," I told him. "You'd better figure out exactly why and how Clem Jensen died, because we both know I'm not responsible. And if you try to bring me up on misconduct charges just to cover your own ass? I'll prove it and make Jimmy Madigan's lawsuit look like pocket change."

NINETEEN

"What's all this?" Garima asked when she found me in the diner that evening. After going toe-to-toe with Strack, I'd snuggled Rowan while Charlie napped, covered an alarmingly slow shift at the hardware store, and helped Riley with her homework. Then I'd escaped the house, preferring to work on Clem's papers away from the prying eyes of my family.

Now I sat in the cracked red vinyl booth, surrounded by stacks of invoices and order forms.

"Clem's business," I said. "I still can't figure out how he was paying for his grandson's medication. His cash flow's been pretty steady over the last few years, but CJ's Apracetim bills should have totaled more than ten thousand dollars. Where was he getting that kind of money?"

"Someone could have given him a bonus," Garima suggested, slipping into the seat across from me. She'd changed from scrubs into a maroon silk blouse and navy skirt, casually elegant even in the diner.

"People give bonuses to employees they see regularly— housekeepers, or hairdressers. Not the guy who power-washed their deck one time."

"He doesn't have any bigger customers?" She perused the menu.

"A few. He works for a motel out on the interstate, and he seems to bill them pretty regularly. But I don't see them giving him a midyear bonus, do you?"

"Probably not. Why not call them and ask?"

"I plan to," I said as the waitress set my order in front of me—chocolate chip pancakes and a side of bacon.

Garima eyed it warily. "Are you having breakfast for dinner?"

"I have had a trying day. This is soothing."

"You may be on to something," she said, and ordered her own stack. "I'll give you this, Frankie. You've got a knack for fighting with people nobody likes."

"Why don't people like Strack? I applaud their instincts, of course." I tucked a napkin into the front of my green plaid shirt. I was running out of clean clothes, and I wanted to avoid doing laundry—it felt like an admission I was settling in.

"Not everyone is excited at the prospect of a sale. Strack stands to make a lot of money if the hospital sells—all of the upper-level administrators do. He'll be able to climb even further up the corporate ladder. Stock options galore."

I made a face, then forked up a syrup-drenched bite of fluffy carbohydrates. "I take it the rest of the staff is not so thrilled?"

"It's like any other merger—a lot of people lose their jobs in the name of redundancy, and the ones who are left have to pick up the slack. Plus, it's a long drive to the next closest hospital."

"So why sell in the first place? The board doesn't have to pursue this."

"Consolidation's the name of the game," she said. "Strack wields a lot of influence over the board. You've seen how tight he is with Hardy, and Hardy's wife is on the board of trustees. It's like a club, and he's convinced them this is the way to go."

"Is this Cardiodyne trial really such a big deal?"

"It is if they win FDA approval. It will boost the hospital's reputation alongside Hardy's, bring in more partnerships with Pharmagen and other companies."

"Which is why Strack and Hardy are so buddy-buddy," I mused. "Would you stay, if the hospital sold?"

"I've put a lot of hours into building that maternity ward. I'm not going to turn it over to someone who only cares about the bottom line." She gave me a sly smile. "Not everyone feels the need to flee Stillwater at the earliest opportunity."

"I didn't flee," I protested.

"Pfft." She sipped at her tea. "You took off after high school, and whatever sent you running out of town has kept you away for more than a decade. Maybe it's time to come back and deal with it. Or him, as the case may be."

"This isn't about Noah," I said, feeling the truth of it in my bones. Noah was a symptom. A symptom I had genuinely loved. The underlying problem was all me.

"Then what is it about? Your mom? Charlie?" She folded her hands in front of her and met my gaze squarely. "Your dad?"

I dragged my fork through a pool of maple syrup, appetite vanishing. "I never wanted the store. That's why Noah and I made so many plans. We were going to travel. You know how portable a nursing degree is, and he was going to get a job working construction. We'd be able to go anywhere we wanted. When his dad took off, his mom couldn't deal, and our plans . . . vanished. Suddenly we were talking about staying in Stillwater, and my mom was thrilled. It was exactly what she'd wanted all along—me, taking over the store, producing the next generation of Stapletons. My whole world was narrowing down to the view from the store counter, and I could feel it getting narrower, and narrower, and I couldn't breathe." My hand went to my throat, remembering the sensation. "I was afraid that if I didn't make a clean break when I had the chance . . ."

"You'd never leave. Inertia would take over."

I nodded, grateful that someone finally seemed to understand. "It was like I needed a running start." What a start it had been—the final fight with Noah, declaring to my mom that I'd rather be dead than stuck in the store for the rest of my life.

According to the laws of physics, an object in motion stays in motion. Three broken engagements later, I was living proof of Newton's laws.

Maybe it was time to figure out how to stop running.

"Will it be hard to leave again, once Charlie and Rowan are well?" Garima asked.

"I have a job to get back to," I reminded her. "Assuming I don't lose my nursing license."

"Which is why you're so invested in the Jensen case," she agreed, gesturing to the pile of papers at her elbow. "You know what I can't figure out? You're a good nurse. You knew better than to administer medicine without authorization, especially in a new hospital. You knew better than to lift someone Clem's size. Why didn't you ask for help?"

"Nobody was around to ask," I said. "Everyone was handling the bus crash."

"The ER was right there, Frankie. Twenty yards away. Why didn't you simply alert the staff and keep on walking?"

"Because I could help him." Because that's what my impulse and my training had conditioned me to do.

"Because it was a rush," she said. "I saw the look on your face. You love being the one to save the day."

"You sound like Strack."

"I sound like someone who watched you climb the water tower after the homecoming game because Mark Burris bet ten dollars you couldn't do it."

I grinned. "Ten bucks buys a lot of cheese fries."

"I said it before: you're an adrenaline junkie. There's no shame in it. It makes you good at what you do, keeps you from burning out in a job that has broken plenty of people. But if you don't find a way to clear your name, you won't be getting your adrenaline fix at Chicago Memorial—or any other hospital."

"I'm hoping I managed to stall Strack this afternoon."

"By threatening to sue?"

"Lawsuits make the hospital less attractive to potential buyers, right? If he thinks I'm willing to dig in for a long legal fight, he might hold off reporting me."

"If you say so," Garima said, but the doubt was clear in her voice.

TWENTY

The next morning, I drove out to the motel Clem had worked for, windows down and music blasting, singing at the top of my lungs about wide-open spaces and free-falling. The sunlight spilled over the land like molten gold, unlike the light outside my apartment, always fractured by buildings and streetlights and planes.

Thanks to the paperwork Laura and I had gone through, it had been simple enough to make a list of Clem's recent clients, call them to pass along the sad news, and ask a few discreet questions about Clem's state of mind and his financials. None of them had anything useful or unusual to tell. But the last number on the list, for The Piney Woods Motel, rang endlessly.

With Riley and my mom at the hospital and Matt manning the store, I decided to drive out and see the manager in person. Piney Woods was far and away Clem's most reliable source of income, and I was hoping all the time he'd spent there meant they'd have some insight into his sudden windfall.

Piney Woods Motel was a one-story U-shaped building with a sign advertising "free cable + housekeeping."

There were, indeed, pine trees all around—sad, spindly looking conifers that dropped yellowed needles and stubby cones along the patched and crumbling asphalt. Unsurprisingly, the vacancy sign was lit. I locked my car and ducked into the main office.

Behind the stained laminate counter, a girl with pink- and yellow-striped hair looked up from her phone and blinked slowly.

"Hi." I gave her what I hoped was a confidence-inducing smile. "I was wondering if I could talk to the manager? Or the owner?"

She blinked again. "You need a room?"

"No," I said. "I just wanted to talk to the person in charge."

Her pierced eyebrows lifted a fraction of an inch. "You gonna complain?"

"No," I repeated, forcing my smile to stay in place. "I had a few questions, that's all. About someone who—"

"We don't give out information about our guests," she drawled and went back to her game. She didn't glance at me as she tacked on an insincere, "Sorry."

"It's not about guests," I said. "I had a question about an employee."

"We don't have employees."

"Aren't *you* an employee?"

She sighed and dragged her attention away from the phone. "My dad's the owner. So I work here, but I'm not really an employee. Which *sucks*, because it means he doesn't have to pay me overtime."

"You could get a job somewhere else," I pointed out.

"Around here?" She scoffed. "Anyway, we don't have employees."

"What about contractors? Clem Jensen was doing some work for you?"

"Clem?" She sat up. "Yeah, he's our handyman."

"When was the last time he was here?"

She shrugged. "A week ago, maybe? There's always stuff for him to do. I mean, my dad thinks he's handy, and so he tries to fix it, and he screws up, so my mom calls Clem."

"What was he working on this time?"

She grimaced. "Plumbing stuff."

I flashed back to the invoices I'd studied. "A hot water heater?"

"Yeah, it—" she broke off, eyes narrowing. "How did you know that? Why do you want to know about Clem?"

"Clem passed away," I said gently, and the girl reared back, the phone slipping out of her fingers with a clatter.

"But . . . he was here last week." She looked utterly bewildered and suddenly very young.

"I know. He died Sunday morning. His daughter asked me to notify his customers. How did he seem to you, when you last saw him?"

She blinked more rapidly now. "Alive."

"I know it's a shock." I waited a beat before pressing her. "Had Clem's behavior changed at all recently? Did he seem stressed or worried?"

She shook her head mutely.

"Are you sure?"

"He was *happy*," she said, almost accusatory. "I mean, he was coming down with some kind of cold or flu or something."

Laura had said the same, but I knew better—Clem had felt badly because of the drug switch; he'd probably suffered at least one minor heart attack before the one that sent him to the hospital. People assume heart attacks are as dramatic as they see on TV, where people clutch at their arm or their chest, but oftentimes, the first symptoms look like the flu: clammy skin, nausea, and fatigue.

The girl continued, urging me to believe her. "He was still whistling and joking around and stuff. He was . . . happy."

Something about the way she said it snagged my attention. "Was that unusual? Was he in a bad mood most of the time?"

"Not bad," she said. "He was kind of gruff. You know how old guys are, but he'd warmed up lately. He would tell me all about his grandson. And he . . ." She blushed. "He gave me advice about my boyfriend."

"That's really sweet." Still, I didn't think Clem's money came from moonlighting as an advice columnist. "Was he doing a lot of work for your dad?"

"Not really. I mean, he had the big painting project, but that was early in the summer." She frowned, finally recovering from the shock. "Why are you asking all these questions?"

I hesitated. "His daughter asked me to help settle his affairs."

That sounded official. The sort of thing someone might ask if they were legitimately helping out.

"How did he die? Was it an accident?"

"No. It was . . . unexpected."

I could have said, "It was murder," but that sort of news tended to derail a conversation.

The girl was quicker than I had given her credit for. "Unexpected how? Like, a heart attack? Or . . ."

"We're not sure yet."

"Well, I'm not sure I should talk to you," she retorted. "What did you say your name was?"

"Her name's Frankie," came a familiar voice behind me. "Is she giving you trouble, Bianca?"

The girl—Bianca—turned. "Deputy Noah! I didn't see you there!"

"You two know each other?" I asked.

"Bianca's always very helpful whenever I have a question about a guest," Noah said, giving her a fond smile. Bianca preened a little, smoothing her pink-striped hair and leaning over the counter.

"Must be nice," I said, unable to keep a sour note from creeping into my voice.

"He's the police," Bianca said. "How do you know each other?"

"Old friends," Noah said, turning his attention to me. "You looking for new accommodations? All the units here are on the first floor. You wouldn't have to climb out any windows."

"Our windows don't open," Bianca put in. "It's a safety feature."

"Very sensible." To Noah, I added, "I'm helping Laura. Clem was the handyman here, so I thought I'd stop by and—"

"Be *nosy*," Bianca said. "She was asking a ton of questions."

"Why don't I take Frankie off your hands?" Noah said easily. "Let you get back to work."

"Did you want a cup of coffee?" she offered, pointing to the pot behind the counter. Judging from the scorched smell hanging in the air, it had been sitting on the burner all day.

"Maybe later. Come on, Trouble," he said, and led me out the door.

Once in the parking lot, I said, "Friend of yours?"

"She's a little young for me. Nice kid, though. I don't like thinking about all the things she probably sees here."

I tended to agree; any place that charged hourly rates was probably giving Bianca a far different education than the community college.

"What are you doing here, Frankie?"

"I told you, I'm helping Laura," I said, making my eyes go wide and innocent. "She wanted me to talk to her dad's customers, let them know he'd passed away. What are *you* doing here?"

"Swung by the store to see how Matt's doing. You know, bring the new father a cigar. He mentioned you were coming out here, so I thought I'd stop in and make sure you found the place okay."

"How thoughtful," I muttered.

"Funny thing, though. I also ran by the library this morning, said hi to Laura Madigan."

"Aren't you the social butterfly?" I snarked, heading toward my car.

"Community relations," he said with a grin. "I got the distinct impression Laura believes her dad died of natural causes. If you're convinced Clem was murdered, why not tell her?"

"It's not something you can drop into a conversation," I said. "We're having coffee this afternoon, and I was going to tell her then. I wanted to be sure before I said anything, because the next step is to have her request an autopsy."

"Autopsies are hard on the family," he said, turning serious. "Do you really need to put Laura through that?"

"You're the one who said I needed proof."

"What if the autopsy proves you're wrong?"

"It won't."

"Because you're never wrong?"

I looked up at him. "I've been wrong about plenty of things. And I'm sorry for them. But I am not wrong about this, so you can either help me or get out of the way."

He considered me for a long moment, those steady green eyes taking my measure. Then he shook his head, rueful. "You were always stubborn."

"Focused," I replied, and then the strange, tense moment was gone. We circled around the property, walking close enough that our shoulders occasionally brushed. Clem had been here in summer, according to Bianca, painting the exterior of the motel. Out of curiosity, I inspected the trim. Not bad. Neat enough brushwork, and he'd taken the time to cut in around the windows and doorframes. The paint didn't seem to be superhigh quality, but based on what I'd seen already, Bianca's dad wasn't the type to pay for quality—and paint was one of those areas where you get what you pay for.

"Iron Ore," I said. Noah's eyebrows shot up, and I added, "The paint color. I remember it from the invoices, because he ordered so much." I bent and scraped at the siding, close to the ground where it wouldn't be noticeable.

"He did two coats. Nice work. My mom thought he was legit."

"Lila has good instincts," Noah said.

"I suppose." She'd liked Noah too, despite his family's reputation. "I'd thought maybe he was overcharging people, and that's where the money was coming from. I guess not."

"You're still focused on that?" He shrugged. "So the cash came from somewhere else."

"But where?" I dug in my bag for my sunglasses, annoyed to find I'd left them atop my head. "Everyone says the same thing—Clem was all about work, fishing, and his grandson. That's it. He wasn't investing it, he wasn't winning at the casino. There wasn't a single lotto ticket in his house. None of it explains how—"

Across the parking lot, the door slammed open. A bedraggled brunette stepped outside, blinking irritably at the sunlight and tottering over to a convertible on impossibly high heels.

"Aw, baby," said a voice inside the room. "Don't be like that!"

I recognized the voice and on instinct pulled Noah into a cluster of trees.

"Hey!" he said, bewildered.

I clapped a hand over his mouth and peered past him. A moment later, Jimmy Madigan strode out of the room, pleading with the brunette. She ignored him, gunning the engine and driving off in a spray of gravel.

Jimmy swore, ran his hands through his hair, and glanced around.

I felt Noah smile against my hand, and I dragged him deeper into the pines, but it was too late.

Jimmy's gaze snapped to us, caught by the movement or—more likely—my lime-green backpack.

"Well lookee," he sneered. "You're the girl from Crossroads."

"You remember," I said. "Glad I made an impression."

"I never forget a face," he said, ambling over. I could smell the beer on his breath from fifteen paces, and it wasn't even noon. "I've heard plenty about you, though. You're that nurse. The one who found my dear, departed father-in-law. How come you're not wearing one of those uniforms? Bet the deputy would like that, wouldn't he?"

"Excuse me?" I said, ice in my voice. Next to me, Noah tensed.

Jimmy laughed, a coarse, ugly sound. "Nurse and the cop at the no-tell motel. Did you get a good rate? They give you a break if you stay for more than four hours."

"Looks like you won't be needing that long," I said. "Shocking."

Jimmy scowled, puffing out his chest. "This is my place of residence. I'm paying weekly."

"That so?" Noah asked, eyeing him. "I thought you were living over on the south side of town."

Interesting that Noah knew where Jimmy lived. I wondered if he'd been keeping tabs on Jimmy all along, or if he was finally taking my suspicions seriously.

"Moving on up," Jimmy said.

"To a sleazy motel?" I asked.

"Can't beat the view. I see all sorts of interesting things. You wouldn't believe the people who sneak off here for an afternoon." He waggled his eyebrows. "You two aren't doing a great job of sneaking, no offense. Not that I blame you for wanting to show off the little nurse," he told Noah, and looked me over. "Girlie, you'd raise my temperature, too."

Before Noah could respond, I stepped in front of him and met Jimmy's eyes.

"Call me girlie again," I said pleasantly, "and I will show you exactly where to put that thermometer. We both know I'm good for it."

He took a step backward and held up his hands. "I didn't mean nothing."

"How long have you been living here?" I asked.

"A few months, give or take."

"You must have run into Clem a few times," I said. "I hear he wasn't your biggest fan."

Jimmy snorted. "We weren't exactly heading over to the riverboats together. I tried to be civil, of course."

"Of course," Noah said dryly. "You're the civilized sort."

"When's the last time you saw Clem?"

He shifted. "A couple of weeks before he died. Why?"

A couple of weeks would have fit the timing of the medication. "Did you two talk?"

"Not much. Last time he bothered to say more'n five words, he was telling me how Laura was going to get rid of me. Like I was going to let that happen."

I elbowed Noah discreetly, and he gave the barest of nods.

"The man never gave me so much as a kind word, let alone a dime. But thanks to him, hospital's going to be handing over a whole lot of cash."

"Glad to hear it," Noah said. "Because your car's got expired tags, and that's a two-hundred-fifty-dollar ticket."

Jimmy's face turned dark with rage.

"Go grab your license," Noah said, unperturbed. "Meet me over by the cruiser, and we'll get this settled. Frankie, stick around. I'd like a word."

I sighed. Probably more than one word, and many of them would have to do with my snooping.

Noah wrote out the ticket and stalked back over to me, scowling as Jimmy disappeared into his room.

"Now do you believe me?" I asked.

"That Jimmy killed Clem? I can see why you like him for it, but . . ."

"But he's dumb as a box of rocks?"

His lips twitched. "Lazy, too."

Hearing Noah confirm my own late-night fears was dispiriting. But my gut said Jimmy was involved in Clem's death. There had to be some kind of explanation.

"Maybe he had help," I suggested. "That brunette looked fit to kill."

"You're reaching, and you know it." Noah headed back to his cruiser. "If I asked the sheriff to open an investigation right now, he'd laugh me out of the station. And the DA would, too. Everything you've got is circumstantial."

"That doesn't mean it's wrong."

He sighed as he got in, starting the engine and rolling down the window. "Talk to Laura and convince her to request the autopsy. Once the results are back, we can talk. Until then, leave Jimmy Madigan alone—he's a weasel, but weasels bite when they're cornered."

I wanted to scream with frustration, to reach inside the cruiser and throttle Noah, to shake some sense into him. He knew I was right, and I knew the stubborn set to his jaw better than anyone. He wasn't going to budge. "Why can't you trust me on this?"

He jammed his sunglasses on and gave me a long, inscrutable look.

"Because I'm not seventeen anymore," he said, and drove away.

TWENTY-ONE

I found Laura in the library, reshelving books after a pre-school story time.

"I loved this one when I was a kid," I said, picking up a sticky copy of *Bedtime for Frances*.

"It's a classic for a reason," she said. "I thought you were coming by later. Did you want to join the book club?"

I paused, and she read the answer on my face.

"This doesn't look promising," she said, and sank onto one of the child-sized plastic chairs. For a moment, she held her hands to her face, then folded them in her lap, threw back her shoulders, and met my eyes. "I'm ready."

Was she? There was no good way to tell her that her father had been murdered. Usually, the doctors notified family members of a patient's death, and I was simply there for support. This felt alien and infinitely worse, like I was ripping open an old wound in the most jagged, brutal way possible.

"You know the hospital is investigating me in relation to your dad's death."

She nodded. "It's ridiculous. I'm so sorry—it's because of the lawsuit, isn't it?"

"Partly. If they can show I was responsible, not them, they might not have to pay as much money—or none at all, depending on how they handle it. Regardless, I might lose my nursing license."

"Jimmy wants money, and he doesn't care who the lawsuit hurts."

"Jimmy is a problem." I drew a chair closer and sat across from her. "But I'm telling you this is because I need you to understand why I've been investigating, too. On my own."

She frowned. "What is there to investigate? He had a heart attack, Frankie. You tried to help him, the doctors tried to help him, but . . . it was just his time."

"That's the thing," I said. "I don't think it was your dad's time. Dr. Hardy had already put the stent in; he was stabilized and his vitals all looked good. There was no reason to think he wouldn't recover."

"They said I could wait until morning to see him," she murmured.

"Everyone expected him to make a full recovery. I think the reason he didn't was because someone interfered. Deliberately. I think that's what killed him."

Blood drained from Laura's cheeks, and she swayed like a tree about to topple. Just as I reached for her, she straightened, refocusing on me.

"Murdered."

The word sounded so wretched when she said it. So violent and incongruous in this cheerful primary-painted room, surrounded by puzzles and picture books.

"They told me it was a heart attack," she said. "Dr. Hardy said—"

"I know. But your dad's blood work showed that he wasn't taking his medication, and when I had the pills analyzed—"

"When you *what?*" she demanded, loud enough that one of the other librarians glared at us.

I swallowed, fighting off the sensation that the conversation was rapidly veering off course. "I had a pharmacist look at the pills yesterday, and according to him—"

"My father's pills? How did you—oh," she said. "Oh, I am so *stupid*. We went to the cabin. I took you there. I invited you in."

"I know it's a lot to process," I began.

"That's why you've been so kind. So thoughtful— dinner invitations, and helping with the business, and everything else you've done. You don't actually care. You were using me to clear your name."

I kept my voice soft, the same soothing tone I used to calm patients. "I helped you because your dad seemed like a good person."

"He was. But you aren't. You *lied* to me, Frankie. You let me believe you were my friend."

"I am!"

"A friend wouldn't lie, or hold back this kind of thing. A friend would have told me from the first time we met."

"I didn't know! The first time we met, I was . . ."

I was checking for clues inside Clem's hospital room.

"It was a feeling I had," I explained. "Instinct. But if you'd asked me that day, I wouldn't have said it was murder."

"What would you have said?"

"Medical error, maybe? Negligence? Once the hospital came after me, I figured I would sound like a crazy person if I started shouting murder, so I didn't say anything."

"You did say something. You said, 'Let me help you, Laura. I understand how you feel, Laura.' But you didn't, not really."

"I understand what it's like to lose a father. The last thing you needed was me stirring up more trouble, especially if there was nothing to show for it."

"Do not presume to tell me what I need." She stood and glared down at me. "You have no idea what I need or how I feel."

"I'm sorry," I said, my voice small. "I wanted to help."

"I don't want your help!" After a moment, she seemed to gather herself, though her eyes were bright with fury. "You're right, though. I do think you're a crazy person. Who would want to kill my father?"

I took a deep breath. "How about your husband?"

Shock is a strange beast. It can kill a person—once a patient goes into shock their entire body can shut down. But if they're not in immediate *physical* danger, shock can break the mind as swiftly as any blow to the head.

Judging from Laura's laughter—holding-her-side, breathless, verging on hysterical laughter—that's exactly what my news had caused. I should have cushioned the words a little more. Led up to it, used a softer tone. I'd misjudged the situation, unsettled by Laura's anger and my own discomfort.

So I waited and watched, and when she finally slowed down to the occasional giggle, I put my hand on hers. "I know it's terrible to hear."

"It's ludicrous," she said, shaking me off. "Jimmy . . . no. He's not a prize, but he's no killer. Why would he do such a thing?"

"Money? If your dad dies while you two are still married, he'd get half of the inheritance."

"What inheritance? A falling-apart van? A cabin in the middle of nowhere? My father wasn't exactly wealthy."

"But he wasn't broke, either. And for someone like Jimmy, even a little money might be a motive." I'd seen people knifed over ten dollars. Sometimes it wasn't the dollar amount triggering someone's greed, but the mere fact of the disparity: the killer saw someone who had something—anything—they didn't, and in that moment, sheer wanting warped their judgment into something violent and possessive.

"Jimmy's one of those guys who feels like the world owes him something. Owes him everything. He figured out your dad was helping you save up the money to divorce him and wasn't going to let that happen."

"I don't believe it," she said, but the waver in her voice told me her resistance was softening.

"Your dad was the handyman at Jimmy's motel. According to him, your dad said something about how it wouldn't be long before you were done with him. He probably knew your dad didn't lock the cabin, and he'd know when your dad was working on a project at the motel, so he'd have time to get out there and switch the pills."

She massaged her temples. "What was wrong with his medication?"

"They weren't what his doctor had prescribed—at least one of them made his condition worse. Without the right meds, your dad was pretty much guaranteed to have a heart attack. I think Jimmy swapped the pills, hoping that's what would happen."

She stared at me, and I rushed on. "I know it's a stretch, Jimmy knowing that much about heart medications. But you can find out all that information on the Internet. One of the drugs he swapped is available over the counter." It didn't explain how he'd gotten a prescription for Thrombinase, but I had a feeling that, when it came to illegally acquiring controlled substances, Jimmy contained hidden depths.

"The hospital treated him after his heart attack," Laura whispered. "They said after he had the stent put in that his prognosis was good."

"It was," I said. "Once Jimmy heard your dad had made it to the hospital, he must have worried that he would be caught, so he went in to finish the job. The security at Stillwater Gen is terrible. He could have snuck in during change of shift, and . . ."

I trailed off. I was giving Jimmy a lot of credit—more than he deserved. How had he known what time shift change happened? For that matter, how had he managed to sneak past Marcus in the dead of night? How had he found out Clem had been admitted? How had he known how to tamper with the monitors, or give Clem a poison that wouldn't trigger the coroner's suspicion?

Jimmy wasn't that smart.

And neither was I, apparently.

"What if he had a partner?" I asked. "Someone at the hospital who was feeding him information? Helping him get access? Does he have any friends who work there?"

"He might," she said slowly. "A few years ago, he got a job there as a custodian. They fired him after a few months, but he might have stayed in touch with some of the guys."

I stared at her. "Jimmy worked for the hospital? Why didn't you tell me?"

"I didn't think it mattered." The laughter was gone now, the disbelief leaching away and anger taking its place. "I didn't know my father had been murdered, remember?"

Fair enough.

"If Jimmy did have a partner inside the hospital, they could have called him when your dad was admitted." Even in the chaos of the bus crash, talk of my confrontation with Paul Costello had spread quickly. Jimmy's partner would have heard about it within hours, at most. A custodian could have moved freely in and out of Clem's room, even in the middle of the night. They were so familiar as to be practically invisible, with access to every department. They'd be familiar enough with the monitors to put them in hospice mode.

I explained all of this to Laura, how neatly it fit, and her pale cheeks flushed with anger.

"Do you think Jimmy . . . suffocated him?" She covered her mouth with a white-knuckled fist, then said, "Did he suffer? Did he know what was happening?"

The thoughts of Clem's final moments had kept me awake at night, too. But I kept my voice gentle. "I don't think so. The medical examiner would have picked up any signs of a struggle, and there's nothing about it in the postmortem."

"How?" she asked hoarsely. "How did they kill him?"

"Poison, probably. Some kind of drug. But we won't know for sure unless they do an autopsy."

"Haven't they done one?"

I shook my head. "Hospitals don't perform autopsies unless there's a reason—or a request. That's where you come in. I need you to talk to Walter Strack and ask for an autopsy. Once we have the results, we can go to the police."

"The police," she echoed. "They'll arrest Jimmy?"

"They'll open an investigation," I said. "Bring him in for questioning, go over all the evidence. Once they've got enough, they'll arrest him, and his partner."

"For killing my father." She stood up so quickly she knocked over the chair. "You said he's at a motel?"

"Piney Woods," I said. "But Laura, you can't confront Jimmy. He's dangerous."

"Not as dangerous as I am," she said flatly.

"If you tip him off, he might run. He might hurt you, or CJ. Be logical."

"Logical? My husband left me, then killed my father rather than give me a divorce, and I'm supposed to be *logical*?"

"If he runs, he can't be punished. If you hurt him, *you'll* be punished, and then what happens to CJ? All you need to do is tell the hospital you want an autopsy. The police will handle the rest."

She looked away from me, fingers twisting the hem of her sweater. "The medical examiner?"

"It has to come from you," I said. "You're the next of kin."

She nodded. "I'll handle it."

"Do you want me to come with you?" I didn't like her color or her fast, shallow breathing. Shock, I thought again. "You shouldn't be alone right now."

"You've done enough, Frankie." She glanced past me, toward the doorway, and forced a smile. "And I'm not alone, because here are my Busy Bee Threes! We've got a great story time today . . . come on in!"

Round-cheeked preschoolers swarmed around her, and she met my eyes even as she passed out hugs. "We'll talk later," she said, a clear dismissal.

I left, trying to ignore the alarm prickling along my spine. The autopsy would prove me right, save my career, put a killer behind bars. It was exactly what I'd wanted.

So why didn't I feel better?

TWENTY-TWO

I didn't hear from Laura for the rest of the day. I called, three separate times, and each went directly to voice mail. Rather than brood, I hung out with Riley, playing endless games of Go Fish and War and Life, which took a lot longer than I remembered from my own youth.

The next morning was Saturday, our busiest day. My mom asked me to open, so Riley and I rode over together—Riley on her bright-purple two-wheeler with a flower-studded basket and me on my ancient red ten-speed, the tires remarkably still good after I'd pumped them up.

Bent on racing me, Riley poured on speed while I coasted behind her, steering with one hand and clutching coffee in the other, a box of doughnuts in my backpack. My bike in the city had a basket, a water bottle holder, and even saddlebags on the back, all for easier commuting, and I thought longingly of it.

Funny, but aside from my bike—and my own bedroom— I wasn't longing for anything else about my old life. The messages from Peter had tapered off, and all I felt was relief. Even the temptation to call the ER and catch up with

Mindy again had faded. Clem's death and Rowan's birth were providing plenty of excitement.

Riley called something undecipherable from around the corner of our building. "What?" I asked as I coasted into the back parking lot. She'd already left her bike leaning against the railing, and I paused to lock them together. Stillwater wasn't the kind of place where people stole bikes, but it wasn't the kind of place people were murdered, either.

"There's a cat in the store." Riley was balanced on her tiptoes, peering through the glass pane set high in the door. "He looks *mean*."

"A cat?" I straightened. "Is he orange?"

"Very. I think it's a cat. Maybe it's something else. What do badgers look like?"

"Good grief." I nudged Riley aside and fitted my key into the lock, squinting. "It *is* a cat. How did he get in?"

In truth, I was more concerned with his exit than his entry. "We need to catch him and then scoot him out, okay?"

"I'm not touching him," Riley said. "He has fangs. I saw them."

"He doesn't have . . . okay, he might. We can't have him in the store, though. Grandma will pitch a fit. You keep an eye on him while I grab a broom, and we'll shoo him outside. Got it?"

"Got it," Riley said with a nod. I opened the door, annoyed again at the lack of alarm, and took a deep breath.

The store smelled . . . wrong. Beneath the usual familiar odors of paint thinner and mineral spirits and fresh-cut lumber was something else, something . . . fetid and sticky. My stomach clenched. Because it was a familiar scent, but not the kind of familiar I associated with caulk guns and garden supplies.

The cat was sitting now atop the counter, haughty and slit-eyed.

"Tell me you caught a mouse," I said to the cat. "Tell me you caught a mouse, and I will buy you a can of tuna."

The cat blinked and stretched.

"Do you think Mom would let me have a cat?" Riley asked.

"Not this one," I muttered. "Don't you guys have your hands full right now? Rowan will be home before you know it."

"Yeah, but Rowan is Mom and Dad's," she said. "The cat would be for me. I could put it in little hats and stuff."

The cat laid its ears back and hissed.

"Or maybe just feed him treats," she said hurriedly. "The feed store sells all sorts of cat stuff."

"Mmn-hmn." I placed a hand on my stomach, trying to quell the swirling sense of dread. "I'm going to get that broom. Stay here. In fact, why don't you hold the door open for me."

Riley nodded and skipped back to the door, the bell jingling cheerfully. "Here, kitty-kitty-kitty."

"Come on, kitty," I said sourly. "Time to go."

Instead, the cat padded to the far end of the counter, looked back over its shoulder at me, and yowled. Twice.

"I'm not picking you up," I said, drawing closer. "I am not a cat person."

The cat jumped, landing on the wooden floors lightly, and waited for me to catch up.

I followed him past the aisles of electrical supplies, of paint chips and varnish and sandpaper. My unease grew with every step, and so did the smell. "You want to go out the front door? Be my guest."

Instead, with a swish of his crooked, matted orange tail, he settled himself at the end of the hand tools aisle.

"Shoo," I said, knowing he wouldn't move, knowing that whatever he was guiding me toward was nothing I wanted to see. "Please."

He stared at me, his tail thumping.

I looked at my watch. It was almost nine o'clock. Customers would be arriving soon, hoping to get a jump on their weekend projects.

I'd never liked the way this corner of the store was shadowy, the light from the big front windows not quite reaching to the back. It was too easy to let my imagination take over. My tendency to see the worst possible scenario was handy when dealing with a critical patient, less so when it was what I very much hoped was a vermin issue. "Riley, hit the lights."

A moment later, the fluorescents flickered on with a low hum. The cat yowled again.

"Fine," I said. "But don't think this is job security. We sell mousetraps, you know. Aisle seven."

I reached the end of the aisle.

Vermin indeed.

Jimmy Madigan was lying face up on the wooden floor, eyes sightless, blood pooling beneath him, skin the color of old oatmeal.

And in my professional opinion, very, very dead.

★　　★　　★

The cat chirruped, as if curious, and I snapped into crisis mode. "Riley, go to the diner."

"What about the cat?" Her voice drew closer.

I scrambled around the corner, blocking her from the sight of Jimmy's body.

"Diner," I said firmly, and walked her back to the door, digging in my backpack. "Here's some money. Get yourself a good breakfast."

"I had a good breakfast. Remember? Grandma made scrambled eggs."

"Fine. Get yourself a doughnut."

"Didn't you already bring some for the customers?" She took in my expression and quit arguing. "What kind do you want?"

"I don't. Stay at the diner until your dad gets there, okay?"

"Aunt Frankie . . ."

"Go." I scooted her out the door and raced back to Jimmy, tugging out the spare latex gloves I kept in a side pocket of my backpack. Teeth gritted, I knelt, searching his neck for a pulse. Unsurprisingly, there was none. His skin was cool to the touch, with the clay-like feel of the recently dead. I lifted his hand. Not quite rigor mortis, not yet, but any chance to save him was long gone.

I stood, intending to get my phone, and then hesitated. The store had been locked when I arrived. How had Jimmy gotten in, and more importantly, *why*? Was he looking for me? Noah had warned me he was dangerous. Maybe Laura had told him about my theory—maybe she'd confronted him, and he'd come looking for me to plead his case. Or more likely, looking for revenge.

Revenge. *I'll handle it*, Laura had said.

My nausea returned and my knees went weak. I forced myself to breathe slowly, through my mouth. Ignoring my phone, I crouched down next to Jimmy's body. No question about the weapon. Dozens of tools were scattered on the ground, as if there'd been a fight and someone had been thrown into the shelves. But only one of them was covered in blood. A chisel—top of the line, I noted, from a company in Tennessee named Whiskey River Tools. It had a hand-forged beveled edge with a polished maple grip, ideal for woodworking.

And apparently, murder.

I inspected Jimmy carefully, peeling back his quilted flannel jacket, lifting his blood-soaked T-shirt, noting the wounds as if I was making a report to my attending: a single inch-long laceration between the ninth and tenth ribs, no lacerations on the arms or hands or face, nothing to indicate any defensive injuries.

If there'd been a struggle, he'd been winning until the thin blade of the chisel was driven into his heart.

Hard to tell any more without a more thorough exam, but nothing I'd seen set my mind at ease about Laura. I couldn't quite understand why they'd met here, but I could picture it perfectly: she'd accused him, they'd fought, and Jimmy had overpowered her, tossing her into the array of tools. Laura had grabbed the first weapon that came to hand.

It was self-defense. Surely the police would see it, too. Surely Noah, of all people, would understand. He'd witnessed plenty of similar scenarios, growing up.

But something about it bothered me. Bothered me in the same way Clem's death had—something vague and nebulous but important. Something other than the fact there had been a murder in my store.

Not my store, I reminded myself. Charlie's. I was just visiting, and soon I'd be able to put all of this behind me.

Unfortunately, soon was not the same as now.

The cat paced at the end of the aisle, his tail brushing against the end cap.

I straightened, peeling off my gloves. "That was *not* a mouse. No tuna for you," I added, reaching down to pet him, wanting some degree of comfort.

He swiped at the back of my hand with a needle-like claw. I yelped as the blood welled up and glared at the cat as he scampered out the still-propped-open door.

I wiped my hands on my jeans, then went to retrieve my phone. Time to call the police.

TWENTY-THREE

"Well, this is a hell of a mess," Noah said mildly, leaning against the counter as half the deputies in the county swarmed through the store.

"Tell me about it," I said. "We're going to be closed for most of the day. My mother's going to kill me. At least that'll be an easy one to solve."

"I don't think it'll hurt business any. Everyone's going to stop in. Rubbernecking." He shifted his gaze to me, assessing. "You seem pretty calm."

"It's not the first time I've seen a stabbing victim. Not even the hundredth."

"First time it's on your turf, though. Any idea how he got here?"

I shook my head. "Riley and I came in to open, and he was lying there." I didn't mention the cat.

"Where's Riley now?"

"I called Matt to pick her up from the diner. She shouldn't see this."

"That kind of thing tends to scar a kid," he agreed, and there were shadows in his green eyes that hadn't been there a moment ago.

I looked away, the sudden silence an acknowledgment that we'd both seen too much, too early—me, huddled in the corner of my father's hospital room while the staff tried to save him, Noah, taking care of his brothers and sisters when he was still a kid himself. It shouldn't have surprised me that he'd become a police officer. He'd stayed in Stillwater to protect his siblings; it was only natural that he'd eventually make a career out of it.

The ME bustled over. "It's not an exact finding, but based on rigor and lividity, I'd say he's been dead approximately three hours. At least two, certainly no more than five. Single wound between the ninth and tenth ribs. I'll have to open him up to be sure, but based on the angle and blood loss, I'm guessing the weapon pierced the right ventricle."

Exactly what I'd thought. I tried not to feel smug.

Another deputy, listening in, said, "Signs of a struggle, but limited to the immediate area. Maybe he was here on a burglary?" He looked me over. "Anything missing?"

"No," I said, then considered it more carefully. "I don't think so, anyway. He wasn't here to rob us."

"What *was* he here for?" Noah asked. "Can't imagine the answer's any good."

"I don't know," I said, trying not to think of Laura. "I don't even know how he got in."

"Any idea who'd want to kill him?"

I hesitated a second too long. "A charmer like Jimmy? Half the town, probably." I shoved my hair out of my face and forced myself to meet his eyes.

"Probably," he agreed. "But why now?"

"Who knows?" I wound a lock of hair around my finger. The crime scene technicians were gathering evidence, taking pictures, and slipping the fallen screwdrivers into evidence bags. Everything was covered in fine black fingerprint powder. Charlie was going to be furious: inventory screwed up, lost business, bloodstains covering the floor. It would take me forever to put the store back together, but all I wanted to do was find Laura.

It was my fault. The details didn't really matter. Laura had confronted Jimmy because of my accusation, and he'd responded with violence. I wondered how badly she was injured, wondered how hard it would be to make the case for self-defense. My stomach twisted. I might not have stabbed Jimmy, but I'd set Laura on this path. In my own way, I was just as guilty.

Noah caught my hand, disentangled it from my hair, and inspected it. "How'd you hurt your hand?"

I glanced down at the rusty red smear against my skin.

"There was a cat when I came in," I said. "He took a swipe at me."

I left out the part where the cat led me to Jimmy's body. Telling Noah that his only witness was a feral cat wouldn't improve his mood any, not that I should be worried about Noah's moods.

"In the store?" Noah asked, plainly disbelieving. "Your mom let . . ."

"He's a stray. He followed me home a few nights ago. I might have fed him. A few times."

"Might have."

"He's very skinny," I said. "You know us Stapletons. We're always worried people haven't gotten enough to eat."

Noah had spent plenty of time at our kitchen table, fending off third or fourth helpings from my mother.

"I remember." He frowned. "We're going to need to take a sample."

I paused in the middle of pulling out the first aid kit from beneath the counter. "Excuse me?"

"You found the body, and you're injured. We're taking a sample."

"It's a cat scratch!"

"It's standard procedure. I can get a court order, if you're going to be a pain about it."

"Fine," I said, and he called over a tech to take the sample while I huffed and rolled my eyes.

When we'd finished, he said, "Go over it again."

I recounted my grisly discovery, stopping periodically as Noah asked questions, helping me reconstruct the morning in minute detail. He was a good listener, waiting for natural pauses before he interrupted, asking skillful questions that drew out information I didn't realize I knew. The entire time, I was aware of Jimmy's body behind me, the pool of blood, and the now-familiar, irritating sensation I was overlooking something.

"And then you guys got here," I said, finishing up, wondering how I was going to get to Laura before the police did.

"Mmn-hmn." Noah tapped his pen on the top of his notebook. "What aren't you telling me?"

"I just gave you a blow-by-blow of everything I saw."

"True. But that's not all you know, is it? You're holding something back. Don't lie to me, Frankie. We both know you can't pull it off."

I hesitated, then offered up the only thing I could without implicating Laura. "There's something wrong. I don't know what it is yet. I just know there's something . . . not right about Jimmy's body."

"His body."

"Yes. No." I drummed my fingers in frustration. "The body? The crime scene? The weapon? I don't know, and my head is buzzing, and I can't place it. But it's off. It's not what it looks like."

Just like Clem.

"Frankie," he said in a low voice, "that's exactly what people say when they're caught at the scene of the crime."

"I wasn't *caught*," I said. "I called you here. And I'm not saying it to defend myself, because I don't need to defend myself. Something here doesn't fit."

Noah sighed. "That's what's bothering you? Something in the crime scene doesn't fit? That's it?"

"The dead body in aisle four isn't helping my mood any."

"I see. You talk to Laura yet?" he asked.

"Laura Madigan? No. Why would I talk to Laura? You were the first person I called. Check my phone, if you don't believe me."

His eyebrows lifted. "I meant about the autopsy."

"Oh. Yeah." There was no point in lying about something Noah could easily verify.

"How'd she take it?"

I rolled my shoulders, trying to loosen the knotted muscles there. "I told her someone had murdered her father, Noah. How do you think she took it?"

"Did you tell her that someone was Jimmy?"

Before I could answer, a voice carried across the store. "This is my building, Travis Anderson, and I don't care if it is a crime scene. My tax dollars pay your salary, young man, so you either let me on my property or I can come back with your mother."

"Guess Riley told my mom."

Noah sighed deeply. "Let her through, Anderson."

My mother appeared a moment later, smoothing her hair back into its bun. "Noah. Glad to see someone in the sheriff's department has an ounce of sense."

"Mrs. Stapleton. Deputy Anderson is right, ma'am. This is a crime scene. You shouldn't be here."

"This is my building, my business, and my daughter. Where else would I be?"

I could think of several million other places, but Mom brushed Noah aside with a sweep of her enormous purse. "You're hurt, Francesca!"

"I'm fine, Mom. Literally a scratch."

"Has she received medical attention?" she demanded of Noah.

"Yes. My own," I said. "Mom, honestly. It's nothing. Noah and his team will be finished up in . . ." I glanced at Noah, eyebrows raised.

"As soon as possible," Noah said. "Frankie's free to go. She's answered all our questions. For now."

"Questions? Don't say you suspect her!"

Noah didn't reply, instead addressing me directly. "You're not heading back to Chicago anytime soon, are you? Fiancé's not expecting you?"

I paused and shook my head. My mother's eyes narrowed.

"Glad to hear it." The firmness in his voice made it clear that he was speaking in a professional capacity, not a personal one.

My mother crossed her arms and looked over Noah with an expression that made me cower. "Someone's going to need to clean up this blood," she said. "Mops are in aisle seven."

With that, she took me by the elbow and marched me out the door.

TWENTY-FOUR

Mom hustled me into her enormous Buick, but instead of driving home, she pulled into the parking lot of the Lutheran church down the street, out of sight of the police.

"Francesca, why is there a dead body in my store?"

I sank lower in the seat. "Because someone stabbed him with a three-quarter-inch Whiskey River chisel."

"Don't be smart," she snapped.

"Trust me, I'm not," I said. "I don't know why he was there."

"Or who killed him?"

I stayed silent, and she eyed me speculatively. "Who was he?"

"Jimmy Madigan."

"Laura's husband? The gambler?" She folded her arms and stared at the white clapboard steeple. "I see."

And she did, I was certain.

"Mom, there's no sense in taking me home. I'll go back and wait until Noah and his team are done, then lock up."

Her eyes widened in horror. "We're not closing!"

"The store is a crime scene," I said. "We can't exactly open for business as usual."

"You're right," she said. "We'll need more people. Matt and Riley can help; I suppose Uncle Marshall can pitch in, too."

I drew back. "What? No. We need to stay closed for today. Tomorrow, too, maybe. Out of respect."

"For a gambler who cheats on his wife and doesn't take care of his child?" she snorted. "What's to respect? We've already lost the Saturday morning crowd. We can't close for the whole day."

"Nobody's going to shop at a crime scene," I said, aghast.

"Of course they are," she replied. "This is better than advertising. By lunchtime, every person in Stillwater is going to remember some sort of urgent home repair they need to take care of. As soon as the MacLean boy leaves, they'll be on our doorstep, looking for gossip and spackle."

"That's . . . mercenary."

"That's business," she said airily. "And good business, to boot. I'll pick up extra doughnuts. You make sure there's plenty of coffee."

"I can't," I said. "Someone needs to tell Laura."

She raised her eyebrows. "Are you sure she doesn't already know?"

I didn't answer, which was all the admission my mother needed. "Andrew Kleeman is supposed to be quite a good defense lawyer. Remind her not to say anything until he gets there."

"You have hidden depths, don't you, Mom?"

She smiled. "I'm so glad you finally noticed."

★　　★　　★

I headed to Laura's tidy white cottage, my steps dragging. Would she even be home? What if she and CJ were already on the run? The police would come calling soon enough—they always looked at the spouse, especially if it was an *estranged* spouse. Would I be considered an accessory after the fact, once Noah realized I'd known it was Laura all along? I hadn't lied, exactly. I'd just wanted to make sure she had someone on her side, after everything she'd been through.

And then my feet stopped completely as an entirely different possibility presented itself.

What if I'd been blinded by sympathy—I'd taken Laura's meekness at face value, but what if she'd been manipulating me all along? What if she and Jimmy had planned Clem's death together, and she'd turned on him when I got too close to the truth?

Is that what I'd missed?

A moment later, CJ came around the house, holding a rake that was far too tall for him. "Hi, Miss Stapleton!" he called, spotting me. He trotted over. "Did you bring Riley with you? I have to rake leaves, but we could jump in them when I'm done."

"Sorry, it's only me," I said, forcing a smile. "Is your mom home?"

He nodded. "She's inside."

"Are you having a good weekend?" I asked, feeling guilty. Small-talk as interrogation technique, especially small talk with a third grader, made me want another shower.

CJ nodded enthusiastically. "We had movie night," he said. "Popcorn and pizza and ice cream sundaes. It was fun."

"Sounds like it." Jimmy had been killed in the wee hours of the morning; Laura wouldn't have left CJ alone, would she? Somehow, I doubted it. And considering CJ's cheery demeanor, the police hadn't made it over here yet.

Which meant I'd have to break the bad news.

Again.

"You'll have to let yourself in," Laura said through the screen door, "I'm baking bread."

"Smells good," I said.

She stood at the counter, hands covered in flour, kneading a mound of dough with fierce, efficient movements. There were three loaves already cooling on the counter. "You've been busy."

"It's therapeutic," she said grimly.

I couldn't help it—I scanned her hand and arms for bruises or scratches, searched her face for any sign that she'd been in a fight. She looked tense and unhappy and decidedly frosty despite the heat of the oven, but unharmed.

Deftly shaping the loaf, she said, "I spoke to Walter Strack, at the hospital, and requested the autopsy. He's not happy about it, but it's not as if he could say no."

"Great." There was no sense in mincing words. Noah would be by any minute to break the news—and ask questions. "Something's happened, Laura. Something bad."

She slipped the loaf into its pan, hands shaking slightly. Then she crossed to the sink, rinsing off flour and checking on CJ through the green-curtained window. He was throwing armfuls of leaves in the air, undoing any progress he'd made with the rake.

"No offense," she said over her shoulder, "but every time you show up, the news gets worse."

"Well, let's hope this is the last of it," I said. "Jimmy's dead."

She stared at me.

"It happened early this morning, we think. At the hardware store."

"Jimmy's dead?" Her gaze flew to CJ again. "You're sure?"

"I was the one who found him."

She sat down at the table with a thump. After a moment, she said, "Why was he at the hardware store?"

"I don't know," I said. "It looks like there was a fight, and he was stabbed."

She let out a long, shuddering breath. Then her hands clenched in her lap, and she looked up at me, flushing. "I'm glad."

"Laura—"

"No," she said fiercely. "I'm *glad*. He murdered my father. He was a terrible husband. He treated CJ like he was . . . damaged. His own son."

"You can't talk like that."

"Everyone knows it's true. You think I don't know what people say about us? The pity in their eyes? I'm tired of being pitied."

"Well, what do you think people are going to say now? The police don't know what Jimmy was doing in the hardware store after closing. They don't know who killed him. And nobody had a bigger motive than you."

"That's ridiculous," she protested.

"Has that ever stopped the rumor mill in this town? The only way we're going to clear you is to find whoever did it." I'd been so certain Laura had been defending herself that I hadn't even considered other suspects. "It has to be his partner, right? That's the only thing that makes sense."

She massaged her temples. "I guess, but why do it now? If they were going to split the settlement money, wouldn't they wait until after the hospital had paid up? And why do it at your store?"

"The police are wondering the same thing," I said. "They're going to want to question you, by the way. You need a lawyer."

"I can't afford to—"

"You can't afford *not* to," I said. "My mom knows somebody; I'll call him. Noah's not unreasonable," I added. "It shouldn't be too hard to make him see sense. The lawyer will have you home by dinner. CJ can stay at our house until you're home."

"What if we're next?" she asked, her face suddenly bone-white. "First my father, now Jimmy. What if the killer is after our whole family? CJ could be in danger."

They both could.

Laura scrambled out of the chair, calling for CJ, ushering him into the living room to watch a video, barely concealing her panic.

"What do I do?" she asked, her voice low and strained. "Should we call the police?"

"Laura," I said, "think very carefully. Can anyone verify that you were here last night?"

She blinked. "Well, CJ. We watched a movie."

"After that? Once he was in bed. Did you send any e-mails or make any phone calls? Visit with a neighbor?"

"An alibi, you mean?" She shook her head. "I didn't realize I would need one."

"Me neither." I dug my keys out of my backpack. "New plan. You guys are going on a trip."

"What?"

"You've been under lot of stress, you're mourning your father, you wanted to get out of town for a bit."

"Frankie, I can't . . ."

"You can. You have to." I slid my house key off the ring and pressed it into her shaking hands. "I'm not using my apartment. It's a day's drive, a great neighborhood. There's a taco stand just down the block. Think of it as a vacation."

"You want us to hide?"

I scribbled my address on a sheet of paper. "Just until we catch whoever killed Jimmy. It's the safest thing for CJ and for you."

"But . . ."

I spoke over her. "Your husband was found dead in my family's store. You have no alibi. If you're taken into custody, the police will call family services to take care of CJ. I don't know who they'll place him with, but I would rather not find out."

Her eyes filled with tears, her breath coming in short, sharp gasps.

"Go pack a bag. And do it quick, because I'd estimate you've got thirty minutes before Stillwater's finest show up on your doorstep."

It took Laura and CJ fifteen minutes to leave; it took me another five to turn off the oven and lock all the doors and windows. Four minutes later, I was rounding the end of the block just as Noah's squad car pulled up to the house.

Twenty-four minutes. I'd been an optimist.

TWENTY-FIVE

I figured the last place Noah would look for me was back at the store, so after a quick stop at home for a shower and not-bloody clothes, I returned to the literal scene of the crime.

My mother had been right. The store was packed—a constant flow of "customers" all gaping at the freshly scrubbed floor. I handed out Styrofoam cups of coffee, rang up bags of clothespins and paint trays, and deflected countless questions.

"I never knew the little old ladies in this town were so bloodthirsty," I muttered between sales.

My mother smiled, nodded, and handed over a bag of light bulbs to the latest snoop. "Pity people don't die in here more often."

"Are you listening to yourself? It's a little disturbing. Not as disturbing as the number of chisels we've sold, mind you."

"Everyone wants the murder weapon," she said and patted my arm. "Better restock while it's quiet."

I headed into the basement and grabbed another box, arms straining under the weight. When I resurfaced, my mom was in front, merrily ringing up another purchase—and Noah was leaning against the back counter, scowling.

"Quit that," I said. "You're scaring the customers."

"You tipped off Laura Madigan," he growled, looming over me.

"I notified Jimmy's next of kin in a timely fashion." I set the box on the floor and rubbed the reignited ache in my back. "It seemed like the decent thing to do."

"Where is she?"

"I really couldn't say." I kept my face blank and began restocking the display.

"You really could," he said. "Or I could arrest you."

"For what?" I shot back.

"Obstruction of justice."

I'd been expecting this. "If Laura killed Jimmy, then I didn't tip her off—she already knew he was dead. But she didn't kill him, Noah. She was home with her kid all night."

"Can she prove it?" I didn't reply, and he shook his head. "What was he doing here?"

"How should I know? We weren't buddies."

Noah seemed to read my mind. "Well, you're the one accusing him of murder. Maybe he came here to confront you."

"Here? In the middle of the night? Do I look stupid enough to agree to that?" When Noah didn't answer, I shoved him aside, none too gently, and began hanging up chisels. "Maybe he had an urgent home repair and decided . . ."

I trailed off and stared blankly at the display in front of me. Row after row of hand-hammered murder weapons, hanging at eye level. Despite their exorbitant price tag,

Charlie had given them a prime spot in the store, hoping they would stand out. "Decided . . ."

"Decided what," prompted Noah. "To steal a screwdriver?"

I'd been about to suggest exactly that, but the screwdrivers weren't the problem. I glanced around to make sure nobody overheard. By the front door, my mother was loudly nattering away, trying to distract the busybodies.

"We are idiots. Both of us. Come here," I told him, and walked over to where I'd found Jimmy. My stomach churned at the knowledge I was standing in the same spot he'd bled out, but I faced the center of the aisle, my heels against the shelves. "Pretend to strangle me."

The corner of Noah's mouth twitched. "Gladly."

He put his hands around my neck, his fingers warm and gentle, his thumb brushing the hollow of my throat, and my pulse skipped.

"Frankie . . ." he said softly, his breath ruffling my hair.

"Pay attention." I reached behind me, stretching out my arm. "I can't reach the endcap."

His hands slide to my shoulders. "It's five feet away. A gorilla couldn't reach the endcap."

"Exactly." I twisted away, forcing myself to recall every detail of this morning. "When I found Jimmy, there were tools all over the floor, like someone had been knocked into the shelves."

"Right," said Noah. He plucked one of the screwdrivers off its hook, tested the edge with his thumb. "Whoever killed Jimmy—assuming it wasn't you—managed to grab one of these and stab him."

"No, they didn't. The killer used one of these high-end woodworking chisels, and those are only kept on the end-cap. Nobody could have reached from here."

"It was premeditated?" He strode over to the display, brow furrowed. "If that's the case, why didn't Jimmy have defensive wounds?"

"You know how cocky Jimmy was, and how clueless. He probably thought he could handle whoever he was meeting. They took him by surprise."

"Doesn't rule out the wife." He scowled down at me.

"Oh, come off it," I said, annoyed. "Laura didn't kill him. She was home all night with her kid. Besides, she's not the type."

"I know," he said, but he didn't sound happy about it. "Let's take this outside."

Taking my elbow, he led me down the back steps and over to the shed, where we kept the bags of mulch and potting soil.

"What's your problem?" I asked, tugging free.

"You had to touch the crime scene, didn't you? Couldn't resist checking it out."

"I *found* the crime scene. Of course I checked it out. But I was careful not to contaminate the scene—I wore gloves."

"I know," he said. "We found them in the trash, covered in Jimmy's blood. Where'd you get them?"

"I work in a hospital, Noah. I always have a spare pair of gloves on me. What's the big deal?"

He spoke with exaggerated patience. "Your prints aren't on the murder weapon."

A middle-aged couple walked by, eyeing us curiously. When they'd gone, I hissed, "Of course they aren't. I'm not the killer."

"There are no prints on the murder weapon, Frankie. And there should be. Maybe not yours, but Charlie's. Matt's. Your mom. The handle is totally clean, which means the killer either wiped it down, or they wore gloves."

"You think it's me?" I couldn't help it—I laughed, and Noah's expression darkened. "Be serious."

"You were investigating Jimmy Madigan. You'd fought with him; he'd threatened to blackmail you." The memory of Jimmy's sleazy innuendos at the motel rose up, and I winced as Noah continued, "His lawsuit was going to result in the suspension of your nursing license. And then . . . someone let him into the store. Someone had the key to get in, and the alarm code. Someone who could plausibly get Jimmy to come to the store in the dead of night. And the only person I know who fits those categories is you."

He took my hand in his—a comforting gesture, until he ran his thumb over the bandage covering my cat scratch. "And you were bleeding."

"Noah, come on. You know me. You know I wouldn't do this."

"I knew you," he said softly. "I don't anymore."

My cheeks went hot. "The alarm's not working. Charlie let the contract lapse. Anybody could have broken in, and the system wouldn't have made a peep."

"They didn't break in," he said. "There's no sign of forced entry, which means Jimmy—or the killer—had a key."

"There you go," I said. "I haven't had a key to the store in years. I have to borrow it from my mom every time I come over. Are you saying my mom snuck in here and jammed a chisel into Jimmy Madigan's ribcage? Really?"

He glanced at the store, as if she might have heard me.

"I certainly wouldn't cross her," he said. "But no, I don't like Lila for this."

"Oh, lovely. Me, then."

He stared at me for a long moment, then sighed. "No. But if that's the case I can build after a few hours, imagine what the district attorney will do. You need to take this seriously."

"Do I look like I'm playing around? Someone was murdered in my store." My family's store, I corrected myself, but it didn't stop the hot rush of anger. It was my store too, at least for the time being.

"Why here?" Noah asked. "Why go the trouble of making it look like self-defense?"

"To cover their tracks," I said automatically. "Same as they did with Clem's heart attack. They just . . . weren't as subtle this time."

"I'd say so," Noah agreed. "But they weren't covering their tracks. They were laying false ones. Someone's trying to frame you."

"Well, they're doing a terrible job of it," I retorted.

"Pay attention, Frankie. The killer had a key, and they weren't worried about the alarm, which means they're familiar enough with this place to know it wasn't operational. If it wasn't you, it's someone who can get to you. Or your family."

A wave of dizziness crashed over me as I finally understood what he was getting at.

"The killer had a key." I braced myself against the shed wall to keep from swaying. "How did he get a key?"

"Has anybody lost one recently?"

"I don't think so. I used my mom's this morning. Charlie's is probably at the hospital, with the rest of her keys."

I clapped my hand to my mouth as nausea swelled. I fought it back, saying, "Laura and I think that Jimmy had a partner—someone in the hospital who helped him get access to Clem. Someone who could move around without being noticed. Someone who had access, even to restricted areas."

He held my gaze. "Areas like the maternity ward?"

"Rowan," I breathed, and then sprang into action, sprinting across the lot toward Noah's cruiser. "Lights and sirens, Noah. Now."

TWENTY-SIX

"If they took Charlie's keys," I said as we raced toward Stillwater Gen, "they could get into the house, too. They could get to Riley. Or my mom."

Rather than answer, Noah radioed in a request for a car to be sent to Matt and Charlie's immediately, as well as a search of the house. After he'd signed off, he muttered, "Can't wait to explain this to Lila."

"She'll love it," I said, fighting for calm. "Her tax dollars at work, and another bump for the store."

He cracked a smile and floored the accelerator.

I jumped out of the car as soon as he slowed, tearing through the lobby and jamming my finger against the elevator button, pounding on the security door. Garima stopped in her tracks as the nurse buzzed me through. "What's wrong?"

"Jimmy Madigan's dead," I said, sprinting toward the NICU.

"I heard," she said, matching my pace. Behind us, I could hear Noah's footsteps. "But—"

"Someone got into the store," I said. "They could get in here, too."

"Frankie," she started, but I wasn't listening. The thought of someone hurting Rowan, so tiny and defenseless, made me want to black out. Garima caught my arm moments before I reached the NICU door.

"Settle down," she snapped, blocking my way. "I'm not letting you upset the patients."

I forced myself to breathe. Noah caught up to us, and Garima's eyes widened for a fraction of a second.

"Rowan is fine," she said. "I checked on her half an hour ago. Charlie, however, is livid. I'm surprised you couldn't hear her in town."

"I need to see them."

"You can, once you calm down," she said firmly. She steered me down the hall, voice low. "This is the most secure ward in the hospital. We have cameras everywhere. Nobody goes in or out of the NICU without prior authorization, and if anyone tried to take a baby out of the room, much less off the floor, it would trigger an automatic lockdown. Rowan's safer here than anywhere."

Noah rested a hand on my shoulder. "She's right. Before we put the entire hospital on alert, how about we check on those keys?"

"Can we get into Charlie's room?" I asked Garima.

"I can't authorize that." She held up a hand as I protested. "I am going to get a cup of coffee. I can't stop what I don't witness."

As soon as she'd rounded the corner, we dashed toward Charlie's room. Her purse was tucked away in her nightstand, and I rifled through it while Noah searched the pockets of her coat, hanging in the closet.

"Nothing," he said grimly.

"They're not in her purse, either." I sank to the floor, fear sapping my strength. "That's how they got in. They've got keys to the house, too."

"I have an officer there now," he reminded me, and pulled me to my feet. "He'll stay until you can change the locks. Good thing you know how, huh?"

"Fabulous," I said. "Total silver lining."

"Come on," he said. "You talk to Charlie, I'll go alert security."

"What if the killer is one of the security guards?" I asked as Garima returned. My control, already tenuous, was slipping. "How do we know who to trust?"

"You trust me," he said, and it was more order than question.

I nodded, my panic easing slightly.

"I know some of these guys pretty well. I'll mention it to them, and they'll make sure Charlie's covered. We'll keep her safe, and Rowan, too."

"Hospital administration will need to be notified," Garima warned. "There are protocols to follow."

Noah dipped his chin in acknowledgment and left. I turned to Garima. "Charlie knows about the store?"

"Matt called her as soon as he picked up Riley. She would have called you, but she won't leave Rowan, and we don't allow calls in the NICU." She held up her keycard. "I will let you inside, but if either of you makes a scene, I'll order security to remove you both. Got it?"

"Got it."

Charlie's head snapped up as I entered. Before either of us could speak, Garima repeated her warning, then settled herself nearby like a referee.

"Why was there a dead body in my store?" Charlie asked through gritted teeth.

"I don't know yet. I'm working on it."

"A dead body," she repeated. "What did you do?"

"Nothing! It wasn't me."

"It has something to do with you. It's that patient, isn't it? The one who died? Matt said the hospital is blaming you. They're trying to take your license."

"Clem Jensen," I said. Suddenly, saving my license was the least of my concerns. "You knew him, right?"

"I did. But . . ."

"He was murdered. The body in the store was his son-in-law, and I think they're connected."

"So naturally, you got involved. Why couldn't the police handle it? Why did it have to be you, Frankie? You're supposed to be here helping *me*, remember? Your sister? You are supposed to be taking care of my daughter, not showing her dead bodies!"

From the nurse's desk, Garima coughed.

"Riley didn't see anything," I said. "I got her out."

"What a relief," Charlie hissed. "God, Frankie, can't you give it a rest? Can't you leave the drama alone, at least while you're here?"

"I didn't plan this!"

"You didn't avoid it. You're like an addict, the way you chase thrills."

"This is not a thrill." I bit off the words.

"Oh, please," Charlie retorted. "This is like everything else in your life—the job, the weird sports, the revolving door of boyfriends. You like the rush, but you can't handle the reality. You bailed on the store—on *us*—because it was more reality than you could handle."

"This has nothing to do with the store. And I didn't bail."

"This has everything to do with the store. There was a dead body in aisle four!"

Garima hummed a warning, and Charlie paused for breath, glaring. "You totally bailed, by the way. I'm not sure if you noticed, but it's Stapleton and *Sons*. Plural."

"I'm not sure you noticed, but *we aren't boys*. It is great that you're carrying on the family tradition, Charlie. Really. But not everyone wants the same things! You're good at running the show, keeping everyone in line. You do it all the time, and you make it look easy. Hell, you were running things from your hospital bed. But that's not me. I don't want to stand behind a counter and help people decide between eggshell and semigloss, or figure out which sort of pavers to use for the back patio. I need something different."

"Well, this qualifies, doesn't it?" She rested a hand on Rowan's isolette. "Do what you want, Frankie. Just keep it away from my family."

"They're my family, too."

Her gaze was as flat as her tone. "Then start acting like it."

TWENTY-SEVEN

Noah hadn't returned, and it was clear Charlie didn't want me around anymore. With nothing else to do, I headed back to the pharmacy.

It wasn't fair to say I'd hit a dead end. I had plenty of clues—from Clem's chart to Jimmy's body—but they were so tangled together, I couldn't put them in any sort of order. I needed to untangle them, and the only way I knew how to do that was to wiggle a single thread free, in the hopes it would lead me to the truth.

The pharmacy was closed up tight, but I knew someone had to be inside. Hospitals need medicine all the time, not just during business hours. I knocked on the window, waited a few moments, and knocked again. And again. And then I knocked until my knuckles were sore.

Finally, the side door opened, and Nestor the pharmacist appeared again, mouth pursed with annoyance. "Another question about your father's medication?"

"I'm sorry," I said. "I know you're closed."

"Indeed."

"I'll be quick, I swear."

He sighed deeply.

"You told me Apracetim is only available through special order, correct? So you probably don't fill a whole lot of scripts for it."

"Very few," he admitted. "We haven't placed an order in months."

"That's not possible. My friend's son is taking it."

"I'm sure he is, but we're not dispensing it."

"This is his hospital," I said. "I'm sure he's having it filled here. Could you check? Please? CJ Madigan."

He drew back, offended. "I'm not at liberty to discuss patient records with you."

I gripped the edges of the counter. "How about this? You tell me if you've filled a prescription for Apracetim in the last year. You don't say who it's for. Just whether or not you've supplied to anyone. That would be okay, wouldn't it?"

Grudgingly, he nodded. "I suppose so."

I fidgeted while he looked up the information, fighting the urge to lean over and check the monitor.

His frown deepened. "According to my records, the last time that prescription was filled was five months ago."

"So where was Clem getting it?" I said, thinking out loud.

"Perhaps your friend got a sample from the manufacturer? Though . . . it's far too expensive to be giving it away for free."

I didn't think that medication was free. I was pretty sure that somehow, it had cost Clem his life.

"Miss Stapleton," said a voice from behind me. "Cease badgering my staff."

I turned. Walter Strack stood only a few feet away, and if anyone looked capable of murder, it was him.

The pharmacist glanced between us. "I believe I'll get back to making up those IV bags," he said, and vanished.

"The pharmacy is closed," Strack said, jowls flushing. "I have had enough of you waltzing around this hospital as if you owned it. Effective immediately, you are banned from Stillwater General. I've given your description to our security staff, and if you're spotted inside this building again, I will have you arrested for trespassing."

"You can't do that! My sister is a patient here."

"Your sister is welcome to stay for as long as her physicians deem necessary. You, however, are not receiving treatment, and your visiting privileges have most assuredly been revoked. Now get out, or I will call the sheriff's department. In fact, I believe there's a deputy in the building as we speak. Shall I have him paged?"

He looked triumphant, eyes gleaming nastily, and my shoulders slumped, then straightened. I wasn't beaten. Not yet, no matter what he thought.

"Nice chatting with you, Strack," I said, keeping my voice pleasant. "Let's do it again once the autopsy comes back."

TWENTY-EIGHT

The police cruiser Noah had posted outside our house was still there the next morning, to Riley's delight. She lobbied hard for a ride to school, but Matt took her instead, and the squad car followed my mom and me over to the store. I'd replaced all the locks last night—at home and at the store—but it didn't keep me from inspecting every aisle before I waved my mother inside.

Business was still good, but Mom seemed more tired than the day before.

"I'm not used to being on my feet all day," she finally admitted late in the afternoon. "It's been a while since I spent so much time here."

"Charlie should be home soon," I said. "She'll take over again."

"I suppose you'll leave the moment she does," she said sourly, then turned to take care of another customer. My phone rang, the sound piercingly loud.

I snatched it up, noting the unfamiliar number. "Stapleton."

"Frankie? It's Laura Madigan."

"Laura! Hold on," I said, and made my way up to the office so we could talk without my mother listening in. "How are you doing?"

"As well as can be expected," she said. "What are the police saying?"

"They know you didn't do it." I filled her in on everything else that had happened.

"Maybe we should come home," she said uneasily. "I can't abandon my job."

"Give me a few more days," I said. "We should have the results of the autopsy soon."

"That's why I'm calling," she said. "The medical examiner e-mailed me the autopsy findings this morning."

"Did you read it?"

"No," she admitted. "I couldn't bring myself do it. I was hoping you could look at it first. Could I e-mail it to you?"

"Of course," I said and rattled off my e-mail address. Autopsies could be graphic; Laura didn't need to read detailed descriptions of her dad's internal organs. "Hold on while I go downstairs."

I used the store's computer, fidgeting while the molasses-slow connection downloaded the file, printing a copy and taking it back to the office. "Got it. Are you ready?"

"I think so," she said softly.

I struggled for a moment with how much I should tell her. Because Clem *had* been murdered—cruelly. I could soften the impact, but I couldn't stop the blow entirely.

I took a deep breath. "Your dad went into heart failure because of the respiratory arrest. His cardiac muscle had been damaged, but the stent had restored blood flow. With the proper medication and careful follow-up, he would have been fine. But when his lungs stopped working, his heart couldn't get the oxygen it needed."

"That's what the medical examiner told us before," she said. "Does that mean he died of natural causes?"

"I'm sorry," I said. "The ME wasn't wrong the first time, but your dad's lungs didn't stop working on their own. The respiratory arrest was chemically induced. Someone gave your father a drug that the hospital would never administer to a patient recovering from a heart attack."

"He was poisoned?"

"Basically. The drug is called vecuronium. It's a paralytic agent used in certain surgeries to make sure the patient's lungs don't interfere with whatever they're doing."

"It paralyzes the lungs?"

I didn't reply. Laura was smart; she'd understand the implication, she'd realize just how excruciating her father's last minutes had been.

"He couldn't breathe," she said, pitch rising. "How long?"

"Laura . . ."

"How long, Frankie? How long does it take someone to suffocate to death?"

"It depends. Seven, eight minutes," I said after a long pause. "He probably lost consciousness much earlier, Laura. A minute and a half, at most."

"Ninety seconds," she said. "For ninety whole seconds, he would have known he was dying. He would have suffered. Alone."

I bent my head, and the tears I never allowed myself couldn't be denied.

"How did it happen?" she demanded.

"I'm guessing it was in the IV—either mixed into the bag or injected directly into the line."

"Could it have been a mistake? I've heard about that happening."

"Not likely," I said, remembering how Charlie's nurse had replaced her IV bags. "All the IVs have a barcode on them. The nurse scans the barcode and checks it against the doctor's orders to cut down on those kinds of errors. And Marcus—your dad's nurse that night—he's good at his job. I can tell when nurses cut corners, and Marcus isn't the type."

"Maybe the doctor prescribed the wrong thing, or the person who filled the bag made a mistake. Maybe they couldn't read the prescription—you know how bad doctors' handwriting is."

"Anything's possible," I said slowly. "But I've met the pharmacist. He runs a pretty tight ship; he wouldn't let an order go out if he had a question about it. Laura, I know you want this to be an accident, but I am virtually certain it was intentional."

She took that in, and when she spoke again her voice was razor-edged.

"What about the doctors? Didn't they try to save him?"

"By the time they realized his numbers were dropping, they couldn't have reversed it, even if they'd put him on a ventilator."

The sheer cruelty of it—the coldness—was mind-boggling. Laura must have thought so, too, because we sat in sorrowful silence for long minutes. Finally, she asked, "Who would hate him that much? He was a good man, Frankie. He loved us. He sacrificed so much for us."

"I don't know," I said honestly. "I keep coming back to CJ's medicine. You were filling it at Stillwater General, right?"

"Yes, but—"

"There's no record of your father filling a prescription for Apracetim at the hospital pharmacy. There's no record of him buying it anywhere else, either—no cancelled checks or charges on his credit card."

"Maybe he paid cash," she said. "His business was booming."

"Not according to the records in his cabin," I reminded her. "I've talked to his clients—he wasn't taking on more jobs. If anything, he was cutting back so he could spend more time with CJ. If we can figure out how he was getting the medicine, we'll figure out who killed him."

"What about Jimmy's partner?" Laura asked. "If he works at the hospital, maybe he's the one who was giving Dad the Apracetim."

I mulled over the idea as I paced the room. What if I'd had it backward? What if Jimmy's killer had been the one to initiate their partnership, not the other way around? If that was the case, then maybe it wasn't about Clem's estate after all? Maybe it was about the Apracetim. But why kill someone who was paying you for expensive drugs?

Unless Clem wasn't paying for them.

That didn't fit, though. Apracetim was expensive, as Nestor had pointed out. Nobody would give it away for free.

"There's got to be a connection between your dad and Jimmy," I said. "Something more than you, I mean. Something the killer was trying to keep quiet."

"Duct tape wouldn't keep Jimmy quiet," Laura said. "There's no connection, believe me. They weren't even on speaking terms."

"Not according to Jimmy. He's staying at the Piney Woods Motel, and your dad did a lot of odd jobs for them. They've run into each other plenty."

"Dad never mentioned it," she said.

I thought back to my run-in with Jimmy at the motel. I'd been so certain he was guilty, and so irked by his needling comments, that I hadn't listened closely. Now I tried to recall every word.

I see all sorts of interesting things. You wouldn't believe the people who sneak off here for an afternoon.

Was it possible Clem and Jimmy had seen the same thing? Someone having an affair, and they'd thought to profit? I could believe it of Jimmy, but . . . Clem?

"Laura, this is going to sound crazy. Is it possible your dad was blackmailing someone?"

"What? My dad?"

"Hear me out. He had a big job at Piney Woods over the summer. He was there painting every day. What if he saw someone doing something . . . incriminating, or having an affair, or whatever . . . and realized he could use it as leverage? Stillwater runs on gossip. If someone had managed to keep a secret—a true secret—they might be willing to pay to keep it that way. They paid for the first few months, then decided they'd had enough."

"No," she said. "My father was a *good man*."

I believed her. Everyone I'd talked to had said the same thing: a good man, loved his family. He'd do anything for them.

Anything.

"Your dad wanted CJ to be well, and he wanted you to get away from Jimmy, and this was his way of taking care of you. As far as he was concerned, the ends justified the means."

"No," she said again. "That's not who he was. You're wrong, Frankie, just like you were wrong about Jimmy."

I wondered if Jimmy had figured it out, too, if that's what killed him.

Laura spoke, her voice so low and hoarse it was barely recognizable. "It was easier when I thought it was a heart attack. You never should have looked into this."

"I wish I was wrong. But I don't think I am."

It happened that way sometimes, in medicine. Minor symptoms revealed a terrible disease. I'd once had a patient come in with what they thought was pinkeye. By sunrise he was dead from a brain infection. A woman with hiccups needed a lung transplant. And a grandfather's act of devotion revealed a motive for murder.

"Do you? Really? Because if someone murdered my father, you get off clean, don't you? It all works out fine for you."

"Laura . . ."

"Thank you for the use of your apartment," she said stiffly. "We're coming home tomorrow, and I am finally going to bury my father. Congratulations on keeping your license, Frankie. Enjoy getting back to your real life."

And then all I heard was dead air.

★　　★　　★

"Was that CJ?" piped a small voice from the stairwell.

I turned. "Hey, Riley. Who brought you over from school?"

"Daddy. He was going to the hospital, so he said Grandma was in charge." She rolled her eyes and popped one of our complementary donut holes in her mouth.

"Good," I said. "I don't want to be in charge."

She sat down at the table, heels kicking the rungs of the ancient dining room chair. "Was that CJ?" she repeated, spraying powdered sugar across a pile of invoices.

"CJ's mom," I said.

She finished chewing, then said, "We were supposed to go fishing. He promised he would show me the best spots."

"Sorry, kiddo. I think they're coming home soon." Not that Laura would allow her kid anywhere near me or my family. "Maybe I could take you instead. How hard can it be? A couple of worms, a couple of fishing poles . . ."

"CJ doesn't use *worms*," she said loftily. "They use flies."

"Riley, I will dig worms with you, but I'm not collecting a bunch of dead flies. There are limits."

She laughed with the delight of a child who has bested an adult. "Not *fly* flies," she clarified. "Fishing flies. CJ and his grandpa made them out of, like, feathers and stuff. He said they took a lot of work."

"Did he?" I said absently, scrolling back through the autopsy report. Where would the killer have gotten vecuronium? That kind of substance was tightly managed in a hospital. I couldn't see Nestor handing it over without a good reason, but I wasn't going to be able to get back in and ask him about it. Maybe Garima . . .

". . . in their treasure box," Riley said, looking at me expectantly.

I refocused on her. "In their . . . what? What kind of box? What treasure?"

She huffed and popped another donut hole in her mouth. "That's what CJ and his grandpa called the box they kept their flies in. The treasure box. Because they're so valuable. CJ said he puts cool rocks in there, too, sometimes."

Something tingled at the base of my spine. "I see. Where do they keep this box? At CJ's house? At his grandpa's cabin?"

Her gaze slid away. "It's a secret. You can't just tell people where a treasure box is, Aunt Frankie. They'd take your treasure."

"This is true. That's very wise. You could give me a hint, though. Like a treasure hunt. We could even bring the box to CJ when he comes home. That might make him feel good, don't you think? It would be like having his grandpa nearby, even though his grandpa's gone."

Of all the things I'd ever done in the name of helping patients, manipulating an eight-year-old in order to uncover a blackmail scheme and catch a murderer was a new personal low. But I hadn't lied. I could examine the treasure box before passing it along to CJ. I wouldn't be breaking my word, only bending it.

Riley considered this. "I promised I wouldn't tell," she announced, and my shoulders sagged. "But if you guessed it, that would be okay. Then I'd be keeping my promise."

I was in no position to fault her logic.

The box wouldn't be at CJ's, or Riley wouldn't be excited about bringing it over. "Is it . . . in Clem's cabin?"

She shook her head.

"In Clem's barn?"

She hesitated, but shook her head again. Warmer, then. "His van?"

"You don't use a van to fish," she said, wrinkling her nose in disdain. "It's no fun if you don't really try."

I was not finding this fun at all. "Fine. His boat."

"Yes!" she shrieked, clapping her hands together like a demented fairy. "Can we go get it now?"

"You're not going anywhere until homework is done," my mom called from the stairwell.

I peered downstairs. "Were you eavesdropping?"

She sniffed. "I was checking on Riley. Homework, young lady."

"But Aunt Frankie said . . ."

I thought about the last time I'd gone to the cabin—the sensation we were being watched, the swapped medication. Charlie's accusation that I'd put Riley in danger.

"Grandma's right," I said, ignoring Riley's look of wounded outrage. "I'll bring it right back here, and we'll take it to CJ as soon as he's home."

Assuming his mother would let us in the door.

TWENTY-NINE

I might be reckless, but I'm not stupid. I waited until morning to drive to Clem's cabin. Laura wouldn't answer her phone, so I left her a message asking for permission and headed out, checking my rearview mirror over and over again to make sure I wasn't followed. The road was clear, no one behind me, and I felt my lungs ease.

I turned into Clem's driveway, teeth clacking as I navigated the bumps and ruts. It was a beautiful day—deep-blue sky, puffy white clouds, the autumn colors of the trees brighter than I'd seen in ages.

A beautiful day to catch a killer.

I parked the car and made my way toward the river. I heard the current before I saw it, smelled damp earth and decaying leaves before I spotted the rush of cold, clear water. It didn't just look different from the murky waters of the Chicago River, it smelled different—bracing and clean and alive.

I walked along the banks of the river for another twenty minutes, stepping over fallen branches and avoiding marshy spots, looking for a boat. Somehow, I'd pictured a little white sailboat, bobbing serenely in the open water. What I found instead was a battered green canoe, tugged up onto a sandy bit of riverbank, almost hidden beneath a willow tree. Tucked under one of the wooden bench seats was a scraped and dented tackle box.

"Hello, treasure," I said softly, pulling it out. "What have you got for me?"

I flicked open the latches. The first tray held nothing but intricately tied flies, bits of wire and feather and thread meant to entice fish. Gently, I lifted each one out of the box, marveling at the precision. You could tell which ones CJ had tied—the knots weren't as tidy, the feathers slightly crumpled—but there were two of each. Clem had walked him through every single one, the same way my dad had taught me how to tie every knot in the Boy Scout Handbook.

Treasures, indeed.

The second tray held supplies and, as Riley had mentioned, a few rocks and arrowheads and old coins. Unlike the top tray, this one was wedged securely inside the box. As if something was jammed beneath, holding it in place.

Happily, no girl raised in a hardware store goes without a Swiss Army knife. It's surprising how often I used mine, from opening bottles to picking out splinters. I unfolded the pry bar, slid it along the inside wall of the box, and levered out the tray, mindful that CJ would not appreciate me damaging this connection to Clem.

The tray came free with a popping sound and the crinkle of heavy paper. A manila envelope lay on the bottom of the box. I snatched it up, tore it open, and shook the contents onto my lap.

Pictures.

A neat set of glossy-finish 4 × 6 prints, the kind you might make at a do-it-yourself kiosk at the drugstore. The first few were pictures of Piney Woods Motel—areas that needed sanding and priming, window frames that needed repair, all the details that make a simple paint job more expensive. They were the kind of pictures a repairman took when he was putting together a bid for a job. Clem must have printed everything on his camera's memory card.

Next was a shot of the parking lot, and two expensive-looking cars, and a couple on their way into a room.

The shot was taken from high up and far away, as if Clem was on a ladder. I squinted at the picture, tilting it to reduce the glare off the water. The man looked vaguely familiar, something in the angular way he held himself, but it was too distant and blurry to be certain.

I looked at the next picture, and suddenly it all made sense.

Clem had figured out how to use the zoom. The lanky figure was Alexander Hardy. In this shot, he was *leaving* the room. Behind him was a slim blonde in a navy-blue business suit, one hand clutching a briefcase and the other smoothing her hair. Ashley Ritter. She and Hardy were smiling at each other, Hardy with an arrogant tilt to his head, Ashley preening and smug.

I flipped back to the previous shot—according to the timestamp, the pictures had been taken two hours apart.

More shots followed, tracing them to their separate cars, glancing around as if making sure nobody was watching. I wondered, cynically, how much of Ashley and Hardy's affair had to do with her buttering up the doctor who would give their drug a passing grade.

Clem would have known that Hardy was married. He'd been turned down for Hardy's drug trial, and he'd spent plenty of time at the hospital. He would've seen the formal portraits of the hospital board members in the entrance— including the one of Hardy's wife.

Regardless, Clem must have realized the opportunity this presented. Hardy flaunted his wealth, with his custom suits and luxury cars and taste in fine wine. It might not have been noble, but compared to adultery, a little bit of blackmail to help his grandson would have seemed like the far lesser of two evils.

Except that Hardy would have grown tired of it. I knew men like him—their arrogance, their sense of entitlement, their belief that they were somehow above the unwashed masses. Hardy and Clem both worked with their hands, but Hardy would never have seen the similarities. He would have loathed the fact that anyone, especially a "mere" handyman, had bested him.

Not to mention, Hardy had plenty to lose. If Mrs. Hardy was the vengeful type, she might demand a divorce and alimony. She might demand his resignation. No matter how gifted a surgeon he was, if the board wouldn't write him a recommendation, it would be hard to find a position like this one, his own personal fiefdom.

Hardy could have easily swapped Clem's medication; he had access to a variety of pills and would have known how to alter the meds to resemble Clem's prescriptions. He could have accessed Clem's medical records in the hospital's computer system, so he could time the swap properly—making sure the change in drugs wouldn't show up in Clem's routine blood work. Most importantly, he would have plenty of opportunities to administer the vecuronium and alter the monitors.

I sprang up with a whoop, startling birds out of trees, rocking the canoe. Between the autopsy results and these pictures, I finally had the proof I needed.

THIRTY

Before heading to the hospital, I made a few stops—one to the local drugstore, one at the sheriff's department to leave a message for Noah, and one to Stapleton and Sons to drop off the tackle box with my mother. She wrinkled her nose. "It smells of fish. Much like the cat that keeps hanging around outside the store."

"Riley and I will return it to Laura tonight, I promise."

She snorted. "What about the cat? I know you're the one who's been feeding him, Francesca. You're a soft touch."

"Not that soft," I assured her, and headed for the hospital.

Technically, I was banned from Stillwater Gen, and I didn't doubt that Strack had circulated my picture to the security staff.

They would be looking for a civilian. I grabbed the spare set of scrubs I had stashed in my trunk and changed clothes at the store. Now I looped my stethoscope around my neck and followed the advice of one of my college professors, who'd been blunt about what it took for a newbie nurse to get respect from a ward full of doctors.

"Walk like you own the place," she'd told us. "It's your floor, too. Don't ever let them convince you otherwise."

So I walked into Stillwater Gen like I owned the place, and nobody glanced at me twice.

Until I arrived at Walter Strack's office, that is.

The secretary looked at me over her reading glasses, eyebrows shooting up, mouth forming soundless words.

"I know," I said. "And yet here I am. Could you please call Dr. Hardy? Tell him I've got something he should see."

Not taking her eyes from me, she picked up the phone and pressed speed-dial.

"Thanks. I'll see myself in."

Strack's face turned a mottled, murky shade of red when he spotted me. "Miss Stapleton. I thought I made myself understood. You are no longer welcome in this facility."

I sat down in the steel-and-leather chair facing his desk. "Your security is terrible, Strack. A killer could waltz right in."

"Get out," he sputtered. When I didn't move, he shouted, "Nancy, call the sheriff's department. Inform them we have a trespasser, and we want to press charges."

"I already asked Deputy MacLean to join us," I said, wondering if Noah had gotten my message yet. "Not sure when he'll get here, though. All these murders are keeping him pretty busy."

"I'll have security throw you out," he said, eyes flicking to a folder on his desk.

I nodded at the folder, neatly labeled with Clem's name. "You've read the autopsy, haven't you? You won't be able to cover it up much longer."

"Cover up . . . what, exactly?"

I sat up straight now, feet on the floor, and leaned in. "Clem Jensen's murder. I know, I know. You're offended that I would suggest such a thing. Dosing Clem with vecuronium was a tragic error. Even if that was the case— which it isn't—your buyer's going to develop very cold feet when the news gets out." I paused. "Especially considering the damages Laura Madigan could be awarded."

Strack's color had faded to a queasy puce.

"Walter, what's this about?" Alexander Hardy stood in the doorway, and I spun to face him. He held himself rigidly, refusing to look in my direction. "I have an offsite meeting in thirty minutes."

"Pharmagen?" Strack waved him off. "Go, go. I'll handle Miss Stapleton."

"I think Dr. Hardy will want to stay for this," I said. "I mean, what's the going rate at Piney Woods? Surely you can afford another hour or two."

His hand tightened on the doorknob. "I beg your pardon?"

"That is where you're meeting her, I assume?"

"Her?"

"Ashley Ritter. From Pharmagen? Do you two have a special room? Does that make it not tawdry? Or do you *like* it tawdry?" I shrugged. "Some guys do."

Hardy wasn't looking good, I noticed. The bow tie was crooked, the collar of his shirt looser than usual, as if he'd lost weight, and his white coat had lost its crispness. Over-work or a guilty conscience?

"Miss Stapleton, I don't know what you think you know . . ."

"I know a lot," I said. "Fortunately, I'm in the mood to share."

"Alexander?" asked Strack, his gaze darting between us. "Do we have a situation?"

"That's one word for it." I pulled the pictures from my backpack, tossed them onto Strack's desk one at a time like I was dealing cards. "Dr. Hardy. Ashley Ritter. Piney Woods Motel. It doesn't take a genius to figure out what was going on."

Hardy's face was a mask of outrage, but I could have sworn that, for a split-second, relief had broken through.

Strack bent closer to peer at the images, then glanced up at Hardy. "Really, Alexander? With so much on the line? I mean, she's quite fetching, but . . ."

Hardy bowed his head, seemingly unable to speak. Finally, he said, "I'm sorry, Walter. I wasn't thinking."

"Clearly," Strack said with a dour expression. "Miss Stapleton, I assume you have a point?"

"Your wife's on the board of trustees, isn't she, Dr. Hardy? I have to imagine she'd make your life miserable if she saw these pictures—personally *and* professionally."

A curt nod.

I turned back to Strack. "Clem Jensen took those pictures. He used them to blackmail Dr. Hardy into supplying his grandson's epilepsy medicine for free. But Hardy didn't like paying, and he *really* didn't like letting someone else run the show. So he teamed up with Jimmy Madigan—I'm guessing you knew him from when he'd worked at the hospital—and convinced him to swap Clem's medication with clot-promoting drugs, knowing they'd induce a heart attack. Jimmy hated Clem, so it probably didn't take much convincing. When that didn't work, the good doctor tampered with the cardiac monitors, pumped Clem full of vecuronium, and let him suffocate to death."

Strack sank back into his chair. "That's quite an accusation."

I shrugged. "The proof's all there. The autopsy showed vecuronium, the monitor tapes show the alarms were compromised; your own pharmacist identified the placebos. Hardy knew there'd be an investigation, so he made sure his report painted Clem as a noncompliant patient, and the coroner had no reason to disagree." I turned to Hardy. "The lawsuit was your idea, wasn't it? Give Jimmy a reason to stay quiet, give the hospital an incentive to wrap up the investigation quickly."

Hardy's eyes glittered with malice. "You're grasping at straws, Miss Stapleton."

"I don't think so," I said. "Was Hardy the person who told you I was in Clem's room that night?"

Strack nodded before he could stop himself.

"He saw me the first time he went to kill Clem, and he had to change the plan, try again later. Then Laura Madigan told him I was looking into Clem's death, and he realized I might cause some real trouble. He encouraged you to go after me. Misdirection, so you wouldn't realize what he'd done."

"When did I commit this murder?" Hardy sneered.

I paused. Hardy was like so many surgeons I'd met—their veins ran with arrogance instead of blood. But rather than weaken in the face of so much evidence, Hardy seemed to be gaining confidence. I ignored the twinge of doubt and pushed on. "Sunday morning. Based on the monitors, I'd guess just after seven, to take advantage of the shift change."

"Interesting theory," he said. "Unfortunately, I was in the emergency room, helping Paul Costello. He'd been on duty since the night before, handling the bus accident, and I offered my assistance. Understandable, of course, that we wouldn't have crossed paths—it was after you'd been kicked out of the emergency room."

"You could have snuck out," I said. "Ten minutes would have been enough."

"The entire Emergency Department will swear that I didn't leave the department until after eight," he replied. "Should we call Dr. Costello now?"

"No need," said Strack with obvious relief. "I don't see why we should trouble Dr. Costello; the accusations are baseless."

"They're *not*," I said. "Look at Clem's charts! Look at his autopsy! A man was murdered in your hospital—by one of your doctors! Then he killed Jimmy Madigan, in my store, to cover his tracks. Are you honestly going to sit by and do nothing?"

I could hear myself growing shrill as my confidence deflated.

"Walter, if I'm not needed further . . ." Hardy said, ignoring me. But he was pale, his mask of arrogance growing more wooden by the minute. No doubt he'd tell Ashley all about my accusations, and the two of them would share a cozy moment mocking me.

Strack stood, smoothing down his tie. "Of course, Alexander. My apologies. I can deal with Miss Stapleton."

When Hardy had left, Strack wheeled to face me again, his words clipped with fury.

"There are countless explanations for Mr. Jensen's death—and none of them involve murder. Based on the autopsy results, I've launched a fresh investigation. I'm confident that it will reveal Mr. Jensen's death was nothing more than a tragic error, and we will institute new procedures to prevent future mistakes."

"It wasn't medical error," I snapped. "It was murder."

"You're grasping at straws, Miss Stapleton. Dr. Hardy is hardly the first man to stray from his wedding vows. Whatever we may think of his private behavior, it has no bearing on this situation."

"Somehow I think the Sheriff's department will disagree," I replied.

He smirked at something over my shoulder. "Why don't we ask Deputy MacLean, shall we?"

I whirled. Noah strode in, jaw clenched, eyes hard. "Frankie. Mr. Strack. What seems to be the problem?"

Strack paused. "Despite being told that she was no longer allowed on hospital property, Miss Stapleton barged into my office, spouting wild accusations about one of my staff members. We've refuted them, and now I would like her to leave."

"You'd like me to arrest her for trespassing?" Noah asked. He made a show of studying the pictures on Strack's desk, then met his gaze squarely.

"I—" Flustered, Strack swept up the pictures and flipped them face-down. "I don't know if that's strictly necessary. If she can promise to drop the matter and stay off hospital property, there's no need to press charges. An apology wouldn't go amiss, naturally."

He wanted to keep me quiet. Assuming Hardy's alibi checked out, he was innocent of murder, at least. But as Strack had pointed out, adultery wasn't uncommon. Why, then, was he so desperate to keep the news from coming out?

Then it hit me: The hospital sale. The Cardiodyne trial. It was a symbiotic relationship. Strack needed the prestige of the drug trial and Hardy's reputation to lure a buyer; Hardy needed the hospital's permission to continue the trial. It was too late in the approval process to try to relocate, especially if Mrs. Hardy decided to destroy her cheating husband's career.

My silence was more important than seeing me punished.

"Frankie?" prompted Noah.

I didn't like it, and I sure as hell wasn't going to drop it, but the smart move now was to beat a retreat. "I'm sorry. I should have thought this through more carefully."

"Indeed," said Strack drily.

"And as for the affair . . ." I continued. Strack tensed, his hand covering the photos. "That's your business, I guess."

Strack tapped the stack of pictures. "I'll dispose of these."

Fine by me. I'd made duplicates.

★   ★   ★

Noah escorted me out, frustration pouring off him in waves. When we reached the parking lot, he said, "Have you lost your *mind*?"

"You saw the pictures. Hardy's guilty."

"Of adultery. He has an alibi. You're lucky he doesn't sue you for slander. He might, you know."

"He's guilty," I repeated, folding my arms. "I know he is."

"That's what you said about Jimmy, and look how that turned out." He dragged his hand across his face. "Frankie, leave this alone. I know you have good intentions, but you're out of your depth. Now that the autopsy report has come back, the Sheriff's Department has formally opened an investigation into Clem's death, along with Jimmy's. We will handle it from here."

"I can help!"

"You've helped enough. Charlie should be coming home soon, right? Once she does, I think the best thing for you to do is go back to Chicago."

"Are you joking? My patient was murdered, and I'm the only one fighting for him, and you want me to walk away?"

Noah, however, didn't look like he was joking even a little bit. "He wasn't your patient, Frankie. And yeah. Walking away is your specialty."

The words were a gut punch—and after the initial burst of pain, outrage took over. So much easier to take refuge in anger than face the barb of truth in his words.

"That was twelve years ago." My words sounded shaky to my own ears. "Ancient history, and it has nothing to do with this case. I can't believe you're still holding a grudge. You should have moved on ages ago."

"Oh, I have, believe me," he shot back. "Except that now I've got two murders—one of them in your store, which makes you a suspect."

"I didn't kill Jimmy. You know that. You know *me*."

His expression twisted. "I know you're a liar."

I drew back. "That's not. . . ."

That's not true, I wanted to say. But I couldn't lie twice over, and he knew it.

He stared down at me. "How's your fiancé, Frankie? You two set a date yet? Picked out china?"

I flinched.

"Exactly," he said, cold and contemptuous. "You must think I'm an idiot. I mean, even more so than you did back then."

"I never thought—"

"I knew you weren't engaged. No ring, dodging questions, and you did the thing with your hair." He made a move as if to touch the curls falling into my face, then drew his hand back. "Matt didn't want to talk about it, either, so I figured you were . . . I don't know. Ashamed, or something. I thought you were afraid I'd make a move if I knew you were single again. Maybe I am an idiot, because I thought it was personal. Now I think you're a liar."

"Noah—"

"Deputy MacLean."

"Fine," I said, dragging my hands through my hair. "Deputy. I didn't tell you about my engagement, and that *is* personal. But if Alexander Hardy isn't your killer, then you've got a murderer running around Stillwater. Why don't you worry less about my wedding plans and more about doing your job?"

"Don't talk to me about protecting this town, Frankie," he said. "I'm not the one who turned my back on it."

With that, Noah climbed into his car and drove away.

My breath caught in my throat, not at the unfairness of his accusation—but how right he was. By the time I'd recovered the power of speech, he was gone.

THIRTY-ONE

I was running out of options—and allies. Despite my apology, I still believed Alexander Hardy was guilty. It was hard to believe he hadn't slipped away from the ER in all the chaos and made his way back to Clem's room.

But wouldn't Marcus have noticed him on the floor? Hardy wasn't the type one would overlook.

Maybe he hadn't gone to Clem's room. It would have been safer to give Jimmy a syringe full of vecuronium and a custodian's uniform. Then he'd killed Jimmy and framed me. I didn't need to break his alibi for Clem's death, only Jimmy's. The question was, who would help me?

An offsite meeting, Hardy had said. Would he really be so arrogant as to meet Ashley at Piney Woods again? Or was that part of his plan? The net was closing; he was tying off loose ends. Maybe he considered Ashley a loose end.

I made it out to the motel in record time. Through the front office window I could see Bianca, pink- and yellow-striped head bent over her phone. But I was more interested in the cars. Hardy's Lexus sat directly next to Ashley's

Volkswagen. I parked behind a moving van, made my way to a nearby stand of trees, and settled in to wait.

It didn't take long. Hardy left first this time, and I took a grim pleasure at his shaken expression. If Hardy panicked, he was more prone to make a mistake. I set off across the parking lot, hoping I'd given Ashley enough time to get dressed, and knocked on the door.

There was a pause. Then I heard the scrape of the chain and the thunk of the deadbolt, and a moment later, Ashley stood in front of me, wary, dismayed, and—happily—fully dressed.

"Frankie?" she said, leaning past me to scan the parking lot. "What are you doing here?"

"I need to talk to you about Alexander Hardy. Can I come in?"

She shifted from one foot to the other, and I brushed past her.

It was a strange place for an affair. Small, shabby room. Ugly bedspread on the neatly made bed, cheap carpeting covered with unidentifiable stains. A scarred wooden table covered with paperwork, Ashley's briefcase leaning against it. In her neat blue suit and tasteful makeup, Ashley seemed out of her element, flushed with embarrassment.

"I'm guessing Hardy told you what went down at the hospital today. About the pictures." I met her eyes, and she tilted her chin defiantly.

"It's not like that," she said.

"Like what? Cheap? Clichéd?" I fought the urge to reach out and shake her. "You're meeting your married boyfriend at an hourly motel in the middle of the day. Do you know how many times I have seen this exact thing?

Older, married doctor and his bright young thing? Did he tell you he loves you? He's going to leave his wife?"

She turned away, and that was all the answer I needed.

"He's playing you."

"He's not," she said, her voice thick with emotion. "This is different."

"I know this is hard to hear," I said, putting an arm around her shoulder and guiding her to the desk chair, "Hardy is responsible for Clem Jensen's death. Jimmy Madigan's, too. He's a very dangerous man."

Her head snapped up. "What? Alexander?"

"Yes, Alexander. That's what I wanted to talk to you about. Do you know where he was early Sunday morning?"

"Home, I suppose," she said with a shrug. "I don't see him outside of work hours."

"And you still think he cares about you?" My patience snapped. "Stop being so naïve, Ashley."

She bristled. "I'm not naïve. He told me about your theory. He told me all sorts of things about you. You're desperate. You want people to take you seriously—you can't land a husband, you're just a nurse, and not even that, pretty soon." She tipped her head to the side, all faux-concern. "You need to fix your own life instead of trying to ruin other people's. You should look at this as a wakeup call."

Nothing makes me lose my temper faster than the words "just a nurse." Before I could tear into Ashley, something else in her words resonated.

"Wakeup call," I murmured. "These rooms don't have phones."

"So?"

"So Jimmy was staying here. If Hardy called him to set up the meeting at the hardware store, he would have had to call Jimmy's cell—the cops can pull the records and find proof they were working together."

Ashley gaped at me, and I smiled sweetly. "Not bad for 'just' a nurse, huh?"

THIRTY-TWO

Noah sent my calls straight to voice mail.

"Be that way," I muttered. I was tired of trying to convince Noah. Tired of pleading with him to take me seriously, when he'd doubted me all along. Tired of feeling guilty for leaving, for taking so long to come back. Tired of running and tired of lying and tired, most of all, of being wrong. I pulled into the driveway, scowled at the squad car still sitting outside, and stomped into the house.

Riley's mood matched mine, I saw. She was sitting at the kitchen table, glaring at her math book.

"What's wrong, kiddo? Multiplication got you down?"

"Everything," she said, slumping dramatically. Her heels drummed a sulky rhythm on the chair legs. "CJ wasn't in school again, and Grandma says the treasure box isn't mine, so I don't get to look inside, and I hate fractions, and you promised me a sausage biscuit, and we haven't gone and it's been almost a whole *week*."

I staggered slightly at the onslaught of words. "Ah."

"You said you didn't lie, Aunt Frankie."

"I don't!" The words came out sharper than I intended, and Riley's brown eyes filled.

"You *said*. You promised, and I haven't told anyone about the boy in the garden."

"What boy?" asked my mother, coming into the kitchen. "What's wrong with my garden?"

"Nothing," I said quickly. "The garden looks great. Riley was reminding me that we wanted to have a breakfast date. How about tomorrow?"

Her chin jutted out. "Tomorrow's Wednesday. I have school."

"This weekend, then."

"That'll take forever," she groaned, sliding down farther. "Please, Aunt Frankie? CJ and his grandpa went all the time. Not just for breakfast."

I sighed. "Did they?"

She nodded. "But they didn't go to the diner. They liked the ones from the truck stop, out on the highway. CJ said they're delicious."

I knew the truck stop she was talking about; I'd passed it on my way into town, but it was a good thirty minutes away.

"You'll spoil your dinner," I said.

"It can be breakfast for dinner! You love breakfast for dinner!"

Which was true, and after the day I'd had, I loved it even more. "Grab your coat," I told Riley.

"Francesca, honestly? Breakfast for dinner?"

"I promised," I told Mom, as Riley slid her grubby hand in mine with a look of triumph. "And I keep my word."

★　　★　　★

Judging from the look of bliss on Riley's face, the sausage biscuit was as good as she'd heard. But even though my pancakes were golden and fluffy and dripping with syrup, I had no appetite.

"Your phone's ringing," Riley said eventually.

I checked the number: Chicago Memorial.

"Frankie!" cried Mindy when I answered. "I totally forgot to send you those numbers. It's been crazy here."

"I know the feeling," I said.

"When are you coming back? We miss you, and you've got to be getting desperate, right? Aren't you homesick?"

"I am home," I said without thinking.

Mindy was silent for a moment. "Well, you know what I mean. Do they have sushi in that town? Or even a first-run movie? You must be bored to death."

"I'm managing," I said, and Mindy launched into a description of the weekend's cases, the kind of nonstop chaos I'd always thrived on. I let her prattle on while I poked at my meal, still mulling over how to break Hardy's alibi.

"Frankie?" she said, worry creeping into her voice. "You there?"

"Yeah," I said. "I'm listening."

But I wasn't. The jealousy and loneliness I'd been struck with during our last conversation had faded alongside the itch to get back to my "real" life. Things here felt plenty real. Absently, I reached out to ruffle Riley's hair. "Actually, Min, I need to get going. Can you text me the number for HR, though?"

I continued to stew as Riley chatted up the waitress. "My friend and his grandpa come here, too," she said. "I mean, they used to come here. CJ's grandpa died."

"CJ?" the waitress said. The penny dropped. "Clem's CJ? Clem died?"

Riley nodded solemnly.

"Oh, that's terrible! Roger," she called to the cook. "Clem's passed. This little girl is friends with CJ."

"You knew Clem?"

"Sure we did. He was here every day. Sometimes twice, if he brought CJ. Sweet little boy." She leaned in confidingly. "Pity his daughter's such a pill."

"What?" Laura was quiet, sure, but I'd hardly describe her as a pill.

"Oh, Clem talked about her like she was a saint, but the few times she came in here, it was like she smelled something bad the whole time, the way her face pinched up. Always sat like she was afraid to let her suit touch the seat."

The back of my neck prickled like the temperature had dropped twenty degrees. "And Clem said she was his daughter?"

"Well, he didn't come out and say so. But who else would she be? A girlfriend? A girl that young would only go with someone Clem's age if there's something extra in it for her." She winked broadly, and Riley looked perplexed.

Hands shaking, I dug in my backpack for the duplicate set of pictures, the ones I'd printed at the drugstore before confronting Strack. I took out the clearest shot and slid it across the counter. "Is this her? Clem's . . . daughter?"

The waitress pursed her lips, held the picture of Alexander Hardy and Ashley Ritter inches from her face. "Sure is. Judging from that car, it looks like this guy's got that something extra, doesn't it?"

"He does," I agreed.

Hardy had an accomplice.

THIRTY-THREE

Needless to say, I tipped generously.

Then I hustled Riley out of the restaurant, mind racing, trying to fit the pieces together. Clem had been blackmailing both Hardy and Ashley? It didn't make sense. Ashley wasn't married, so she had no spouse to conceal the affair from, unlike Hardy. Her Pharmagen bosses wouldn't care, as long as Cardiodyne got FDA approval. Shepherding such a profitable drug to market would be a career-maker for someone as driven as Ashley.

Strange, then, that she would muddy the waters by sleeping with Hardy. I'd gotten the distinct impression that the only thing Ashley was truly passionate about was her work. Hell, she'd even brought her laptop to their latest "meeting"—hardly the sign of a torrid affair.

I snatched up the picture again as Riley buckled into her booster seat.

Who takes a briefcase to a hookup in a cheap motel? Both Ashley and Hardy looked as if they were heading into a meeting, not an afternoon between the sheets. None of the pictures showed them touching, not even a brush of hands, or looking into each other's eyes. This was not the way illicit lovers acted. Thinking back, I'd never seen a hint of attraction between them at the hospital—Hardy had seemed almost paternalistic, and Ashley had seemed annoyed.

This wasn't a romantic meeting. It was all business. But why go to Piney Woods when Hardy had an office on the hospital grounds? They'd certainly held plenty of meetings in Strack's office, too.

Unless these meetings were secret.

For a drug to pass FDA approval, it needs to show that it is both effective and safe. What if Cardiodyne wasn't? What if it wasn't effective, or worse . . . what if the side effects outweighed the benefits? All of that information would be revealed in the trial, scuttling Cardiodyne and Ashley's career alongside it.

Finally, horribly, it all clicked together.

They hadn't killed Clem to cover up an affair—they'd done it to cover up a problem with Cardiodyne. Their meetings were to falsify data.

"Riley," I said, throwing my car into gear and speeding down the highway, "Get my phone out of my backpack, please. Call the Sheriff's Department."

Then I thought about Noah's face in the parking lot and the calls he'd sent to voice mail.

"Hold on," I said as she scrabbled in my backpack. "Forget that."

Noah wasn't going to listen to me unless I had tangible evidence. A clear connection between Clem's death and the Cardiodyne trial.

Drugs, I realized. It all came down to drugs. Pharmagen didn't just make Cardiodyne. According to the pharmacist, they also made Thrombinase, the drug swapped for Clem's true medication. Most big pharmaceutical companies made a generic version of vecuronium. What were the odds that they made Apracetim too?

Easy enough to check with a quick Internet search. Once I had proof, I could go to Noah with my head held high.

"Call Grandma," I said. "Ask her if she's at the store or at home."

Riley obeyed. "Store. She's closing tonight."

"Fantastic. I need to use the computer at the store, so tell Grandma we'll swing by. She can take you home, and I'll close up. That should give you time to finish your math homework, shouldn't it?"

"I guess," She relayed the message, looking less than thrilled at the prospect. I, on the other hand, had never been so eager to get to Stapleton and Sons in my life.

★   ★   ★

"Since when are you so happy to close?" my mother demanded.

"You wanted me to help out more," I said, setting my backpack next to the front register. "And aren't you the one who said you weren't used to being on your feet all day? Go home, hang out with Riley. She's already eaten her weight in processed meats, so you won't even need to feed her. You can have a nice, quiet night."

"I do need to finish my novel for book club," she admitted as I helped her into her coat. She waggled her eyebrows. "It's a spicy read this month."

I prayed she was talking about a cookbook. "Well, here's your chance."

She gathered up her purse and took Riley by the hand. "Make sure to lock the windows this time, Francesca. And don't let that cat in."

"I won't." I shooed her out the front door and locked it behind her. Through the plate glass window, I watched them head for home, the ever-present squad car trailing behind. At least Noah hadn't been so angry he'd canceled our protection.

The store was deserted. Wednesday nights were notoriously slow; in fact, we usually closed early. Despite the lack of sales, I was grateful for the quiet, the familiar creaks as the building settled, the whoosh of the furnace kicking on. The notoriety of Jimmy's death had started to fade.

I'd gotten it backward. Jimmy wasn't the partner or the mastermind. Jimmy was a patsy. Hardy and Ashley had killed Clem, then encouraged Jimmy to file the lawsuit as a way to divert attention. No doubt Jimmy had reacted with his typical overconfidence—shooting his mouth off, assuming he had power when he was only a pawn. Rather than risk him spoiling everything, or asking for more money, they'd killed him and tried to frame me.

I made quick work of locking up and closing out the registers. The rest of the tasks—restocking the shelves, sweeping the floors—could wait.

Settling in at the computer, I pulled up Pharmagen's website, clicking the tab labeled "Our Products." Cardiodyne was listed as "coming soon," and the product page was filled with links explaining how huge the market for this type of drug was, how the company would leapfrog its competitors and make record profits.

Not if the drug didn't work. Not if it endangered the very people it was promising to save.

I clicked around the website, and just as I'd thought, Apracetim was one of the first Pharmagen products listed. Thrombinase and vecuronium were there too. Ashley would have had access to all of it.

No wonder I'd found no sign of Clem's newfound wealth, no pharmacy receipts. The drugs themselves had been the payment. Ashley had diverted samples of CJ's medication each month in exchange for Clem's silence.

I hit print, and on the bottom shelf the printer whirred to life, spitting out page after page of black-and-white, irrefutable proof. Crouching to gather the pages, I murmured, "Gotcha."

The store seemed to hold its breath in response, utterly still and silent, as if acknowledging the moment. All my searching, all my questions, all my doubt and fear . . . it was over. All that was left was to tell Noah, and then I could go home.

I could go back to Chicago, just like he'd told me, and go back to my old life, which . . . I hadn't thought about in what felt like days. It had slipped away like water, replaced by Riley and Rowan and the rest of my family, maddening and mine and more important than I'd realized.

Something deep within the store creaked, breaking the silence and my introspection. I shook off the sudden melancholy and headed up to the front register, where I'd tossed my backpack and my phone.

They'd vanished.

I'd put them on the counter. I distinctly remembered setting them on the counter when I was talking to my mom. I'd tucked the night's deposit into my bag, ready to deliver to the bank. Then I'd gone back to the computer, leaving the bag—and the phone—in plain sight on the front counter.

They were gone.

A shadow moved, at the very edge of my peripheral vision. I whirled, my shoulder exploded, and I crashed, face-first, into the floor.

"Gotcha," trilled Ashley.

THIRTY-FOUR

For a killer, Ashley Ritter looked remarkably well put-together. I, for example, would have worn something comfortable if I was going to spend the evening indulging murderous impulses. But Ashley looked as tightly wound as usual, from her flat-ironed hair to her glossy manicure to her boxy, all-business suit. The only thing out of place was the pry bar she'd hit me with and the glint of madness in her eyes.

"You," I gasped, twisting to face her. "You killed Clem. And Jimmy."

"I did." She gave a what-can-you-do shrug.

"We changed the locks. How'd you get in?" It wasn't the question I meant to ask, but shock had scattered my concentration.

"I know. I was here earlier, with your mom. Your basement, by the way, is disgusting."

I scrambled backward, my shoulder throbbing. If I hadn't twisted away, the blow probably would have shattered my scapula. As it was, my entire shoulder blade felt like it was on fire. Blinking away tears of pain, I rasped, "Where's Hardy? Is he down there, too?"

"Alexander? No, he didn't come tonight. Thanks, by the way, for making such a scene this afternoon. You convinced the police and the hospital administration that you're an absolute lunatic."

I struggled to my feet and snatched a rubber mallet from the nearby shelf, brandishing it with my good arm.

She inched toward me, continuing, "Alexander doesn't have the nerve—or the brains—to handle this situation. You know surgeons. They like to keep their hands clean."

"He's still an accessory to murder." My nose was dripping, the coppery taste of blood filling my mouth.

"There you go underestimating me again," she said. "He's only an accessory if I get caught."

"You're already caught," I said. "I told the police about the phone records, and it's going to lead right back to you."

"Do I look stupid, Frankie? Whoever was calling Jimmy Madigan used one of those prepaid phones you can pick up everywhere. Kind of like this one." She pulled a cheap little phone out of her pocket and held it up. "Hard to prove who owns it. It could be *yours*, for all anyone knows."

She slipped it back in her pocket. "We're a month away from turning in our final Cardiodyne report to the FDA, and I am *not* letting anything—or anyone—interfere with that."

"You're falsifying data, aren't you? Does the Cardiodyne not work, or are the side effects too severe?"

She shrugged, took a lazy swipe at me with the crowbar, smiling when I jumped backward. "A little of both. The drug works—it improves the cardiac cells' response to electrical impulses—but for a small number of patients, it also kicks the immune system into overdrive. Their antibodies attack their own organs."

"They die."

"Everybody dies," she said. "They were terminal patients when they entered the study."

"That doesn't mean they signed up to be killed."

"We're not killing them," she protested. "We can't definitively tie the rejection to the Cardiodyne. For the rest of the patients, it really did make a difference."

"Sure, until their liver stops working. Or their kidneys shut down. You have no idea if you're helping these people or harming them. But you don't care, do you? As long as you get your approval, and . . . what? Stock options? A corner office?"

"Among other things."

"Hardy signed off on this?"

"Alexander Hardy is desperate to be out of this pathetic little town. So am I. So are you, from everything I've heard. Cardiodyne is our ticket."

"What about Strack?"

She snorted. "Please. Walter has no idea—he's too worried about finding a buyer. Why do you think we had to meet away from the hospital? Everyone at Stillwater Gen knows everyone's business, and we needed to keep this quiet."

I glanced around, trying to figure out an escape route. The front door was closer, but it was locked—by the time I got it open, Ashley would be on me. She was blocking the back door. The basement was a dead end. But if I could get to the apartment staircase, I could lock her out. I might have enough time to climb through the window.

The stairs, then.

I began to edge toward the next aisle, but she was following me too closely.

"Why kill Clem?" I asked. "He didn't want money—just meds for his grandson, and you had access to as much Apracetim as you wanted. He didn't even realize what you and Hardy were really up to, did he? He thought you were having an affair."

"I tried to tell you it wasn't like that." Her expression twisted for a brief moment before smoothing out again. "Everyone assumes I worked my way up through Pharma-gen on my back."

"You killed him because you were insulted?" No. She'd killed Clem because she was insane. Actually insane, and now she'd fixated on me.

"He would have gotten greedy. Everyone does. I swapped out his medication—it was easy enough to get his address, since it was on his application for the drug trial. I went out to the cabin before our last meeting—I knew he'd be waiting at the diner, so there was no chance he'd spot me. Then all I had to do was wait for him to have that heart attack."

"He made it to the hospital," I pointed out.

"I know. I was hoping he'd just die, but he made it in, and Alexander put in the stent. That's when he should have killed him," she added, shaking her head in dismay. "But he lost his nerve. Once he called me, I knew I'd need to handle it myself, like everything else."

"By injecting him with vecuronium. You left him," I said, thinking about Laura, calculating how many seconds her father had suffered. "You let him suffocate to death alone?"

"I stayed as long as I could." She smiled then, and the faint trace of madness I'd glimpsed earlier shone bright and unfettered. "I wanted him to know who had the power."

I pressed my fist to my stomach, trying to quell my growing nausea.

"Anyway," she said cheerily, taking another swing at me, talking all the while. "We figured that would be the end of it. Heart attack, oh-so-tragic, these things happen. Alexander even tried to tell the daughter there was nothing to be done—he had a guilty conscience. But when you asked him for the chart, he realized that might not be the end of it. I found Jimmy and told him to sue; and Alex went to Strack right away and complained about your interference."

"You killed someone and decided to ruin my career as a diversionary tactic?" The anger pulsing through me dulled the pain.

"Better yours than mine," she said. "You didn't do yourself any favors yelling at Strack, or that ER doctor. I wanted to know how much you'd figured out, so I left my purse behind. It gave me an excuse to run into you."

That day in the cafeteria, when I'd been on the phone with Laura. I'd thought I was being so clever, returning her purse, but she'd set me up. "You heard me ask Laura about her dad's medication."

She nodded. "I needed to switch his meds back, but you beat me to the cabin. After you left, I went inside, but you'd already taken the pills."

"What about Jimmy?" I said, backing down the paint aisle.

"Jimmy was greedy." She kept pace with me, pry bar swinging loosely in her hand. "We knew the hospital had a ceiling—an amount they'd be willing to settle for. Any more, and they'd take their chances in court—which would mean a full investigation. I was very clear with Jimmy that he couldn't ask for a larger settlement, but once you started asking questions, he wouldn't listen. I told him you wanted in on the deal, and he agreed to meet us at the store to talk it over."

"And then you stabbed him with a chisel."

"That was a nice touch, wasn't it?"

Nice was not the word I would use. "Why make it look like self-defense? We figured out pretty quickly that you staged it."

"Because it made you look like you were trying to cover it up. I didn't realize you and the cop were an item."

"We're not," I said quickly.

"I know that *now*," she replied. "It seemed like a good idea at the time."

"Really? There was a point in time where you thought any of this was a good idea? From where I'm standing, every single move you've made has been a bad one."

"Only because you're still standing," she said with an eerie calm.

With her free hand, she withdrew a syringe from her suit jacket.

"Vecuronium?" My heart stuttered. "Ashley, don't be stupid. I'm thirty-four. They're not going to believe this was natural."

"Everyone knows you've been under a lot of stress—the investigation, the broken engagement, the high-pressure job. You've publicly accused a well-respected doctor of murder and had another falling out with your high school sweetheart. The guilt of killing Clem Jensen finally pushed you over the edge. Poetic, that you'd use the same drug—and in the same place you killed Jimmy Madigan."

"You have lost it." I'd talked down plenty of mentally ill patients before, and I used the same no-nonsense tone now. "I'm bleeding all over the floor. You've wrecked my shoulder. Suicides don't have defensive wounds, you idiot."

"Not a problem," she said. "We won't leave a body for them to examine."

"What do you mean?"

She tapped the shelf with the syringe, ran it lightly along the cans of turpentine and paint thinner and mineral spirits. "Look at that. Highly flammable, highly flammable, highly flammable. Seems silly to keep all this in a wooden building. What aisle do you keep the matches in?"

She'd do it. There was no talking her down. She'd burn the store to the ground and me along with it, whether she got away with it or not.

I bolted, pulling over floor displays as I raced for the stairs. I made it to the second step, but before I could close the door behind me, she was there, reaching out for me. I slammed the solid-oak door, pinning her arm. She screamed, pain and frustration mingling together.

I slammed the door again and clambered up the stairs, but she caught my ankle and yanked, sending me tumbling back into her. I landed on my side, felt a muscle in my back tear, and saw lights like tiny fireworks float across my vision.

Cursing and spitting, Ashley leaped on top of me, syringe still clutched in her hand. The pry bar had fallen, and she reached back for it while I struggled to get away, pulling her hair, digging my knee into her stomach.

I'd seen countless fights in the ER; rarely did a night pass without an argument turning physical. I'd been attacked by patients, too, but there'd always been security on hand, ready to intervene. Never had I been so alone and so desperate and so . . . furious.

It was the fury that finally made me snap. I gave her a vicious kick, freeing myself just as her hand closed around the pry bar. Gasping, I ran for the supply room, weaving around pallets of lumber and racks of copper pipe, heading for the fire alarm on the far wall. Seconds before I reached it, she tackled me from behind. We both went sprawling on the floor.

I scuttled away, pushing along the floor, weeping as she pinned me again. My energy was ebbed, the pain in my back nearly paralyzing me. She drew back, arm lifted, and I saw the syringe was uncapped. There was nothing I could do but thrash weakly, flailing in a pile of sawdust I hadn't swept up yet.

"Quit fighting," she panted, her face pale and manic. "This will only hurt for a minute."

My fingers clenched, the sawdust gritty against my palm, and the survival instinct I had witnessed so often— people pulling themselves back from death through sheer force of will—took over.

I threw the sawdust into her eyes, a fistful of fine, splintery powder. Ashley screamed, clawing frantically at her eyes. The syringe fell, and I twisted to avoid it, dragging myself up to my feet as she followed me, half-blinded.

My fist came up in a smooth, strong arc, clipping the side of her jaw, rage and adrenaline giving unexpected force to the punch.

Ashley staggered and fell, head bouncing on the concrete floor.

She lay still, her chest rising and falling, but no fluttering of eyelids. She was well and truly unconscious.

The first thing I did was stamp on the syringe, feeling the plastic shatter beneath my feet. The sawdust soaked up the vecuronium, leaving only a damp, sandy circle. I breathed, deep and long and slow, savoring the feeling of my lungs expanding and contracting, knowing how close I'd come to never feeling it again.

Every muscle in my body protesting, I hobbled to the spools of rope on the south wall and cut several lengths of clothesline. I tied Ashley up, binding her hands and feet as tightly as I could. Only then did I stumble to the back counter and call 9-1-1, opening the door so the police wouldn't break it down when they arrived.

Then I slid down to the floor and waited, keeping an eye on Ashley's still-unconscious form. A soft noise, almost a chirrup, came from the doorway. Blearily, I turned my head.

The orange tabby, filthy as ever and now missing part of an ear, watched me from the stoop.

"Sure," I mumbled. "Now you show up. Where were you when I needed those claws?"

He padded inside, crossed over to inspect Ashley, and then returned. Slowly, he settled next to me, the tip of his tail just brushing my thigh. A rumbling noise—a purr or a growl or some combination of the two—emanated from his chest. I got the distinct impression he was guarding me.

We stayed like that, two survivors side-by-side, until the police showed up.

THIRTY-FIVE

I passed out in the ambulance—which seemed like a perfectly reasonable response to narrowly escaping death. When I came to, the first face I saw was the last one I wanted.

"I told you to stay out of my ER," Paul Costello said, standing over my gurney with a scowl.

"Wasn't my idea," I muttered, and then I saw Noah in the corner, solid and stone-faced, and the pain was swamped by fear. "Where's my family? Is Riley okay? My mom?"

"They're safe," he said, crossing the exam room in three quick strides. "They're on their way over. Riley's finally getting to ride in the squad car. Lights and sirens, even."

"Hardy's out there." I tried to shake off Costello, who was examining a cut along my forehead. "He might—"

"Hold still, Stapleton," Costello ordered, but his hands were surprisingly gentle as he cleaned the wound.

"My guys picked him up five minutes ago," Noah said.

"You're sure? You checked on Rowan and Charlie?"

"Do you ever stop talking?" Costello said. "I need to suture this. You want to look like Frankenstein's bride?"

"I'll tell everyone it was your work," I shot back.

"Frankie," Noah began, but Costello stood up.

"Out," he said. "I need to fix up my patient and you're distracting her."

Noah's eyes flashed. "This is police business."

Costello didn't budge. "Is she under arrest? No? Talk to her when I'm done."

Despite his bluster, his hands were deft and kind as he patched me back together, only raising his voice when my pain meds were too slow in arriving. When I panicked at the sight of the anesthetic in its slim plastic syringe, he ordered a fresh vial of lidocaine for me to examine, and let me break the seal myself.

When he was finished, he inspected me carefully, then gave a satisfied nod. "I do good work. Let's not do this again."

"I'll try," I said woozily. Before I could thank him, he strode out, and my mother took his place.

"Francesca," she said simply, eyes bright.

"I'm okay." I wasn't sure that was true, and I started to shake.

"Of course you are," she said, tucking the thin blanket more securely around me. "That doesn't mean I can't worry." She took my trembling hand in hers. "I never stop, you know. That's what it means to be a parent."

She eyed me speculatively, and I braced for a comment about how maybe I would understand, if I would only have children of my own. But she didn't. Instead, she bent and kissed the part of my forehead not swathed in gauze. "I'm very proud of you, Francesca. That never stops, either."

I gave her as much of a smile as I could manage, and she straightened, patting her hair into place. "That doctor said I could only stay a minute before he'd make me leave. He seems serious."

"He is," I assured her.

"Hmm," she said and glanced over her shoulder. "I don't suppose *he's* single?"

"Mom . . ."

★   ★   ★

I'd barely had a chance to close my eyes before Noah reappeared in the doorway, looking exhausted and uncertain. "Can I sit down?"

I nodded, and he pulled up the wheeled stool.

"Ashley Ritter and Alexander Hardy are both in custody. You did a number on Ashley, by the way. Impressive."

"Thank you," I murmured, my eyes drifting shut.

"It sounds like they're both making a full confession. Ashley won't shut up, in fact."

I didn't doubt it. "She doesn't like being underestimated."

He exhaled noisily, took my hand. "I should have believed you. I let our history interfere, and you nearly died because of it."

I forced my eyes open. "I lied about Peter. I'm not sure why." I'd let our history interfere as much as Noah had. "But I can't blame you for not trusting me. The whole reason I went after Clem was because my instinct told me something was off."

"It was," he pointed out.

"I know. But I can't get mad at you for going with your gut when I did the exact same thing, can I?"

He chuckled, and then I did, and then I clutched my side. "Ow."

"You okay?" he asked, his fingers tightening on mine. I nodded.

"Maybe we could start fresh? For as long as you're here, anyway."

"I'd like that." I wondered if it was really possible to start over after so much time. I wondered if I wanted to turn my back on all that history, if it meant erasing all the good memories along with the bad. I wondered if there was a difference between a fresh start and a second chance and if I'd be around long enough to discover the difference.

★　　★　　★

Normally, patients are transported by orderlies or nurses. You almost never see a doctor wheeling a patient around, and by the third time Garima had accidentally run me into a wall, I understood why.

"Sorry!" she said again.

"Keep it up and they're going to extend my stay," I said. "I'll leave with more injuries than I came in with."

"Hard to imagine," she said, steering me into the NICU.

Charlie leaned forward in the rocking chair. "You're okay!"

I nodded, wheeled myself closer to Rowan's isolette. "How's our girl?"

"She's doing really well. Want to hold her?"

I glanced at Charlie, whose anxious face held no blame, only relief. "You're sure?"

"Absolutely." Gently, Charlie laid Rowan in my arms, a warm, barely there weight.

Rowan looked up at me, eyes enormous and quizzical. I laid my cheek against her downy hair and inhaled her sweet newborn scent. "Hey, girlfriend. Looking good."

She blinked and yawned.

"Someone should take a picture," Garima said. "Sisters in matching outfits. Very sweet."

"It would be sweeter if we weren't wearing hospital gowns," I grumbled.

"Well, good news," Garima said. "We're springing you both tomorrow. Plan your wardrobe accordingly."

"Really?" Charlie asked. "What about Rowan?"

"Dr. Solano wants to keep her a little longer, but she'll be home before Christmas."

Charlie blinked back tears.

"I'll let you two catch up," Garima said softly.

We sat in silence, the only noise the beeping of monitors and Rowan's squeaks of contentment. Finally, Charlie said, "I'm glad you're not dead."

"Me, too. Sorry I trashed your store."

"Are you kidding? You saved the store. Mom said that crazy woman was going to burn it down."

"Well, I'm still sorry. For all of it."

Charlie touched Rowan's hand and smiled as tiny fingers closed tightly over hers. "Me too. Frankie . . . we might lose the store. I don't know how much longer I can keep it going."

"You'll be back behind the counter next week," I said. "And we're infamous now. Business will pick up."

"Even if it does, Rowan needs me. It's not like with Riley, where I put her in a sling and brought her along."

It was true. Preemies often had weaker immune systems, and winter was prime time for viruses that could quickly turn dangerous. Rowan wouldn't be getting a turn behind the counter until summer at the earliest.

"You could hire someone," I said, but I knew that wouldn't work. Charlie wasn't making enough money to pay herself, let alone a new employee.

"You're going to make me ask, aren't you?"

"Do you know how much paperwork it takes to file for family leave?" I said. "Seems like you could put in a little bit of effort."

"Really? You have to see me squirm?" She huffed out a breath. "Frankie, will you please come home and help out at the store? At least until we're back on our feet."

"Did I mention that family leave is unpaid? What's my salary?"

"You're holding half of it," she said. "And the other half seems to have developed a craving for sausage biscuits. Care to explain?"

"Nope," I said. "But I'll take the job."

"Excellent." She grinned. "We'll even provide room and board."

★   ★   ★

Later that night, someone knocked on the door of my hospital room.

"How do people sleep around here?" I grumbled.

"Morphine," Marcus said brightly. "Brought you a sandwich."

"Real food!" I exclaimed. He passed it over, and I dove in.

"Turkey, bacon, avocado on homemade sourdough," he said as I stuffed my face. "My wife is a genius with sandwiches."

"I love your wife," I said, and he laughed.

"Brought you a visitor, too," he said, and Laura Madigan stepped into the room.

I nearly choked on my sandwich. "I won't stay long," she said quickly. "I just wanted to say thank you, and . . . I'm sorry. My father wasn't who I thought he was, and I took that out on you."

"He was exactly who you thought he was," I said. "Everything your father did was to help you and CJ. To give you a better life. Maybe you didn't agree with his methods, but . . . he did it out of love, Laura. Focus on that."

She wiped her tears. "I'll try."

"That's all you can do," I said.

Because here is what I'd learned: The people we love are the ones who can wound us the deepest, often without meaning to. But they're also the ones who know how to heal us, if only we let them.

★   ★   ★

When all the visitors had gone home and my sandwich had been devoured, I settled in to nap.

Which, naturally, was when a stranger appeared in the doorway. I smothered a groan.

"May I come in?" said the woman. She was in her mid-fifties, I judged, with short silver hair and a well-tailored suit that spoke of discreet wealth. I got the distinct impression that the question was a formality. I nodded and sat up, feeling disheveled in my thin polycotton gown and bedhead.

"I'm Grace Fisher," she said. "I'm the president of Stillwater General Hospital."

"You're Strack's boss?" I blurted. I'd forgotten, with all his threats and his shouting, that Strack was only the vice-president.

"I was," she said with a grimace. "Walter Strack has resigned, at the behest of the board of trustees and myself. I wanted to apologize to you personally. In light of everything that's happened, we will not be making a complaint to the state medical board. Your license is perfectly safe."

"Thank you," I managed, relief clogging my throat.

"I've spoken to several staff members about you," she said. "My understanding is that you're not returning to Chicago immediately?"

"Family business," I said. "In every sense."

"I see." She pursed her lips. "I'll be honest with you, Miss Stapleton. Clem Jensen's death revealed serious problems within my hospital. Some, of course, can be traced directly to Alexander Hardy. But I find it troubling that no one on my staff—at any level—recognized there was anything suspicious in Mr. Jensen's case. Were it not for you, his murder would have gone undetected."

"You're welcome?"

Now she smiled. "You aren't easily intimidated, are you?"

"No, ma'am."

"And you're very good at your job."

I shrugged. "I like to think so."

"We could use someone like you on our staff. What would you say to joining us?"

I couldn't help it. I burst out laughing.

She waited. When I'd finally stopped, she said, "I'm quite serious, Miss Stapleton."

"I'm sure you are. But . . . I'm not working here. I have a job."

"One you won't be returning to for several months, correct?" She arched a brow. "You strike me as the sort of person who doesn't enjoy being bored. We may be small, but we're hardly boring. What about a temporary position?"

"You want me to work in your ER?"

She nodded. "Consider it a trial period, for both of us."

I did consider, and I couldn't deny the appeal. I couldn't work at the store all the time, not if I hoped to maintain my sanity. But . . .

"Have you talked to Paul Costello about this? What did he say?"

"Many things, all of them quite loud," she assured me. "Make no mistake—this may be Paul's emergency room, but it is *my* hospital. Shall we say three months?"

She extended her hand to shake.

I smiled and took it.

"Three months."

ACKNOWLEDGMENTS

Frankie Stapleton isn't based on a particular nurse, but she is a testament to the countless intelligent, dedicated, hardworking nurses I've met. They've held my hand in dark hours and joyous moments, kept my loved ones safe and well, and done it all with extraordinary grace and compassion. If you are a nurse . . . thank you. If you aren't a nurse, thank the next one you see. They've earned it, a million times over.

Hugest thanks to my nursing experts—any medical mistakes here are mine, despite their best efforts to educate me. KC Solano, NICU nurse extraordinaire, is nearly as tiny and fierce as her patients, but her generosity and expertise are vast. While I was writing about critical care nursing, my baby sister was actually *doing* it—and then answering all my questions with patience, good humor, and small words. Thanks, Kris, for showing me a zillion ways to kill people in a hospital. I knew your job was tough, but I didn't realize how much until now. Also, thanks for never once complaining about the Great San Diego Kid Barfing Incident of 2010.

Thanks to the staff of the Williamson Street Ace Hardware in Madison for answering my questions, letting me poke around, and for stocking my very favorite coffee. *All the doughnuts for you, guys!*

Lauren Hilty and the staff of GAPL gave me ample space to work, peace and quiet, and a very inspiring poster of Joel McHale. Jen McAndrews, Joelle Charbonneau, Susan Dennard, Melanie Bruce, Ryann Murphy, Erin Brambilla, and Hanna Martine cheered me on every step of the way. The women of Portland Midwest—Lynne Hartzer, Melonie Johnson, and Clara Kensie—talked me through plot points and character arcs (and, more than once, off the ledge). My porch is always open, ladies.

Loretta Nyhan is a brilliant writer and dear friend, and there are not enough ways and words to say how grateful I am for her, no matter how long the phone call goes. Eliza Evans always knows exactly what to say, what to ask, how to make me laugh, and how to make me get to work. I'm thankful every day that she is in my life.

Joanna Volpe has guided my career with vision and savvy every step of the way. She works hard, dreams big, and believes in me, even when I don't—in short, she's the perfect agent. It is a tremendous privilege to work with her and the rest of the New Leaf team, especially Jaida, Danielle, Jackie, Mike, Kathleen, Mia, and Pouya. Thank you to the entire staff of Crooked Lane, particularly Dan Weiss, Matt Martz, Heather Boak, and Sarah Poppe for giving Frankie such a wonderful home.

Thanks, always, to my family—especially Mom, Dad, and Kris (twice!), plus the extended branches that have supported me over the years. Thank you to my girls, for your excitement, your understanding, and your willingness to eat grilled cheese and baby carrots every night of deadline week.

Most of all, thank you to Danny—for being the person you are and for loving the person I am. I could write a million happy endings, and none would compare to the life we have together.